# A BROTHER'S
## —— GIFT ——

SUSAN CONNELLY

iUniverse, Inc.
New York   Bloomington

A Brother's Gift

Copyright © 2009 Susan Connelly

iUniverse books may be ordered through booksellers or by contacting:

iUniverse
1663 Liberty Drive
Bloomington, IN 47403
www.iuniverse.com
1-800-Authors (1-800-288-4677)

Because of the dynamic nature of the Internet, any Web addresses or links contained in this book may have changed since publication and may no longer be valid. The views expressed in this work are solely those of the author and do not necessarily reflect the views of the publisher, and the publisher hereby disclaims any responsibility for them.

ISBN: 978-1-4401-4934-4 (pbk)
ISBN: 978-1-4401-4935-1 (ebk)

Printed in the United States of America

iUniverse rev. date: 6/11/2009

Cover: *Odysseus and the Sirens*
Author photo credit: Photography © Annie Higbee/ Imagewright

How good that a son be left behind
When a man dies.

*Odyssey 3*

Brothers lost

Acknowledgments

Editors and first readers—
    Maine, Massachusetts, Michigan,
        Patty Lane, Peggy Emanuel, Janet Cohen

The library writers' groups—
    Wiscasset, Maine, and Pembroke, Massachusetts

Friends and neighbors of the peninsula—
    A landfall that is almost an island, a community that sticks together.

# ————— CHAPTER ONE —————

THE DAY I GOT THE LETTER about Luke was supposed to be a day for chores. To me, that word still suggests getting up on the farm at first light to milk cows and pitch hay and plow a few furrows. My own chores were of a somewhat lighter variety—loading the dishwasher, emptying the toaster crumb tray, and possibly ironing that camp blouse that must be just about to come back into style.

It was a Saturday in October and as close to flawless as a day in Boston can get. The sun was out and the air mild, and I had opened every window to let the breeze flow through my small apartment. My cat Woody was in the window that overlooks the street and would be out from underfoot as long as I remembered not to open the refrigerator.

When I clean, I start by filling several grocery bags with the packaging and paper that accumulate during the week on any flat surface. I'd spring for a wastebasket, but I'm trying to recycle for the next generation. As I stuffed a pile of third-class mail into one of my paper bags, it occurred to me that today's mail had probably been delivered. It was just over two months to Christmas, so I probably had a stack of holiday catalogs which could be added without delay to my trash. I got my mailbox key and defeated my deadbolt with a matchbook cover so I wouldn't have to carry my door keys. Security is us.

I was right about the mail. It was more catalogs and entreaties for donations, with a few brown envelopes trying to look official and marked

1

Open Immediately. Most of my important mail, including checks from my clients, goes to the office I maintain for my work as a private investigator. The only communications in this batch that weren't instant junk were my telephone bill and a cream-colored envelope addressed to Ellen C. Prentice.

The cream envelope had come to the right address, but I was still surprised to see my birth-certificate name on a piece of home mail. My friends all call me Nell, and I even have it on my business cards. My bank would never question a check made out to me as Nell Prentice. I looked at the return address. Hines and Fayerweather, PC, with an address in Portland, Maine. Who might they be? I put the letter on top of the slippery catalogs and took everything back upstairs.

Woody was waiting right inside the door—I nudged him aside with my foot so he couldn't make a break for freedom. He trotted behind me and supervised as I put the mail on the table for a quick sort. I was going to need another paper bag for all this junk. The envelope from Hines and Fayerweather was my only correspondence that had not been pre-sorted. I touched the envelope, and decided to wait a while before opening it. This is an old habit of mine which I suppose derives from having an essentially pessimistic nature. I got ginger ale out of the refrigerator (Woody did a quick dance of supplication, but I ignored him) and went into my living room to read the local paper, mailed to me for free. An orange card fell out of the paper—an appeal for me to start paying for my free subscription. I picked up the card and added it to the junk pile.

Once I was settled with my ginger ale and my cat, I skimmed the paper quickly and got to the Personals, which I love. The illustration changes from season to season, but I've noticed it's always a heterosexual couple, both of the same race. The photo for this month had them walking in some fallen leaves. The ads were the usual assortment, some depressingly familiar because they had been in for months. Among the desired attributes were such skills as dining and dancing. I'm above average at the former. No one was seeking a private investigator who read Herodotus in her idle hours and viewed antiquing (a noun metamorphosed into a gerund) as a fate worse than that suffered by Polyphemus when Odysseus gouges out his eye with a heated stick.

I read every ad, wondering what woman would be so lacking in self esteem that she would respond to a guy who insisted on No Kids. I took a second look at the Real Estate ads. Woody had gone to sleep, purring softly, and I thought if I didn't get up I might join him in a nap. I lifted him off my lap and set him on the sofa, where he crossed one leg over the other and fell immediately back to sleep, quite indifferent to whatever was waiting for me in my letter.

The envelope from Hines and Fayerweather was of heavy stock; I had no doubt that the letter inside would be on matching paper. I slid a finger under the flap and extracted a single sheet that had been precisely folded into thirds. The firm's name was in bronze script, above last Thursday's date.

*Dear Ms. Prentice:*

*Our firm requests that you contact us at the telephone number shown above, for discussion of a confidential matter in which we believe you have an interest.*

*Please telephone us at your earliest convenience so that we may provide details of this matter. Thank you for your consideration. We look forward to hearing from you.*

*Very truly yours,*
*Lee Thomson, Esq.*

Ms. or Mr. Thomson's signature was angular and seemed to consist of no more than four actual letters. It looked like an EKG, and I decided that my correspondent was most likely Mr. rather than Ms. Thomson. Or Attorney Thomson. It might be a nice convention if this particular segment of the professional class were to adopt the style of the dead who speak from their graves in Spoon River. This fellow would be Lawyer Thomson, and I guess I would be Investigator Prentice.

I can stall with the best of them. Never mind whether it was Ms. or Mr., Lawyer or Man of the People. What did Lee Thomson want with me? I turned the envelope upside down just to make sure that no Check for One Million Dollars (non-negotiable) fell out. Woody darted over to see whether I was shaking cat treats out of the mail, and I scratched his head.

"It looks as if I'm the one getting the treat, my friend," I said. "If such it is."

I am always a little put off by business mail that arrives on Saturday. I picture the sender in his or her office, the last one there on a pleasant Friday, printing out the letter and metering the envelope in plenty of time to experience a warm sensation of relief. Done—someone else's problem now! And off the sender goes, with a bounce in his or her step. (I am no more partial to weekend neediness from people I know, although there are exceptions. With the repeat offenders, I've learned that if their mission is to Touch Base with me, the problem is emotional. If they want to Run Something By Me, it's money.)

I returned the letter to its envelope and took it into my bedroom, where I keep my briefcase. Out of sight and out of mind until Monday, when I would call the number shown on the letterhead. But the mischief was done. As I worked around my apartment my mind kept trying to guess why this particular Professional Corporation was writing to me. Finally, a little before noon, I decided that a walk and an ice cream cone were what I needed to distract me. I refrained from mentioning my destination to Woody, whose love of ice cream is a match for my own.

Walking in the city can be less than recreational. There are the always-present crowds, the dirt and noise, the curbs and Walk lights every block. When I visit my friend Martha we walk on the beach, which is a treat for me. Our pace is always slow, in part because Martha is eighty-two, but also because she has taught me not to miss things. On days when the weather is ugly and the city impossible, I can close my eyes and be standing barefoot in the wet sand, looking where Martha tells me to, seeing a bird or beach rose that I would never have noticed if I were alone.

Today, I was just glad to be out and about. In another month the early darkness would begin, but for now the only sign that summer was over was the angle of the light. There were lots of people out but I didn't see anyone I knew. The city is like that. A pet-walker went past with five dogs on different colored leashes, and I gave the man an admiring smile. When I was in college I had a cute mutt who was hopeless on a leash. He would pull to one side and lean so far toward the sidewalk that anyone seeing us would stare, then burst out laughing. If I tried to walk five dogs they'd be in a worse tangle than Ares and Aphrodite found themselves in when her husband trapped them in golden chains.

I reached the ice-cream store and found it crowded, but decided I didn't mind waiting. I hoped they had plenty of chocolate chip. While I stood in line I regarded my fellow customers critically. A teenage couple, she in halter and jeans, he in jeans and a tank top, looked close to anorexic but just about everybody else was plump. I hoped they all realized that this was my lunch and not just an indulgent snack.

My ice cream, when I finally got it, tasted wonderful. I took it back outside and walked as slowly as if I were with Martha, savoring the weather almost as much as my delicious treat. When the last crumb of the cone was gone I wadded up the napkins and picked up my pace as I headed for a trashcan that was at least a hundred feet away. There—that should nuke a few calories. All I needed to do on the walk home was to burn off the other thousand or so.

# ———— CHAPTER TWO ————

THE FINE WEATHER LEFT US ON Sunday night, leaving behind the kind of gray chill that is especially hard to take on a Monday. I would need something warm to wear in my office, but my sweaters were still packed away in a box far down in my closet. I do own one sweater that I don't pack away, but it's something I wouldn't wear while escaping from a burning building, much less to the office. It belonged to Michael, whom I married and fully expected to spend my life with. The sweater is striped in red and gray, much too big for me, and so full of holes that Woody has been known to poke his nose into them. It may be that Woody likes this particular sweater because it belonged to Michael.

Four months before he died, Michael went to the mall in search of an anniversary present for me. Outside the pet store, two little girls were giving away kittens. Two cute females and a funny looking male—white with a black tail and a triangular mark on his side. When Michael returned thirty minutes later, having been too distracted by the cats to find a gift for me, the females were gone. Michael picked up the male, who butted against his hand and purred.

When he walked into the house and produced this ridiculous creature from under his jacket, Michael put on a doubtful look.

"Do I have it right?" he asked. "It *is* a cat for the twelfth anniversary...?"

I settled on pleated pants, a turtleneck and a linen blazer that, if I concerned myself with such things, would have been banished into storage no later than midnight on Labor Day. But I have never been known for my fashion flair, and besides, I love any garment that's actually supposed to look wrinkled.

I was in my office by nine, stalling masterfully by listening to messages, returning calls and shuffling papers while the letter from Lee Thomson, Esq. lay just off to one side of my desk. Soon it was time for a coffee break, which necessitated moving the letter to my in-basket to protect it from spills. I wouldn't want the handsome cream stationery stained with coffee when I was actually ready to deal with it.

Up until almost eleven, my work went well. I did some basic accounting and confirmed that there was a little more money coming in than going out. Maybe on my next trip to the grocery store I'd spring for a few packages of those French cat treats that Woody likes. You can tell by looking at my white cat with his black head and tail and black plectrum shape on his side that he comes from generations of rough and ready alley cats, but that has never stopped him from having expensive tastes. I was reaching for a Post-It on which to do a little math when the phone rang.

"Prentice Investigating," I said into the phone, as soon as it had rung twice. After four rings the caller is beamed into voice mail, and I can't afford to lose a prospective client who won't talk to a machine. The two rings are to avoid the appearance of eagerness.

"Oh...hi," my caller said. She sounded nonplussed at getting a real person. After a moment she said, " I want to find my husband."

I knew she wasn't talking about a mail-order groom, so I was able from long practice to ask the right questions. I strove to keep the whole sad situation on a professional level, but the caller, whose name (maybe) was Betty Jones, would not cooperate. The straying husband was "that bum," the extra-marital relationship was "the little tramp," and Ms. Jones's burning desire was to "make them pay."

Sordid or not, this is the kind of work I do and I was about to ask Ms. Jones what time would be convenient for her to come to my office when she said, "So can I talk to Mr. Prentice?"

She couldn't have been asking about Michael, because I had never taken his last name. Once, after I'd gotten to know my friend Martha, I made an attempt to wax witty on that decision, saying that keeping my maiden name had been a good move, because I wasn't faced with having to change Woody's surname at the vet. My laughter at this excuse for a joke was way over the top, and Martha had covered my hands with her own and sat there quietly with me. Woody, too, sensed something and jumped into my lap. His worried expression made us both laugh, and the moment passed.

"It's Ms. Prentice," I said now. She had one more chance.

"Are you his wife?" she asked. I suppose she thought that the docile Mrs. P. was helping out at the office while the boss's "girl" took time off to have a baby or join her girlfriends on a cruise.

"This is Nell Prentice Investigations," I said. "I'm Nell Prentice." I couldn't make it much simpler than that.

"Oh," she said. It was the same interjection with which she had begun the conversation. Then, "I thought they said Neal."

I didn't feel it necessary to ask who "they" were. The message was clear, whatever the source. I was speaking to one of my own gender who may have enjoyed being a girl but sure didn't want one working for her. I waited in silence and after a minute or so my caller said that she'd think about it and might be getting back to me.

I spent ten minutes after that call glowering and telling myself that we hadn't really made all that much progress since the days when a victorious warrior had his pick of captured women, to go along with the gleaming tripods and embroidered cloaks he would carry home as his spoils. Finally I was able to put my pique aside by telling myself that I never would have accepted Ms. Jones as a client. I have my standards, and someone who can't spell a name with only four letters is not up to them.

There was one thing to be said for my annoying call—it had used up fifteen minutes, plus ten minutes of fuming about it afterward. It was now almost eleven thirty and I decided to go out for an early lunch before finding out who in Portland, Maine had need of me, and why.


Burger King, my royal choice for lunch, was mobbed, with most of the clientele appearing to be under the age of puberty. Didn't kids go to school any more, I groused to myself, and was at once chagrined by how old-cootish my question sounded. Any minute now I would be plucking the sleeve of some teenager's baggy clothes and telling her how Abe Lincoln and I had toted our one pair of shoes to school. Not even one pair each—we had shared.

I counted twenty-one people ahead of me in the line, the more prudent equipped with something to read. My copy of *The Decipherment of Linear B* was at home, so I studied the Nutrition Information poster and received confirmation that my food choices were exceedingly poor. I was going to have to rid myself of the fast-food habit if I didn't want to end up like Bill Clinton, who had fast-fed himself right into bypass surgery.

When it was finally my turn I looked around to see whether there were any free tables, and seeing that there were not I ordered my lunch To Go. The button for that command must have been too close to the button for Here, because my lunch was presented on a plastic tray and then had to be transferred into a paper bag. During this maneuver several French fries spilled to the floor but I refrained from picking them up. Always a lady, and besides, I couldn't reach them.

Back at my office building I took the stairs up to my office, just in case the elevator was filled with wealthy prospective clients who would change their minds about hiring me if they saw my $3.86 meal. Once I was safely in my office, with the door locked, I arranged my double cheeseburger and fries onto the bag they had come in and ate everything but the bag. I then put the telltale wrappers in the very bottom of my wastebasket and sprayed the area with air freshener, replacing the smell of grease and cheap red meat with the smell of Mountain Wildflowers, or so I hoped.

It seemed it was time to call Ms. or Mr. Thomson.

I placed the letter I had received in the center of my desk (in the same spot so recently occupied by my Burger King dinnerware) and punched in the phone number. On the second ring a professional-sounding female voice said, "Hines and Fayerweather. How may I direct your call?"

"Lee Thomson, please," I said, sidestepping the gender question.

"And who may I say is calling?"

Maybe I'd be put right through if I said it was Neal Prentice. "Ellen Prentice," I said. "Mr. Thomson wrote me a letter."

"I'll connect you," the voice said. Either I had guessed right, or she was going to let me find out for myself that it was Ms. Thomson. There was a click, followed by a new voice, light but undeniably male.

"Ms. Prentice," he said. "Lee Thomson here. You're calling in regard to my letter?"

I sometimes get myself into trouble by leaping to conclusions, and was so impressed by this inbred caution that I felt I should be taking notes on how not to give away too much. "Yes," I said, consulting the letter for its exact phrasing. "Your letter says you want to give me the details of a 'confidential matter' in which I may have an interest."

"To be sure," he said. I was surprised by the formal sounding phrase. "You got it" is considered perfectly acceptable business speaking these days, though not by me. He went on, "But I do need to be certain we are dealing with the right individual. May I please have the date and place of your birth?"

"Mr. Thomson," I said, "you may not. You are 'dealing' with a person who is calling in response to your request and who is certainly not about to reveal personal information to a complete stranger. You tell me what this is all about, and then we'll decide whether I can help you."

"My apologies," he said, after a slight pause. "It's just that any time a law firm is representing a minor, we have to be especially circumspect. Not, of course, that that doesn't apply to all our clients..."

"Who's your client?" I asked. His stuffy phrasing made me want to get straight to the point. Not surprisingly, he balked.

"I really don't think..." he began.

"Mr. Thomson," I said, "I am in my office and am very busy. You wrote to me because you need something from me. We're both wasting our valuable time if you're not willing to tell me what this is all about."

This time the silence was long enough so that I was about to tell him to forget the whole thing. Just then he spoke, having the sense to begin with the two words everyone most likes to hear.

"You're right," he said, and took an audible breath. "Our client is Lucas John Prentice. He is fifteen years old, and we believe he is your nephew."

With clients, or with anyone connected with a case, I have developed a technique of getting all the information I can before making any response. It counteracts that tendency to pole-vault to a conclusion. But I was not at all prepared to hear my own surname coupled with two boy's names, and my self-training deserted me. "I don't have a nephew," I said and added, to this person I had just designated a complete stranger, "I don't have any immediate family."

Lee Thomson was unperturbed. "I'm sure this is quite a surprise," he said, "but we have been most thorough in checking the young man's background before contacting you." There was a pause, and I could hear the sound of paper being moved. "We have a number of documents I would like to send you, but I suppose the most important one is the boy's birth certificate..."

I was in that mental space in which everything is quiet and in readiness. The storm might be just on the other side of the hill, but for the moment all is calm. Later I would have to make sense of what I was hearing, but for now all that mattered was that I knew I was hearing the truth. Mr. Thomson was asking if I had a fax, and I heard myself saying—calmly—"Why don't you read it to me?"

"Certainly," said Mr. Thomson. He seemed relieved that after our initial jousting, he and I were getting along as two business people should. "The certificate is from Penobscot Bay Medical Center in Rockport, Maine... Lucas John Prentice... born February 8, 1989... mother Doris Aguila..." Here he paused, possibly for dramatic effect, then went on, "The father is listed as Edward Sven Prentice, age twenty-four, laborer."

Ned had hated that ethnic middle name almost as much as he'd loved Maine. He'd stay in that frigid water until his limbs were blue and our mother would have to go down to the shore with a towel and call to him to come out *right this minute.*

Mr. Thomson seemed to be waiting for me to say something. "That was my brother's name," I said, "and the age is right." I drew in a breath. "Mr. Thomson," I said, "You do know that my brother is dead?"

"Yes," he said, and seemed to be thinking about whether he should offer condolences. In a moment he went on, "The reason we are contacting you at this particular juncture is that the boy has recently lost his mother."

As I let that information sink in—some juncture—Lee Thomson may have been reminding himself how little I seemed to know about my own family, because after a moment he added, "Your brother's wife."

Ned's wife. So I not only had a nephew, but also—until "recently"—a sister-in-law.

"What happened to her?" I asked.

There was a pause before he answered in a somber tone, "Ms. Aguila had breast cancer. She knew for some months that her time was…limited…which made her refusal to try to contact the boy's father"—he seemed to be searching for a non-judgmental word or phrase—"inexplicable."

It was even more inexplicable to me. This woman had been Ned's wife, but it was doubtful she knew for certain that he was dead at the time she became ill. I was the one who knew that for sure, along with the cause of his death, if not the reason.

What Lee Thomson said next reinforced my supposition. He said, "We found you through your brother's reissued death certificate. From there we took his Social Security number, which led us to his military record. You were listed as next-of-kin."

Ned had told me he was doing that. We both knew that if anything happened to him in the Marines I should be the one to tell our parents, not the other way around. I said, "How much does the boy know about his father?"

"Only that Mr. Prentice is deceased. There was certainly no reason to go into detail."

Amen to that. I asked, "What about other relatives?"

"There's a grandmother, in Puerto Rico. We've had someone look into it… the woman is apparently senile. Certainly in no condition to provide support for an adolescent boy."

I looked around my office. It looked exactly as it always had, and smelled of Burger King overlaid with air freshener. I tried to think of the right way to phrase my question and decided to just come out with it.

"Mr. Thomson," I said, "what do you want from me?"

Mr. Lee Thomson was a pro. He countered my bluntness with a crisp, businesslike tone. "Nothing, Ms. Prentice," he said. "What we want is to represent our client to the best of our ability. In our opinion, that includes contacting any known relatives when a minor child is left without parents."

Fair enough, I had to admit, and felt my first twinge of sympathy for this unknown boy—Ned's son—losing his mother at such a vulnerable age, then almost immediately finding out that his father was dead. Not that it's ever easy. I had been in my late twenties when my own mother died, and will never forget the pain of it. I had lain in bed in Michael's arms, weeping until my head throbbed. I wondered just how much time this other mother had had following her diagnosis. But it was a different question that I asked.

"Mr. Thomson, where is the boy now?"

"In Massachusetts," he replied. "He goes to school in Ashfield. There was some discussion of his taking time off from school, but he wanted to be with his friends."

"Does he know about me?"

"No," said Lee Thomson, and I sensed a bit of disapproval. "It would have been quite inappropriate for us to tell the boy he had an aunt, without even knowing whether you would want to meet him."

So there it was. Except for an old granny who might not even know who her grandson was, I was this kid's only family. Me and Cousin Woody.

"It must be a rough time for him," I said, feeling my way in this conversation. "But of course I would like to meet him...Lucas. Do you have any suggestions for how I might go about that?"

Now Lee Thomson approved of me. His voice took on a note of heartiness. "Very sensible of you to think that way!" he said. "As you say, the boy has been through a lot, and quite recently. How about this: I'll call the boy and tell him to expect a letter from you. How would that be? Introduce yourself, give him a few days to get used to the idea, then see about arranging a visit."

I looked at my corkboard as I reached for a Post-It, my stationery of choice. Fastened to the board were more Post-its, appointment reminders, scribbled notes, and two family pictures—Martha and me in front of her house in Manomet, and Woody napping on a Gateway computer box.

"What's the address?" I asked.

Lee Thomson read the information to me, and said he would mail a copy as well. After we hung up I read over several times the few lines I had written. I couldn't take in yet what this development might mean to my life, but I could be all but certain of one thing. I was going to have to be the one to tell Lucas John Prentice how his father had died.

# CHAPTER THREE

I HAVE TRAINED MYSELF TO GET back to work after an affecting encounter or phone call, but this time it was harder than usual. My thoughts kept returning to Lucas Prentice. What did he look like? What were his likes and dislikes? Surely fifteen was too young for a girlfriend, but Lee Thomson had said he had friends at school. I remembered Ned at that age, quiet and serious, with only a couple of close "buddies." But Ned had come from the same two people I had come from. Half of this boy was a complete unknown.

Fortunately for me, one of my more demanding clients decided to call and see whether I had made significant progress on his case since he had checked in yesterday. He owned several dry cleaning stores, and was sure that an employee at one of them was stealing from him. He was probably right, but he was also a self-satisfied jerk who had inherited his business and never had to sweat behind a counter while customers took him to task for missing buttons. I gave him my full attention, and the problem of Lucas moved to the back of my mind. When I finally got off the phone, I made sure to enter the length of the call in my billing records. I couldn't bill for psychic overhead, but I could certainly make sure that this particular client did not get so much as a free minute.

The rest of the afternoon passed without event. At three, I saw a new prospective client, a man seeking help with an unusual custody situation. The child, a girl of ten, had been adopted by the mother before the mother's marriage to Malcolm Williams, who was now sitting in my client chair angrily telling his side of the story. Mr. Williams had been a father to the girl since she was two, but now that a divorce was in the offing, he had no legal rights to see the child.

"Why an investigator?" I asked. "It seems to me you should be talking to a lawyer."

"I did!" he said, clearly frustrated. "He said that unless something has changed since Alice adopted Katie, I don't have any more rights than I would if Alice and I had just been shacking up."

I wasn't crazy about his terminology, but that was beside the point. I asked, "And has anything changed?"

"Yes!" he said. "Alice is planning to marry—you're not going to believe this—a woman."

Oh. I said carefully, "That's legal in Massachusetts."

"I know that!" he said. "The lawyer said that Alice's *spouse* could adopt Katie if she wanted to. Can somebody please tell me what kind of example that is for a little girl? Two women... doing whatever it is they do."

Mr. Williams did seem to be a man of rather rigid principles, even prejudices, but that didn't mean he didn't care about this child. The one thing I was sure of was that this free consultation was not on its way to becoming a paying case. It was only fair to both of us that I not encourage my visitor any further.

"Mr. Williams," I said, "this must be hard for you. But there's nothing I can do. People are allowed to legally marry members of their own sex. Your ex-wife adopted a child before you came along. As long as she's a good mother, nobody in the court system is going to care who's sharing her house or her life."

He looked so crestfallen that I felt I had to say something more. I waited a moment and then said, "I'm not a therapist or a family counselor, but here's my advice to you. Wait a month or so, then call your ex-wife and tell her how much you miss Katie. Don't say a word about the other woman—just focus on the child. If your ex-wife won't let you visit, then ask if you can send cards and birthday presents. People's attitudes change. If you're patient and don't pass judgments, your ex-wife may come to see that it's best for Katie to stay connected to the man she thinks of as her Dad."

He seemed about to say something, then nodded instead. He looked very dispirited. In a moment he got up, and I rose from behind my desk to shake his hand.

"Good luck," I said, and he nodded again. After he left my office I went to the window and watched as he came out of the building and turned in the direction of the subway station. His head was down, and I supposed he was thinking of the course his life seemed to be taking. Maybe in time that course would reverse itself, but whether it did or didn't, I would probably never know.

It wasn't much after four when Mr. Williams left, and I knew I should stay in my office another hour or so. That big-ticket client might be headed my way in a limo right now, only to get here and find the lights out and the problem-solver gone. But I wanted to be home, where I could sort out this emotional day with the help of my cat, who's my best listener. I straightened things up and at four-thirty I set the phone machine to forward calls to my home number, just in case that major client chose to call.

The outside air felt good, and I decided to defer the ordeal of the rush-hour subway by walking a few stops before getting on the train. My routines are pretty well set, but today's news was so out of the ordinary that I felt the need for a change of pace. The day was still gray and cold, and there was a small, persistent wind. An October wind. It brought to mind a song Michael liked to sing. The song had the sweet melancholy of the dying year, with a woman singing to her baby.

*Leave no ill will to hinder us*
*My helpless babe and me...*

The tune ran in my head for a moment and I was suddenly taken with the thought that maybe I would have a child in my family, after all the years of watching others bring forth the next generation. A moment later, I laughed aloud, causing my fellow pedestrians to start, and then step more quickly while looking anywhere but at me.

*He's fifteen!* I thought. *Helpless babe, indeed! He's probably into groups with names like Crypt Crawlers.*

Restored to sanity, at least for now, I put on the sober face of a city-dweller who was as normal as the next person and walked quickly toward the lighted sign for the Copley Square "T" station.

The train was very crowded, and I realized that most of the crowd was young, students from the nearby high schools and colleges. They were noisy, full of energy, and fun to watch. There were boys with flowing hair and girls with crew cuts. Earrings on everybody, and not a leather shoe to be seen. Baggy pants and black T-shirts, backpacks and bottles of water. I supposed that the age range was somewhere around thirteen to twenty-five, but to me they all looked like children, their clothes and makeup and jewelry unable to hide the essential freshness of their years. I nearly missed my stop, so intense was my interest in this age group I would scarcely have noticed before today. When I got off the train, the sudden quiet of my street seemed unnatural, missing somehow the whirl and dash of life.

Woody was in the window watching for me, and I greeted him with even more affection than usual. It's been more than nine years since Michael reached into his jacket and lifted out this boon companion of mine, my purring, lap-sitting, leg-circling pretty boy. I want him to set a world record for cat longevity. It seemed all I could think of on this strange day was age, and aging. I thought of the way Cicero put it, writing in the last full year of his life:

*The hours and the days, the months and the years slip past—*
*The time that is gone will never return,*
*And what is to follow can never be known.*

I picked Woody up and carried him against my shoulder, opening the refrigerator with one hand and getting out a can of diet root beer to sip while I read the newspaper. It was too early for dinner, although Woody's questioning eyes suggested that he didn't think so. I read the headlines, skimmed through the local news, and finally put the paper aside so that I could scratch Woody's head while I filled him in on the day's events. It was all fine with him, as usual.


I didn't write to Lucas that night. I wanted it all to settle in before I took up the somewhat tricky task of introducing myself by letter to a nephew I had not known about until today. It would be important to strike just the right tone in my letter, friendly but not gushy, letting the boy know that I would respect however he chose to handle the news that he had an Aunt Nell.

"Doesn't that sound *old* ?" I asked Woody, returning again to my new obsession. "Aunt Nell, with her preserves and support hose and bingo night." Woody paid no attention—he is thoroughly accustomed to my nonsense. I wondered again what my nephew looked like, and suddenly saw the perfect way to approach my first communication with him.

"Pictures," I said to Woody, moving him aside so I could get up from the sofa. That particular word was not in his vocabulary of terms relating to food, so he stayed put as I headed for my bedroom closet.

After I told my friend Martha what had happened to Michael—the senseless, unthinkable way he had been killed trying to save a baby—I asked her advice about the pictures I had moved with. "Don't throw them away," she advised me. "Put them in a box and label them and put the box in a place where it can't ambush you." I had taken her advice, adding my own refinement by using two boxes. One, labeled M+N, held the small stock of pictures of Michael and me. I knew Woody was in the last few taken by me, perched on Michael's shoulder, but even after nine years I wasn't ready to look at those. The other was labeled MISC. I reached into the closet and unwedged the second box, then gasped and dropped it as I found myself looking into the dark at what appeared to be the eyes of a very large rodent. A moment later Woody, who had slipped into the closet without my noticing, sprang out and headed for quieter parts.

"Old age, nothing," I said as my heart rate fell back toward normal. "My own cat is going to give me a heart attack long before the bloom of middle age is off me."

I carried the box back to the living room, where I could spread things out. Everything was tossed together in the musty box, making for a strange little world in which the same person would go from youth to infancy to maturity in one stack of photos. Many of the photos were dated in my mother's careful handwriting—"June 30, 1948" was penciled on the back of a photo of her eighth grade class smiling in long-ago sunlight. I set that one aside where Woody couldn't reach it—maybe I would put it on my desk.

I found three photos of Ned that I thought his son might like. In one, my brother had a bow and arrow and was squinting toward a target in the back yard. Another showed him with me; it was Christmas, the year he was born. I was grinning from ear to ear as I held my goggle-eyed two-month-old brother.

The last one was a school picture that had an explanation for the angle at which it was taken. Ned had gotten a dark green bicycle for his seventh birthday. It was too big for him, and he fell off it the day before his second-grade picture was taken. Because of the bump over Ned's left eye, from which he would always have a tiny scar, the photographer had posed my brother in profile. Ned's hair was cut very short, and I was sure he had had no need for the comb the school photographer always gave to each child.

That would do it. Another time I might go through the pictures more thoroughly, but my task had become a heavy one. I carried the box back to the closet and set it inside near the front. Before I closed the closet door I checked for Woody, but his interest in the dark interior seemed to have passed. Just to make sure, I called his name.

"Woody," I said, and for good measure added, "Ready for dinner?" In an instant, he was at my side, purring and winding around me, taking my mind off brothers, nephews, and mothers. It was time to eat—what else in life could possibly matter?

# CHAPTER FOUR

I WAITED UNTIL WEDNESDAY TO WRITE to Lucas. That way, Mr. Lee Thomson had a couple of days in which to give the boy the news. Composing the letter was a daunting task. Dear Lucas? Dear Luke? Nephew? After a full five minutes during which Woody strolled distractingly on my desk, I decided on Dear Lucas Prentice. It still felt odd to pair my own last name with somebody else's first name, but at least I was no longer staring at the date and my street address. Now I just needed to pick up the pace if I wanted the letter to arrive before the boy reached his majority.

Any good book on letter writing will tell you that the first paragraph is the introductory one, if you are corresponding with someone for the first time. It's where you say, *The purpose of this letter is...* or, *I am writing to you because...* After half a dozen tries and deletions I settled on: *Your father and I were brother and sister.* Then some basic information about where I lived and how I had found out that I had a nephew, and an expression of sympathy about his mother. A mention of the photographs I was enclosing. The end was in sight. I fingered my mouse as the cursor steadily blinked. So much easier when one had a pencil to chew on while awaiting inspiration. Finally I wrote:

*Your school is only a few hours from where I live. I would like to meet you. Could you let me know what days family are allowed to visit?*

There was no happy medium between *Love,* and *Very truly yours,* so I printed the letter without a closing and read it over critically before signing it. It seemed stilted and formal but I supposed that was better than too cozy.

I opened my desk drawer and took out one of the stamped envelopes I had bought for just this occasion, addressed it, and held it out to show Woody.

"Done," I said. "Now just let me get it into a mailbox before I decide to go back and ask him what grade he's in."

# CHAPTER FIVE

THE WEEK WAS PROVING TO BE a busy one, full of the kind of routine work that pays the bills and doesn't give you ulcers. I get quite a few small assignments from the insurance company I once worked for—things like surveillance work, checking the physical facts of a claim, or talking to the neighbors. It helps that I am a woman and a couple of years past forty. I always dress for the neighborhood and act friendly but never pushy, and before you can say Concealment, Misrepresentation or Fraud I'm hearing all about how the claimant is working full-time while collecting disability benefits, or that the car that Grandma banged into the house was actually being driven by her unlicensed teenaged grandson. The claimants never seem to realize that they are envied, not admired, for their scheme. And envy leads very quickly to eager tattling about what the schemer is up to.

Several times a day, I would think of Lucas receiving my letter. Maybe he wouldn't respond at all. I would have liked to call my friend Martha and share my news, but I decided to wait until I could casually say, "It seems I have a nephew. I'll be meeting him this weekend..."

By Friday, I felt a real sense of accomplishment, heightened by the fact that Friday itself went well. The thick clouds outside my window had an autumnal look, and I realized that this weekend would bring the end of Daylight Savings Time. The dark months would be here, and the long wait for Spring. I supposed that Lucas was in the Spring of his life. As for me, "that time of year" was approaching faster than I would have liked—Shakespeare was not even forty when he coined that somber phrase. I was deep in these melancholy thoughts when the phone rang, and I had to do an instant shift into my professional demeanor.

"Nell Prentice," I said, picking up on the third ring. There was no reply. I listened carefully and could tell there was someone on the line. It is not at all unusual for my callers to be worried or upset, and I have learned to use my calmest tone in order to keep them from hanging up.

"This is Nell Prentice," I said. "Is there something I can help you with?"

Another short, steadying pause and then, "Nell, it's Sheila."

My circle of first-name friends is small, and I only know one Sheila. Sheila Kramer. Mother of Tom Kramer. I haven't known Tom very long, but he has come to mean a great deal to me. I probably don't let him know that often enough.

"Sheila," I said, "I'm here. What is it?"

Her voice had steadied. It's something women can do, especially mothers. They can put their own troubles aside when the people they love need them. "It's Tom," she said. "He's in the hospital. That's where I'm calling from. They have him in Intensive Care."

I closed my eyes. All this recent obsession about age and the seasons of decay, and here came the jester with his mocking bells. This call was not (thank God) about my friend Martha, who is eighty-two. It was about Tom, who had turned forty-eight this year.

"His partner called me," Sheila was saying, and with that word—partner—I was back listening to Tom just before the first time we made love. He was telling me about the devastating loss of his first partner, in a domestic violence stabbing when Tom was off duty. He and Jack had been on the Boston police force then—Tom later moved to a suburban force, but where lawlessness against those who uphold the law is concerned, the madness can come from anywhere.

"What happened?" I asked.

"They think it's a heart attack. He was on a call and he collapsed. We won't know anything for a while..."

"Which hospital?"

"Mass General," Sheila said. "But Nell, you won't be able to see him. It's just family until... oh, my God, Nell, I didn't mean ..."

"Sheila," I said. My own Calm Tone was there for me. "Suppose I don't take offense? You have quite enough to worry about without me being a jerk over the hospital rules. But I'd like to be with you, if you'll let me."

I could hear her crying now, softly, trying not to. "Okay," she said. "Yes."

"Twenty minutes," I said. "I'll walk—it's probably faster than waiting for the train. Anything I can pick up on the way?" Sheila said no, nothing.

"On my way," I said. And because I wanted to say something just a little bit light before I hung up the phone, I said, " I'd stop and get Woody, but I'm pretty sure they have a hospital rule about *that*."

In less than two minutes I had the phone reset, the lights turned off, and my raincoat on but not buttoned. When I got outside I found that it had begun to drizzle and had to run back upstairs for an umbrella, but I was still on my way up Tremont Street toward the hospital in less than five minutes. I would have liked to ignore the pedestrian WAIT lights that were on every block, but car after car was running the red lights in poor visibility, on slick streets, and I knew that I would not be much use to Sheila or Tom if I ended up dead.

The word "dead" is not one you want taking up residence inside your head at a time like this. I shook my head vigorously, as if to send it packing. Tom was going to be fine. He was trim and active, didn't smoke, never drank more than a beer or two. I resolved that never again would I endanger his health with the sausage omelets we both liked. I would serve salads, with fat-free dressing. Lean meats with the skin removed...

Of course, the issue at hand was not that Tom was basically healthy and didn't deserve this. The issue was that he was intelligent and decent and kind. If anything bad happened to him, the Fates were in big trouble with me.

I had just reached the hospital when the drizzle turned into a downpour. I locked both hands onto my umbrella and made a run for the main entrance. Just as I got there an elderly man stepped quickly aside and I realized I had been about to bowl him over. "I'm sorry!" I said. "My friend is here..." He gave me a nod of understanding and gestured me through the door ahead of him, even though he was hatless and his white hair was streaming with rain. I took a moment to silently but fervently wish him every good thing that could ever befall a human being.

The Massachusetts General Hospital is regarded as one of the best in the world, and is surely one of the busiest. The newspapers love to run stories about billionaires coming from the other side of the world to be treated here, or child victims of land mines getting free care, but in one way it's just like any other hospital. Ninety nine percent of the sick and suffering who come here aren't newsworthy. They're people of all colors, rich and poor, young and old, caught up in the bewilderment of crisis. The main reception desk resembles nothing so much as the scene in Homer where the dead are straining toward Odysseus, but only those who have drunk blood are permitted to speak. Here, it wasn't a cup of blood that could clear the way for you, but rather the right insurance form or ID card, or in many cases an interpreter to state your need in English. I looked around for the red Emergency arrows and set off in the direction they pointed, at a pace fast enough to keep me from thinking.

The waiting area in Emergency was huge, with about a third of the plastic chairs occupied by people who automatically looked up as I came into the room. Seeing that I wasn't a bearer of news, they went back to their magazines or quiet conversations, or to watching the overhead television that was tuned to the local news station. Sheila was way at the back. She had seen me, and was coming toward me. I hurried to meet her, and forced myself not to talk until we had shared a long hug.

"Nell," she said as we finally let go of each other and moved to a couple of free chairs, "I'm so glad you're here." She took a moment to steady her voice, as she had done on the phone. A half-hour ago—was it possible? "Tom's not conscious," she said. "I haven't been able to see him yet but I guess they wanted me to be prepared for that when I do go in..." Her eyes shone with tears, and she brushed a hand across her face. At just that moment I saw the people nearest to us look up, and I turned to look where they were looking. It was a doctor, with a laminated badge clipped to his white coat.

"Mrs. Kramer?" he called.

Sheila reached for my hand and squeezed it. "I'm Mrs. Kramer." she said. The doctor took a moment to speak to a couple who began imploring him for news, then came over to where we were sitting and pulled up a chair. The people next to us turned discreetly away.

"Mrs. Kramer," the doctor said, and looked at me before he went on. Sheila told him we were together. The doctor nodded and said, "Your son is in serious condition, but he's stable. He's had a heart attack. It's unusual for an attack like this to come with no prior warning..."

Sheila said, "There's a family history...."

Tom had never mentioned this. His grandfather? An uncle? I knew that Sheila's husband Mike had died of cancer, when Tom was about the age of the nephew who, until this moment, I had completely forgotten about.

"I see," the doctor said. He then went on to talk about the first forty-eight hours and the latest available treatments. He used the phrase "a good chance," and I saw on Sheila's face the same hope that took hold of me.

Sheila had told me that Tom's sister was on her way, and as the doctor got up I thought I should go, too. I had never met Maura, and didn't want her to think I was usurping her role as Sheila's daughter. Just then Sheila, who in the few months I had known her had proved to be an utterly truthful lady, spoke.

"Doctor," she said, "Nell has to leave. Could she see her brother before she goes?"

We went in together, as soundless as we could be. For my own part, my tiptoeing came from pure superstition—as long as none of the ill-health spirits could hear me, they wouldn't bother with Tom. Sheila had an arm pressed through mine, and I could feel her trembling.

Tom lay in a high hospital bed with the rails up. He was wearing a light blue johnny with a diamond design on it, and his skin was as pale as milk. Rather than look at his closed eyes and still figure, I looked at the various machines and monitors. Beside me I heard Sheila say something in the slightest of whispers. It sounded like "Tommy." We stood there for a minute or two, barely breathing, and then I heard the faint choking sound of Tom's mother fighting back her tears. I gave her arm a gentle squeeze and she looked at me and nodded. We turned together and went quietly out of the room.

I had thought that Sheila would break down as soon as we were back in the hall, but I had underestimated her. She felt in her purse for a packet of tissues and wiped her eyes, then said to me, "Maura will be here any minute. If she sees me crying it will upset her."

"You'll call me?" I said. "Any time. Anything I can possibly do..."

"Of course, Nell," she said. And added, "I'm so glad you were there to call."

The rain had stopped but it was still a damp, darkening evening, filled with city smells, not all of them pleasant. I breathed in the wet air as if it were pure oxygen. There is nothing that quite compares to leaving a hospital under your own power, knowing as the doors close behind you that within are people whose lives are coming to a close.

"Not Tom," I said. And then feeling that I might have sounded peremptory in addressing the spinners of fate, I added, "Please. Not Tom, please."

The heat had been turned on in the subway cars and I endured a long, slow ride home, sweating inside my soggy raincoat, being pressed against by tired and irritable fellow riders. On the short walk from my stop to my apartment, I felt again the strong sensation of being alive and blessed with good health. I looked up at my front windows, expecting to see my cat, but he wasn't in his usual spot. I hurried up the stairs and let myself in. Woody wasn't at the door to greet me.

"Woody?" I called, filled with the dread that this awful day had spawned. Just then I heard the scratching sound that my cat makes when he is cleaning his paw on the edge of the litter box. He flew out of the hall, and began wrapping himself around my legs. I heard myself say, absurdly, "Where WERE you?" The reaction to Sheila's call and the sight of Tom unconscious had finally set in. I was trembling and near tears. I reached down to touch Woody's head, and he arched his neck and purred.

"Treats for you," I told him. "A shower and hot tea for me. We'll have the tea that Martha sent us."

At the thought of Martha, I felt a longing to hear her voice, to know that she was all right. I looked at the phone but decided to wait until morning before calling her. There was nothing she could do, and perhaps in the morning there would be better news.

Fifteen minutes later I was on my couch in a terrycloth robe, drinking tea and petting Woody. I knew I wouldn't be able to sleep and that the only possible distraction would be a beloved book. Woody lifted his head to watch as I went to my bookcase and returned with the Oxford edition of the *Odyssey*. Homer was the only possible choice for me, but in my unquiet state I chose to wander the seas with the Ithacan rather than to suffer the fury and bloodletting of the *Iliad*. I was a scholar once and still take pleasure in working out a translation puzzle. When the answer finally comes to me, I am elated—I feel that I have performed a magic trick with language, and will own forever my small victory. But tonight I just wanted to read for the flow of the story and the poetry. If I missed a word here and there, I'd look it up another time.

Woody settled back against me and I turned to the story of Odysseus's arrival in Phaeacia. My mental vision was still seeing Tom in the hospital bed, and I wanted to replace it at least temporarily with Homer's charming picture of the princess Nausicaa sweetly asleep as the dawn approaches. I followed the girls' journey to the washing pools, their splashing and picnicking and spirited play, right up to Nausicaa's discovery of the grimy, naked Odysseus asleep in the bushes. What a lot of explaining he would have to do in today's social climate.

It was working. My eyes moved over the accented characters and the story they told came alive for me. I finished Book 6 and read on into Book 7, Odysseus's arrival at the palace. Then, without warning, the millennia-old writing hustled me back into the present:

*peisetai hassa hoi aisa kata klothes te bareiai*
*gignomenoi nesanto linoi, hote min teke meter*
...He shall suffer whatever destiny and the harsh Fates
Spun from their thread at the beginning, when his mother bore him.

So there it was. A man of forty-eight, with a family and friends who loved him, the best hospital and the latest techniques...but according to Homer, it had all been decided the day Sheila gave birth to her son. If Atropos was standing there in Tom's room, with her own version of surgical scissors, there was nothing anyone in this world could do.

I flung my book down with none of the reverence I usually show toward

Homer and went to the phone. Patient Information told me that Tom's condition was critical. I asked if he was conscious and got a reply that suggested I had just asked for important state secrets to be faxed to me at once. I meekly apologized—the same person might answer next time—and hung up the phone. Right next to the phone was my small desk clock, and I was surprised by the amount of time that had passed while I wandered in Alcinuous's city.

"Look at the time, Woody," I said, and he responded with his python yawn. I picked him up and carried him into the hall, where he settled into his basket and immediately resumed his untroubled sleep.

# CHAPTER SIX

I WOKE UP EARLY AND HUNGRY, to the sound of rain. It took me a moment to remember why I had skipped dinner the night before. At once I had a surge of guilt—I should have thought of Tom and his family first thing. I checked the phone machine and saw there were no messages. If I pressed the right button I could have this information confirmed by a mechanical voice that would sound a little disappointed at my lack of popularity. I put on some coffee and looked in the refrigerator and cabinets for something to eat. A survivalist I'm not—if there were a catastrophe requiring me to be barricaded in my home for weeks, I would soon be joining Woody in assorted flavors of Iams. There was some oatmeal, and a carton of vanilla yogurt that had only expired yesterday. I was set.

As the oatmeal heated in the microwave I read the text on the box. It directed the consumer to add more water for thinner oatmeal, and less water for thicker oatmeal. I would think that pretty funny, but for the fact that there have probably been mental-distress lawsuits resulting from someone's being forced to contemplate runny cereal.

By the time I finished my cereal, yogurt and coffee, it was 7:30. I needed to call Martha, and Sheila, but it was much too early. It would be OK to call the hospital, though. Chances are this was the time when most friends and family wanted to be sure that someone they loved was still among the living. Breathing the upper air, Homer calls it. It was a lot less complicated then—either your lungs could do the work or they couldn't. Now we have

26

machines that can keep a once vital person in a state of almost-life for months or even years.

This morning Patient Information was manned by a fellow with a deep voice who asked, "How are you today, ma'am?" His friendliness made me sure he would be the bearer of good news, but he had the same ugly word for me as his counterpart had had. Critical. I thanked him and hung up. Woody was standing on me, peering at the phone. He's sociable, and several of my callers like to greet him after they've spent a few minutes talking to me. I scratched Woody's head and he pressed against me as I listened to the rain striking the windows.

Just then, a boom of wind struck, and the power went out. For a moment I felt as if I were in pitch darkness but then my eyes adjusted to the gray morning light and I could see the shapes of my furniture and books. I had a moment of panic thinking of the hospital and its machines, then realized that of course they would have all the equipment necessary to generate electricity. It wouldn't do to have some potentate all ready for surgery only to have the surgeon wandering around feeling for his scalpel. It wouldn't do for those monitors to stop working for my friend Tom.

Woody had gotten down when the power failed. I could see his shape over near the window, looking for some light. "Well, Woody," I said, "I guess Nature has just suggested that I slow down for a while. No lights, no answering machine, no computer. The only thing I can think of is to light the stove with a match and make some hot chocolate. Then we'll go back to bed and read, if I can find where I put the candles."

While the water was coming to a boil I looked out the window to get some idea of how localized the power outage was. I could see that the traffic lights were out for several blocks, the light holders swinging uselessly in the wet wind. As I watched, a police car pulled up to the intersection nearest me and an officer in a black slicker got out to direct traffic. I was glad that from my bedroom I wouldn't be able to see the blue light pulsing on top of the car. A siren sounded, but no other emergency vehicle came into view. Some stranger's trouble, on this rainy day at the end of October.

I made hot chocolate, cooling it with a little milk from the dark refrigerator. My candles were behind the cans of Progresso soup—a logical association, actually. Lack of electricity means no microwave, few food choices except canned soup, and therefore a good place to put the candles. I shone a flashlight over my bookcases and selected an anthology of short stories from several decades ago. I haven't been able to develop much appreciation for the modern prize-stories, in which it seems that everyone's got a parole officer and the speech patterns of a dull fourteen-year-old. I get quite enough of that at work, and prefer to read about less gritty lives.

Carrying my candle, cup and book, I went back into my bedroom. The candle made an unsteady reading light but the silence of my building more than compensated for that small inconvenience. No Saturday cartoons or morning talk shows from the neighboring apartments. I let Woody get settled where he couldn't tip my cup or jiggle the candle, then I browsed in my book until a story caught my attention. At 8:10 the power was restored, and I felt just a touch of disappointment as all my gadgets hummed themselves back into life.

I was rinsing out my cup and breakfast dishes when the answering machine picked up and my voice came on, announcing my phone number. Thinking of Tom, I was about to break my rule of never lifting the receiver until I knew who was calling. I had my hand on the receiver when a stranger's voice said, "Mrs. Benson-Fells? This is Jerry Nolan. Sammy's Dad..."

There was silence then, and I thought that Jerry had realized his mistake. But then I heard a mechanical dialing sequence, followed by more from Jerry.

"Fran? I called that number you gave me but it doesn't sound like Lansing's Mom. I think we're on somebody's answering machine. Look up the number for me again, will you?"

This was a new low. People I didn't know were having a teleconference on my answering machine. I turned the volume all the way down until they finished sorting it out.

"Woody," I said as I rinsed our few dishes, " there just has to be a way we can sign up for the first colony on Mars."

I waited another hour before calling Martha. She's an early riser but I was familiar with her quiet habit of beginning her day in a chair near the window, quilting or sewing by natural light while she drank her second cup of coffee. It was probably too dark a day for that, and I admitted to myself that my hesitation about calling probably had a lot to do with the fact that I was the bearer of heavy news. Martha liked Tom a lot. When Tom and I had visited her in Manomet, it was clear how happy she was for me, how much she hoped Tom and I might have found something lasting.

I dialed her number, and the phone rang a half dozen times before she answered. On the phone Martha always sounds a little breathless and uncertain. It used to worry me until I realized that for a person born four years after the First World War, a phone call means serious, possibly unwelcome, news.

"Martha," I said, "it's Nell."

"Oh!" she said, sounding flatteringly pleased. Then, "Is everything all right?"

"Oh, sure," I said. "We're fine. Woody's right here—the power was out so he's a little nervous..." I paused and swallowed. "Martha, Tom's in the hospital. He's had a heart attack."

At the other end of the line Martha drew in her breath. When she spoke a moment later her voice was tense but without any note of panic. "Tell me, Nell," she said.

I told her as much as I knew, which was very little. I stayed away from the word "critical" and did not describe how Tom had looked lying white-faced in a hospital bed in Intensive Care. "I'll be talking to his mother later," I said, "and then I'll go see him if I can...I'll call you as soon as I have any more news."

I could feel how intensely Martha was listening, and wished we were together so I could share a hug with her and feel a little of the strength she's possessed as long as I've known her. She said, "I'm sure he'll be all right, dear. He's so young. You just take care of yourself and let me know if there's anything I can do."

"Thanks, Martha " I said. "I always feel better after I've talked to you."

I hung up the phone and sat for a moment listening to the on-and-off spatters of rain. I realized that I had completely forgotten to mention anything about Lucas.

There was no answer at Sheila's number, which made me pretty sure she wasn't home. Most people with a close family member in the hospital will answer the phone on the first ring. I had mentioned to Martha that I might try to visit Tom, but now I thought better of it. It was Saturday, and his large family would be sure to be at the hospital taking turns going into his room for brief visits. The last thing they needed right now was someone they didn't know hanging around making everybody feel awkward. For a moment I was filled with self-pity, thinking of the brothers and sisters and nieces and nephews that I didn't have. Then I thought, what nonsense. You're healthy, barely middle-aged, and have a career that will never put you to sleep. You have Martha and Woody, and a part of Ned turning up just when you need it. You have Tom.

I refused to let myself think otherwise.

I felt restless after talking to Martha, wishing I had thought to invite myself down to Manomet for the day, to see my friend in person. We could have gone to the glass museum in Sandwich, or to Heritage Plantation. We could have had a delicious seafood lunch at the Daniel Webster Inn, a place so popular with retired seniors that I always feel like the youngest person there. Most important, I could have had Martha's comfort and counsel. She is my Nestor, the one person to whom my stubborn heart will always listen.

It was still raining hard, with an occasional burst that would sound like gravel hitting tin. I tried to read but couldn't concentrate on anything, whether serious or light. Woody grew tired of my getting up and down so much and went off to sleep on my bed, where I could see him arched in bliss, his toes spread. My apartment, except for some mail clutter, was still pretty clean from a week ago. I thought back to that bright Saturday, and realized that today's mail had probably been delivered. Saturday was notorious for supermarket flyers offering family specials, but sometimes there would be a card from a friend who either doesn't have or doesn't like email. I got up and checked the phone machine again to make sure the volume was turned up, then located my keys and headed down to my box.

The usual junk was there, folded together with a card showing a missing child last seen with a non-custodial parent. I hoped that Mr. Williams, whose first name I could not recall, was aware what serious criminal trouble he would be in if he ever considered taking Katie without permission. It's an unbalanced world we live in, with kids that nobody wants and other kids being fought over like trophies. There were two white envelopes for me. One looked like an appeal for money, hand-addressed by some hopeful working at home. The other was from Lucas.

I studied the address of the school, and the boy's awkward handwriting of my name and address. Carefully I separated the junk mail, including the other white envelope, so that Lucas's letter was on top and could not somehow be lost before I could read it. Once I was back inside my apartment I dropped the rest of the mail on my table and read the short letter while standing at my counter.

> *Hi.*
> *I got your letter and you can come see me if you want to. We mostly have visitors on Saturday and Sunday unless its Awards Day or something. You can come this weekend if you want to. Its from 11 to 5 so that parents can take you to lunch. I don't know if you want to come this weekend, so I'll give you my email.*
> *Bye for now.*
> *Luke*

Under the name he apparently preferred to be known by, my nephew had printed his email address. For Internet purposes he was known as Looper. Automatically, I found myself trying to come up with the Latin equivalent. Orbis? From the strange library shelves of my mind it came to me that "orbus" was an orphan.

I smoothed the letter, which was typed, and read it again. If possible it was even more guarded in tone than my own had been. The Prentice genes at work. I also noted with amusement that the boy seemed interested in lunch, another sign that we were related. Of course it was entirely possible that he just wanted to get his maiden aunt in her orthopedic shoes away from the curious stares of his friends. I looked at the clock above my counter. It was a little after eleven—I needed to make plans if I were going to drive to Ashfield tomorrow. I began drafting a reply on the back of the other white envelope and was concentrating hard enough so that I jumped when the phone answering machine began announcing.

"Nell," I heard, "it's Sheila..." I lunged for the phone.

"Sheila!" I said, "How are you? How's..."

"He's better," she said, and I felt myself actually go weak. "I mean," she went on, "he's still in very serious condition but he's awake and the doctor said we can see him if we make sure not to get him excited."

"Sheila, that's so wonderful," I said. My voice wasn't quite steady, and Woody came to press against me as if sensing my emotions. I couldn't reach down to touch him but I met his gaze and mouthed: *Tom. Better.* To Sheila I said, "Who's there with you?"

"The whole gang," she said. "Maura and two of her kids. Patrick and Frannie. And some of Tom's friends from the police station."

I felt a slightly guilty relief. There was no need for me to go to the hospital. Tom couldn't possibly take a turn for the worse with all those people pulling for him.

"Sheila," I said, "this is the best news. I'm so glad you called me. Would it be all right if I waited a little before I go to see Tom? Of course if you want me to come now..."

"Nell, thank you. You just stay put and relax. Once this mob is gone, you and Tom can have a quiet visit together."

"Okay," I said. "I'll call you. And I'll check my phone messages. Tomorrow... I think I might be going for a drive."

# CHAPTER SEVEN

ENERGIZED BY THE GOOD NEWS ABOUT Tom, I returned to the task of writing to my nephew. When I was satisfied with my opus, I turned on my computer and slowly typed Luke's address into the "To" box. An encouraging underlining appeared. I tabbed down to the subject line and typed Visit, followed by:

*Dear Luke,*
*I'd love to come visit you on Sunday. I'll leave about 9 so I can be at your school before noon. We can go to lunch anywhere you want.*
*Nell Prentice*

I read my composition twice and hit Send. As soon as I had done so, I realized that I should have specified that lunch was on me. When I was fifteen, my finances would not have run to buying a large Coke for a visiting adult. I considered doing a follow-up email, then decided that was unnecessary and maybe even silly. A small child once drew the fine distinction for me between silly, which apparently meant annoying but cute, and very silly, which meant enough already. I was definitely edging toward the latter.

The next thing was to call Martha. She cried a little at the news about Tom, which I understood completely. I thought again about making the drive to visit with her, but I wouldn't be able to spend the night. One of the best parts of visiting Martha was always sleeping under one of her quilts and getting up the next morning to have coffee and breakfast with her, with Woody underfoot and showing clear favoritism towards Martha. I can't fault his taste. But even if I couldn't see her in person, I could share my other news.

"Martha," I said, "do you remember my mentioning my brother Ned?"

Martha listened quietly while I told her about Luke. She seemed to find nothing odd in my nervousness about meeting the boy. She didn't say that this was an absolutely wonderful thing that would change my life. She just listened, and at the end of our conversation she gave me a bit of good, practical advice.

"You may want to bring him some food, dear," she said. "Boys that age are always hungry."

So now I had a mission. I could make a trip to the supermarket and sweep all kinds of interesting items into my cart, in place of the usual bread, cheese, yogurt, Lean Cuisine, and cat food that I could by now pick off the shelves in my sleep. While I was out, I could also look for a book for Tom, to keep him quiet while he recuperated. And maybe some nice gourmet food gift that Sheila could share with her family. Even better— I'd skip the supermarket altogether and start with the gourmet place at the mall. They must have that peanut butter with no additives that costs as much as steak. I pulled my rain jacket from its hook and got my purse. Woody looked disappointed that I was going out, and I had to promise that there would be some kind of treat for him, too. I hoped my credit card was up to all this spirit of giving.

I headed away from the city. In spite of the chilly rain, more than three million people were in Boston celebrating the first Red Sox World Series win since 1918. The mall might not be a pretty sight, either, but I needed to be doing something other than pacing my apartment, unable to concentrate on anything for more than fifty-nine seconds. Water splashed from the potholes as I joined the slow westbound traffic, headed for someplace to get and spend.

My sojourn at the mall was in fact not so bad. Everybody else must be watching the duck boats carry their heroes down the Charles. I came in through the Food Court entrance and saw a scattering of people sitting in the little locked chairs or waiting in line for cinnamon buns or tacos. The bookstore was not crowded and I was pleased to find right away just the book for Tom—a paperback re-issue of *On the Loose*, with its wonderful photographs and often wry text. I wanted Tom to feel as young as these two adventuresome brothers had been, ready to see the natural world close up, opening like a flower. I spent a few minutes looking at the get-well cards but the only choices for men seemed to be bronzed world maps or buxom cartoon nurses. I'd just write him a note that I could tuck inside the book.

Next I located a store that carried all sorts of gourmet foods for the survivalist on an unlimited budget. I walked up and down the aisles, spotting a present for Sheila as quickly as I had found something for her son. It was a cherry shortbread with walnuts, in a handsome tin that showed foreign soldiers guarding a palace. I put the cake into the basket I was carrying and then got to work picking out student snacks. Cheese crackers, chocolate cookies, colorful juices, even a few envelopes of soup that could be transformed into a tasty meal with the addition of hot water. There were some exotic flavors, game and shrimp and escarole, but I played it safe with two packets each of chicken noodle and chicken rice. In the last aisle before the dairy items I found the pet snacks and got Woody three crunchy mouse cookies which would leave crumbs everywhere, but who cared?

I paid for my loot and was given a large shopping bag with handles to tote it all back to my car. Just in time, too. The afternoon movies were starting, and I preferred to be out of the milling crowds before I had to think too much about how I'd like to be at the movies with Tom, instead of buying him a book to read in his hospital bed. The rain had stopped and there was even a patch of blue sky off to my left. I located my car and loaded up the hatch with my packages and was most of the way home when I realized that I hadn't done my own grocery shopping. Oh, well, there was still that Progresso soup on the candle shelf, and maybe the mouse cookies would do as croutons.

With the sun returning the day looked more like the end of summer than a month into Fall. I went through the mnemonic devices as I do twice a year and figured that at two o'clock tomorrow morning it would become only one o'clock so I needed to set my clocks back one hour or risk being early at Luke's school and starting off on the wrong foot. I didn't even take a moment to de-mix my metaphor because it occurred to me that I should set the car clock back so I wouldn't be confused as I set out on my journey. I played with various tiny controls until a truck horn blew a huge blast to remind me that there was supposed to be some connection between my eyes and the road when I was driving.

*Ellen Catherine Prentice, 42. Leaves a nephew, Lucas Prentice. Contributions may be made to the Animal Rescue League of Boston...*

The accompanying short obituary would comment on the poignancy of the fact that I had been just about to make the acquaintance of my orphaned teenage nephew when the tragedy occurred.

Sobered by my Dickensian vision of Equinox Future, I spent the rest of my drive practicing every good road habit I could think of. I left space between me and the car ahead of me, used my directionals, and stayed below the speed limit. Since nobody else was doing any of those things, I was probably putting myself in more danger than if I were driving with a blindfold on, but somehow I made it home, double-parked while I ran upstairs with my purchases, moved the car, and nearly fell into my apartment with relief at being home.

After I called the hospital (condition listed as serious—wonderful word!) I tried Martha. There was no answer, and I wondered how she was spending this Saturday afternoon. She is almost exactly twice my age, but guess which one of us has the fuller social life. Martha's great gift is that she makes whoever is with her feel like her favorite person. For that reason she is always being asked places, and is not at my beck and call whenever I might want her.

While Woody chewed on his cat treats (they were all-natural, and so crunchy it sounded as if my cat was eating a starfish) I checked the larder to see what might do for my own dinner. There was a box of rice pilaf, which should do nicely in combination with some soup. I boiled some water with the liquid from the soup and added the rice, and for the next twenty minutes enjoyed the aroma of my dinner cooking. When there was just a skim of water left on top of the rice I added the rest of the soup, covered the pan, and gave it five more minutes. The resulting concoction was delicious—I hadn't missed a thing by not visiting the Food Court.

After dinner, I was sure I would be able to settle in with something to occupy my mind. The news about Tom had soothed my restlessness, and the hectic atmosphere of the mall had given me an appreciation of the quiet space of home. Woody followed me into the living room and sat back to wait until I collected my reading and writing materials and was ready to invite him to join me.

I had been working on and off on a translation of *Iliad* 18, in which Homer magnificently describes the forging of the arms of Achilles. I had left off at a somewhat sticky passage that told of a public quarrel over a *poine*—a blood-price. The general idea seemed to be to convince the relatives of a murder victim to accept a sum of money as compensation for their loss. In modern terms I guess the *poine* might be translated as "policy limits". The Greek was somewhat elliptic, and I finally reached the point of "good enough" and moved on to the city at war, complete with golden gods and goddesses. Time had shifted for me. With nothing more than a copy of the same book Alexander had carried on his campaigns, I was overlooking a fierce battleground, watching the bronze spears fly and hearing the murderous din.

Woody's jumping down was what woke me. In the midst of a Bronze Age melee, I had drifted quietly off to sleep.

# CHAPTER EIGHT

ON SUNDAY MY NEIGHBORHOOD IS QUIET, and I often take advantage of the chance to stay in bed a little longer, reading and drinking coffee. On this particular Sunday I woke with a panicked feeling, seeing sunlight further across the room than it should be. I looked at the clock and saw that it was close to eight. I had to be on the road by nine. Up I jumped, pushing the button to start the coffeemaker as I made for the shower. Woody watched me, not looking too happy with this change in routine. Where was his breakfast, and his quality time in the crook of my arm while I had coffee? I was in too much of a hurry to explain, but took a moment to pat his head as he settled on the bathroom scale to wait while I showered. When I came out the coffee was ready and I filled a mug, intending to sip from it as I dressed and had a quick breakfast and got ready to leave on my journey. I walked to the window to have a look at the day, and that's when I remembered. The time change. I hadn't reset the clocks. I had nearly two hours before I had to leave.

"Woody," I said, "it seems we have just been handed an hour." I remembered a morning years ago in Newton, when I was home with a stomach bug and Martha made steamed custard for me. She told me I should try to have a nice nap while the custard cooked, adding that it did best if it took its time. Words I would live by if only this rushing world would let me. I put my mug down long enough to feed Woody and towel my hair, then headed back to bed, closely followed by my cat.

A little after eight (the real eight) I got up and picked out some clothes,

36

aiming for a ladylike but not dowdy effect. Usually I don't care whether people like my style of dress or not, but I knew how important it is to a fifteen-year-old that adults not be any more of an embarrassment than they have to. Probably the worst for kids is when the older generation dresses and acts like the kids themselves. I once read about a juvenile court judge who had his robes made up in denim, so the kids would relate better to him. Maybe it worked, but I strongly suspect that more than one young offender had to be carried from the courtroom, howling with derisive mirth.

I gathered up the presents and set them outside in the hall. Before leaving, I called the hospital. Thomas Kramer's condition was listed as serious. I let out the breath I had been holding, thanked the person who had looked up the information, and picked up my purse and jacket. It was time to get going.

There were a lot of people out and about, at quarter of nine on a Sunday morning, and I wondered whether some of them had goofed as I had over the time change. The presents for my nephew went on the floor of the back seat, my purse and jacket beside me, and I was ready. I pulled out of my parking space and settled in for the drive to Ashfield.

A few years before Luke was born, I was at college in western Massachusetts. I met Michael there. During the twelve years we were together we revisited that part of the state at least once a year, usually to see a live production of Shakespeare. That subject—performances of Shakespeare—had come up a few months ago in a most unlikely context. Someone had tried to kill me. The man who abducted me had nothing to lose by taking my life, and a great deal to lose if I lived to tell what I knew. When it was over, the first person I called from the police station was Tom. He came to get me, brought me home, and took care of the things I was incapable at the time of doing. Afterwards, he liked to joke with me that in a nearly unconscious state I had extracted a promise from him to go with me to see Shakespeare.

I thought now of Tom in the hospital and of the uncertain future, and dealt with those thoughts the way a kid younger than Luke might.

"You promised, Tom," I said in the quiet of my car. "You promised."

On a long drive I seldom want or need the diversions that some drivers can't do without. I put the radio on just long enough to find out which route out of the city was the less stalled. ("Some problems," said the jaunty traffic reporter. " A few trouble spots." "A multiple-car accident just being cleared away.") I don't have a cassette or CD player, so audio books are out, and I can't court death-by-distracted-driving by talking on a cell phone because I don't own one. The miles pass easily for me, always with something to occupy my thoughts. It's never much of substance, just a mental puzzle to pass the time. Once I spent a quarter-hour trying to recall whether the ebb and flow in "Dover Beach" was turbid or turgid. Another time I tried to come up with the names of the Freedom Seven astronauts, in the order of their flights.

Today, though, I was unable to think light, insubstantial thoughts. My small circle of close friends rode with me in the car, their troubles mine and their absence bringing an ache to my heart. Tom, Sheila, Martha—each of them someone I couldn't do without. And then there was Luke, my only living relative. I forced myself not to dream up a picture of the sort of boy I wanted him to be. He was whoever he was, and I only hoped that he would not have a mental picture of me that would lead to disappointment.

I had reached the turnpike, running straight through the city and then through the western suburbs until it becomes a wide, impersonal stretch of lanes that could be anywhere. The road was supposed to be paid for decades ago but it never happened, and I had stocked up on change for the tolls. There was not a lot of traffic, and no one around me was using his car as a deadly weapon. In Massachusetts, that state of affairs is Highway Heaven.

Once I was clear of Boston, the mesmerizing effect set in, and miles passed without much going on in my head beyond a pleasant hum and an occasional wisp of song. There was still plenty of leaf color, and I knew there would be even more two hours west of where I now was. Clouds covered half of the sky, and when the sun would reappear from behind them, the leaves would turn to golden fire. I felt energized by the cool Fall day, and more excited than apprehensive about meeting my nephew.

It was eleven thirty when I saw the road sign announcing that I was entering Ashfield. Less than a mile later, a smaller sign pointed me in the direction of the school. I turned up a long driveway with curves and slopes that must be murder in the winter. The speed limit was ten miles per hour, but I drove even slower than that, aware that this was a place full of young boys who might run out into the road without looking.

The road widened at the top of the last small hill, and I got my first look at the school. Straight ahead of me was a brick building with columns and wide front steps. Spread out behind it and off to both sides were smaller buildings that must be classrooms and dormitories. I turned into the visitor parking lot and tucked my car into a space between a Volvo and a Lexus. A tall couple walking toward the brick building turned at the sound of my car door, and both of them smiled at me. The woman was more casually dressed than I was, and looked exactly right. They waited for me to catch up with them, and we introduced ourselves and shook hands. We were halfway up the steps of the administration building when I remembered the packages in my car.

"I have to go back to my car," I explained to the Andersons (Bob and Libby). " I forgot my packages."

Libby Anderson gave me a warm smile and patted my arm. "We do spoil our boys, don't we?" she said. "But who else will if their mothers don't?"

After that, I was relieved that I had to go back to my car. Libby Anderson seemed like a nice woman and I would not have wanted her to be embarrassed at her mistake if she overheard me explaining myself at the reception desk. I waited a few minutes next to the car, then walked slowly back to the building where Luke would be waiting for me.

Inside, the building reminded me of those homey convalescent hospitals in English films. I half expected to see Sister passing by in her starched uniform, on her way to make tea for the pale but recuperating patients. The walls were dark, hung with portraits and awards, and the furniture looked worn but substantial. A woman of about my own age looked up from behind an oak desk and smiled at me. "May I help you?" she said.

"My name is Nell Prentice," I said, a little too nervous to return the smile. "I'm here to see my nephew."

"Oh, yes," she said, still smiling. "Lucas. A lovely boy."

I guessed that she very seldom told relatives that their boy was anything other than a lovely boy. I recognized my own edginess, and put it down to the butterflies suddenly flitting about in my stomach. The woman said, "Lucas is in Doctor Butler's office. Doctor Butler would like to see you for a moment before you meet your nephew."

For a moment I wondered if the boy was ill, then I remembered that in academia everybody is Doctor this or that. I said to the woman, "Fine. Of course. Could you let... Lucas... know I'm here? I'm taking him to lunch and I don't want him to think I was late."

"I'll tell him," the woman said. "Let me call Doctor Butler."

She made her call, and a moment later the door to the inner office opened and the good doctor himself appeared. "Ms. Prentice," he said, crossing the room and shaking my hand. "A pleasure to meet you. I'm Doctor Butler."

Well, I wave guns at people and put them in jail. So there. No sooner had this uncharitable thought come to me than I had a second, less mean-spirited thought. Maybe this guy wasn't just being pretentious. Maybe he had a first name that he didn't want the boys getting hold of. Not that it would make any difference. I know a few things about teenagers and was sure that the kids had already done something suitably disrespectful with Butler. The Doctor was round-faced, with dimples and balding curls, and was wearing a brown suit. He would have borne an unfortunate resemblance to Friar Tuck were it not for the red and brown argyle sweater showing under the jacket.

"I understand you're Lucas's aunt," he said. "A fine boy."

I guessed it was not a guy-thing to refer to a teenaged boy as lovely. I said,

"I'm actually meeting my nephew for the first time. His... lawyer... tells me that Luke's mother recently died."

The smile went, and with it the dimples. "Yes," Doctor Butler said. "Very sad. At such an age."

I couldn't tell whether he was referring to Luke's age, or that of the boy's mother. I said, "How is Luke doing?"

Doctor Butler took a moment to consider my question, then said, "We're having him see the school counselor. That's standard, even when the boy seems to be adapting well, as Lucas does. And he has a tutor to help with the schoolwork he missed. We are also...hopeful...that getting to know his aunt will be a positive thing for him."

He was silent then, perhaps wondering whether he might have insulted me. I picked up the bag I had set down to shake hands, and let him off the hook.

"Only one way to find out," I said. "Will you take me to him?"

# CHAPTER NINE

DOCTOR BUTLER CROSSED THE ROOM TO the door he had come out of, gave it a tap, and then opened it. "Lucas," he said. "Your aunt is here." He beckoned me into the room, and the boy sitting in a chair across from the desk turned towards us and stood.

In Homer, anyone meeting a son of someone he knows always has the same general reaction. *His father to the life! You have his look, his build, his fine brow and clustering curls.* And so on. Maybe the bard had prepared me for the sight of my brother at fifteen, and thereby set me up for a twinge of disappointment. The teenaged boy who was regarding me looked nothing like Ned. At this age Ned had been pudgy, with a shy, reserved disposition. This boy was slender and had a look of being at home in the world. He had dark curly hair (Ned's had been fair and straight) and skin of a beautiful golden shade.

Doctor Butler and I spoke at the same time. He said, "Lucas..." and I said, "I'm..." Doctor Butler nodded in deference for me to go first and I took a breath and started over. "Hi! I'm Nell Prentice."

The boy looked back at me and I saw with a start that his eyes were brown, with an agate-splash of gray. Not Ned's eye color. Mine.

"I'm Luke Prentice," he said, and put out a hand for me to shake.

Of the three of us in the room, I seemed to be the only one who was a little nervous. Doctor Butler was beaming at us, his dimples on full display, seeming as pleased as if he had personally reunited Luke and me. Luke was looking ...what? Interested, expectant maybe, but not at all ill at ease. Doctor Butler, whom I was liking better by the minute, came to my aid. Turning to Luke, he said, "Lucas, why don't you show your aunt your room? Remember to sign out before you leave for lunch."

Lunch! That was the ticket. I gave Doctor Butler a big smile to let him know he had said the magic word. Luke started toward the door.

"It's this way," he said to me. I was about to follow him out of the room when he stood to one side. I realized he had been taught to let ladies precede him.

"Oh," I said, like an idiot. "OK. Thanks..." And out we went.

Once we were out in the corridor, Luke fell into step beside me, walking with that slight lope of an adolescent who is still getting used to his growth. He was wearing chinos, a white polo shirt, and moccasins. We left the building by a side entrance and walked along a stone path to a two-story building with a few steps leading up to it. At the top of the steps Luke held the door for me and I said, "Thank you," again. We had had no other conversation.

Inside the building was a kind of common area, with sofas and chairs that had seen hard service. A boy with thick glasses and black, longish hair sat at a small desk with some kind of sign-out sheet. My nephew spoke for the first time since we had left the administration building, but not to me.

"Benzedrine!" he said. The black-haired boy looked up from the book he was reading and said, "Hey, Loops." Just then a woman came around a corner and said, "Benjamin..." then saw me and smiled. I was about to introduce myself when she turned to Luke.

"Lucas," she said, "I'd like to meet your guest." Her tone was friendly and encouraging, but my nephew ducked his head and for a moment I saw the child, so young, under the self-contained exterior.

"Sorry, Mrs. Hansen," he said, and I heard the other boy make some smirky sound which we all ignored. Luke said, "Mrs. Hansen, this is my Aunt Nell." He paused for a moment and then said, "...Aunt Nell, this is Mrs. Hansen, our housemother."

Mrs. Hansen gave my nephew an approving look. She was a stocky woman with light brown hair and an air of being in charge. She said to me, "How nice to meet you, Ms... is it Prentice?"

"Yes," I said, "but Nell is fine." I thought I had better speak up before she started calling me Aunt Nell. Luke was looking stony, and I suspected that Benzedrine was taunting him in some way while the grownups made social talk. I said, "Luke is going to show me his room and then we're going out to lunch."

"Very nice!" said Mrs. Hansen. "Now don't let us keep you. Lucas, don't forget to sign out."

I was beginning to wonder if they called out the helicopters and search dogs whenever a kid forgot to scribble his name on the sheet presided over by Benjamin, whom I had already pegged as a teacher's pet who probably never had to be prompted to introduce his relatives. As Luke signed his name, I looked steadily at Benjamin to let him know I was onto him. Mrs. Hansen wished us a nice lunch, and we were free.

Luke's room, which was tiny, had matching pairs of beds, chairs, desks and computers, curtains in a green and silver stripe, a gray-green carpet, and boys' litter everywhere. I looked quickly away from a pair of dingy underpants that were hanging from a lamp. "Luke," I said, "which side is yours? I brought you a couple of things."

"Oh, thanks," he said, and pointed. "That one."

I crossed the room in a step and a half and slid the shopping bag under Luke's desk. Above it was a corkboard with several notes pinned to it, a ticket of some kind, and the photograph of Ned with the bow and arrow.

"So," I said, turning to the boy, "Which way to lunch?"

It was a short walk from the residence hall back to my car, but more than enough time for me to visualize said car through the eyes of a fifteen-year-old boy. I own, and have owned for quite a few years, a Volkswagen hatchback, light blue, free of any and all accessories. But I had to hand it to my nephew—if he was disappointed that he wasn't going to be riding in a red sports car he was too polite to show it. Maybe he was just relieved that Aunt Nell wasn't driving a Chevy Nova in tan and beige, with an afghan crocheted to fit the back window.

We got in the car, and Luke fastened his seatbelt without my having to mention it. If having a teenager was this easy I might just invest in a few more. We drove back the way I had come and along a road lined with pale trees. I was pretty sure they were birches. Martha would be able to tell me for sure, but they looked like the raw material for those toy Indian canoes sold along the Mohawk Trail. My parents used to take us for drives up this way, my father driving, my mother in a dress, and Ned and me wrangling for space in the back seat.

I wracked my brain for a topic of conversation. The presidential election was a few days away, but I didn't recall being very interested in politics at fifteen. I thought of the recent Olympics, which had taken place in Athens, one hundred and twelve years after their modern beginning.

"Did you watch the Games?" I asked my nephew. He looked at me enthusiastically, and I felt absurdly pleased. Maybe Aunt Nell was with it after all.

"Sure! They let us stay up for Game Four."

Game Four? Oh. The Red Sox. I scanned my memory banks for any information I might have absorbed about the recent World Series, but decided not to fake it.

"How about the Olympics?" I said. "Did you watch those, too?"

This time the boy's look was considerably more restrained. After a moment he said, "I liked the swimming."

"Do you swim?"

"Yeah, but not as good as Michael Phelps. I'm not as…long."

I laughed, and Luke said, "One of the other guys–his father was a swimmer, too. So he got to start out when he was real little."

I watched the road as I took this opening. "Do you remember *your* father?" I asked Luke. I didn't look at him, and he didn't look at me as he answered my question.

"I guess not," he said. "I was, like, three."

"So you were about three," I said, zipping my lip about the use of 'like' as a jarring bump in an otherwise simple declarative sentence. At least he hadn't used it as a verb of speaking. I asked, "Did your parents get divorced?"

Luke shrugged. "I don't think so. Mom just said he wasn't coming back. I mean later, when I asked her."

So much for not remembering. I hoped that Mom had thought to reassure her child that his father's leaving was not his fault. I took a quick look at Luke's profile—he must have been adorable at three. Before I could ask him anything further he said, "There's Kenny's."

Kenny's was a coffee shop/ice cream shop that was doing its best to look as if its patrons customarily arrived in a hay wagon for a treat of hot chocolate with real whipped cream. The front windows had ads made to look old-fashioned, and there was a striped canopy over the entrance. I was able to park on the street, after getting over my surprise that the area right in front of the restaurant wasn't a Tow Zone or Residents Only or Emergency Vehicles. I said to Luke as I put the car in Park, "Pretty lucky, getting a space right out front."

Luke unsnapped his seatbelt and reached for the door handle on his side. "People mostly go in the back," he said.

I had no reply to that, and we walked in silence into the restaurant. It was about three-quarters full and before we had taken ten steps I heard, "Mrs. Prentice." I could not have been more surprised to have my name called out in the middle of a remote jungle. I looked around and saw Bob and Libby Anderson in a red booth, with a blonde boy across from them. Luke trailed a bit as we went over to the booth and I was introduced to the Anderson's son,

Mason. Both Mason and Bob stood to shake hands with me, and Libby said, "We could get another chair..."

Oh, Lord. I said quickly, "Oh, thank you, Libby, but you're just about finished. We'll just grab a booth over there. Good meeting you, Mason!" I touched Luke's shoulder to steer him toward a booth that was unoccupied but had not yet been cleared. As Luke took one side of the booth and I took the other, I grinned and waved at the Andersons. See! Everything under control! A waitress came with menus, which she put down after clearing and wiping the table. I opened mine and scanned the hungry-student fare, all of which sounded pretty good. Should I set an example and have the Garden Salad? I saw that the waitress had returned and was waiting for our order. "Luke," I said, "what would you like?"

"A hot dog," he said, "with French fries and a root beer float."

I had never heard such a good idea in my life. I looked around quickly. The Andersons were at the cash register—Bob paying the check and Libby standing nearby with an arm around her son. I spoke to the waitress in a lowered voice, as if I were buying pornography.

"Make that two, please."

# CHAPTER TEN

AFTER THE WAITRESS LEFT, LUKE LOOKED out the window next to him as if yesterday's Red Sox parade was passing. He reminded me of Woody, except that Woody actually did find the smallest motion fascinating, while I suspected that Luke was intent on discouraging any further questions about his family. Woody had served me well in the past as an icebreaker and I decided to use him again.

"Do you like cats?" I asked Luke.

He looked away reluctantly from the pageant in the empty street. "I guess," he said, and then more politely, "Sure."

"That's what I have," I said. "A cat. His name is Woody." I paused for questions. There were none. "He's white," I said, with a hint of desperation. "He has a black tail and a mark on his side like a guitar pick."

"Cool," said Luke. That utterance was such a step up in our communication that I beamed at him, inanely I'm sure. A second later he asked me a question that hit me like an avalanche.

"Are you, like, married?"

For a moment I was unable to speak. Pain I had thought deeply buried surged up in me and I bit my lip. I positively would not cry in front of this teenaged kid. Luke was looking at me steadily, just when I would have loved for him to study the parked cars. I took a breath and said, "I was. I'm...a widow."

Luke blinked—in addition to everything else he had killer eyelashes. It was strange to see the same eyes that looked back at me from the bathroom mirror. "Was he in Iraq?"

"No," I said, wondering if to a boy a soldier's death would appear grand and glorious. "He died doing his job. The same job I have now, actually. He was a private investigator."

Saying the words, even in that bland, no-frills way, made my throat catch, and I felt my eyes begin to fill. Luke was regarding me with adolescent embarrassment instead of the admiration my offbeat career might have otherwise evoked. Poor kid. Father decamped, mother dead, and Aunt Nell fresh from group therapy to visit. The boy looked past my shoulder, and I realized the waitress was standing next to our table.

"Two dogs, two fries, and two root beer floats," she said, resting her tray on a small stand. "Will that be all?" she asked as she set the food in front of us.

"Oh, yes!" I said, as if bars of gold had been placed in front of Luke and me. "That's perfect."

When I was Luke's age, there were still chain department stores aimed at the almost-poor, who would shop for shoddily-made clothing, household goods, snacks such as caramel corn, and lunch counter specials. In the small city where I grew up it was Woolworth's. I realized that it was the Woolworth's look which this coffee shop was striving for. My plate was heavy and white, holding a curved hot dog in a steamed bun, a few dozen crinkle-cut French fries, and a bread-and-butter pickle, also crinkled. I couldn't believe I had ordered this meal. When I looked up from my plate, I saw that Luke was waiting for me to start before he tackled his own lunch. I picked up my hot-dog bun, which felt damp, and said to the boy, "This looks good!" He appeared relieved, and began to eat. I joined him, tasting nothing, but making as good a show of it as I could.

We didn't talk during our lunch, and it seemed a long time until the waitress came by again and picked up Luke's plate, empty except for the pickle and a squirt of ketchup. She turned to me and asked, "Shall I take that for you?" My plate looked pretty much as it had when she set it down, except for one bite out of the hot dog and a few French fries missing. For a moment I thought she might ask if everything had been all right. Had the hot dog not been medium-rare? Was the root beer from an indifferent year? I might have giggled most inappropriately had the waitress not said at that moment, "Some dessert?"

I looked at Luke with visiting-aunt enthusiasm. "What about it, Luke? Anything you want."

I could have sworn that the boy was humoring me, to avoid any repeat of my emotional display of a little while ago. He said, "Could I have a sundae?"

Yes, you certainly could. If I had to sell my car to pay for it, you could still order the biggest, gooiest sundae in the world. I said in my most mature voice, "Of course. Do you know how you want it?"

He did. The waitress took down his choices of ice cream flavors, toppings, whipped cream and walnuts and a cherry on top. At least 2000 calories which his boy's metabolism probably wouldn't even notice. I ordered coffee, and in no time at all Luke and I again had food and drink to concentrate on before we needed to try a conversation. I sipped my coffee and watched my nephew eat his sundae with a long silver spoon. There was only a bit of strawberry ice cream left (not my favorite flavor, either) when Luke said, "Aunt Nell, can I ask you something?"

I was still so unused to this form of address that I almost looked around to see who he was talking to. Then I said quickly, "Of course, Luke. What is it?"

"Well," he said, "do you think if...if somebody offs himself, then his kid might, too?"

His hazel eyes were lowered, as was his voice. It took a moment for what he had said to sink in. I closed my own eyes and prayed the non-believer's prayer that I wouldn't mess this up. First the power kick of having to say out loud that Michael was dead, and now the moment I had known would come—Ned's son asking about his father's death.

I reached for the check and made my voice bright and normal. I even smiled at the boy, whose golden skin was tinged with pink. "It's good that you could ask me that," I said. "Could we talk in the car?"

In my distraction I nearly followed a departing customer out the back exit, then saw that Luke was not behind me and remembered that I had parked in front. I gave Luke a rueful look—absentminded Aunt Nell!—and quickly canned it when I saw his serious, strained face. He looked as if he already regretted asking his question. We got into the car and I calculated how much time the drive back to the school would allow us for our talk. I said to Luke, "Is there a park or someplace where we could walk a little?" I did him the favor of not adding any tripe about needing to stretch my legs, or work off the 27 calories in my bite of hot dog. Luke said, "There's the falls, I guess."

"The falls," I said. "Is...are... they close?"

"You go back to the school," he told me, "then the other way. It's not very far."

We rode in complete silence back the way we had come. Luke had his window open, and the breeze blowing in smelled of coolness and decay, like the bottom of a leaf pile that has been left to molder. *From yon far country*, I thought. When I had been this child's age, I thought Housman was the only person who truly understood my sad, adolescent soul.

The falls turned out to be a half acre of bright trees, with a rocky little spillway that appeared to be man-made. There was a bench, and a stone set with a bronze plaque which I read in silence. The spot was dedicated to one Louis Catalano, class of 1960 at Ashfield. He had been a son and brother, and had died in Vietnam almost forty years ago.

Luke was standing near the bench, looking away from me and toward the hazy sky. With the time change, the angle of the sun was very low. I walked to the bench and sat down, feeling its chill through the thin skirt I had chosen as appropriate visiting-day attire. I said to Luke, "Want to sit here?" He turned to look at me, then dropped into a slouch at the other end of the bench. His eyes were on his shoes.

If Luke had been a client, or even just a grownup, I would have eased into the story, first finding out where he had gotten the idea he had, then choosing my words with studied care. But he was a boy, and his question had been a brave one. It deserved the truth.

"About seven years ago," I said, "I had to find your father. I hoped so much that he was OK but of course he wasn't —he had died a few years earlier." Here I paused, framing what I had to say. I wanted to touch Luke, but knew better. Finally I said, "You must have been so worried that if your father committed suicide, you might think the same way when life got bad. But Luke, he didn't. Can you remember exactly what your mother told you?"

"She said he killed himself with drugs."

I felt a stab of pain for him. All those years worrying because of an explanation he didn't understand.

"It's true," I said slowly, " that your father got into drugs." Even as I said it I wondered about Luke himself. I'd heard that drugs were easy to get in private schools. "But he didn't kill himself."

Now he looked at me, wariness in his expression, but a little hope, too. I would have traded in my earthly treasures not to have to tell him the rest. I had the remarkable sense that I was looking into my own, younger eyes.

"Your father," I said, "didn't commit suicide, but he didn't die a ...natural... death, either. He wasn't sick, or in an accident. He was killed."

I had given it my best shot, but I saw at once that Luke still didn't understand. I pride myself on my show-off vocabulary but there was no euphemism for what I was trying to tell him. Finally I added, "...by someone."

Luke looked away from me, but not before I saw him rub a fist across his ear. It was Ned's gesture, and it hit me like a blow. Luke could not have learned it by observation, in the short time he had known his father. It must have been in the Prentice half of his genes.

Luke was facing away from me but I heard his question. "My Dad was murdered?"

"Yes," I said, "He was."

# CHAPTER ELEVEN

MY BROTHER NED WAS TWENTY-NINE YEARS old when he died. He had left home twelve years earlier and from all appearances had found friends and a purpose in military life. Somewhere along the way, he also found drugs. My family's last contact with him had been shortly after his twenty-first birthday, at which point he was on his third new address in less than a year, and then gone. For good, as that peculiar saying would have it.

Until I learned of Ned's death, I had hoped that I was not the last of my family. I still wasn't used to the idea of Luke, or sure how to deal with the anger I felt toward Ned. Not only had he taken a wife and begotten a son, then ditched them both, but he had also deprived my mother of a grandson. My mother had been a woman of sweet, simple joys and would have opened her arms and her heart to Ned's family.

My parents had died within a year of each other, my mother first. My father redid his will, leaving everything to me. I published the required notice in the newspaper and waited the requisite period for Ned to come forward. When he didn't, the court allowed the will. And that was that, until Aunt Margaret died.

Unlike my father, Aunt Margaret had not updated her will after we lost all contact with Ned. Her will provided that all her assets were to be divided equally between Ned and me. If one of us were deceased, the entire estate was to go to the survivor.

I was new at being an investigator, and there was a clear conflict of interest in my being the one trying to find Ned, so I hired an investigator who had been a colleague of Michael's and gave him what information I had. After that, I went back to learning as much as I could about the way Michael had worked. My grief over him was almost paralyzing at times, and the only thing that helped was to know he'd be proud of me if he could see me helping people the way he always had.

The investigator called me from time to time, and I got to like him for the determination he showed for finding me an answer. And find it he did. The insurance company I had worked for was sending some freelance work my way, and I was reading a permanent-partial disability file and thinking about an early lunch when Matt called.

"Nell," he said. And then, "I'm sorry."

What Matt was sorry for was the news he had to deliver. Ned had been dead for nearly four years. He had been shot by person or persons unknown, and buried on Los Angeles city property reserved for those who have no one to claim them.

The last part of the odyssey was up to me. I flew out to the west coast and with Matt's help talked to the right people, wrote some checks and showed my identification, and finally got the information I needed. I went alone to the cemetery and a worker accompanied me to a cheerless space marked by numbered disks. He pointed out the one that was Ned's and walked off, listening to a ball game on a staticky radio. The sounds of the radio faded, and I stood in the smoggy, humid California morning and looked at what I had come to see.

Ned and his luckless fellows were buried in a spot that had no trees. The grass was brown, so those ancient epitaphs inviting the passerby to sit and rest on the green grass would not have made much sense. Nor would the advice and wisdom that the dead have to offer in those same epitaphs. Ned had his milky stone marker with its identifying number, and I had in my purse the official certificate listing the manner of death as Homicide.

The air stirred. It would have been a stretch to call it a breeze. What was passing over this blighted spot felt gritty, and made a sound like paper in the dry grass. What came to me then was not a classical epitaph, but a line from Yeats, who had probably been thinking of a damp, green place when he wrote:

*There is enough evil in the crying of wind.*

So there is, and for a few more minutes I stood there and let the wind cry for the lost brothers of us all.

I stayed in California for another week. During that time I visited several municipal offices and signed my name to all the appropriate documents. Then

I reimbursed the city of Los Angeles for the trouble Ned had put it to, and, on an early morning eastbound flight, I brought my brother home.

Luke was watching me, and for the second time—in the way the boy held himself still, waiting for the other person to go first—I could see a suggestion of Ned. I said, "Luke, your father was a good person. But he got into bad trouble, and died because of it. When he disappeared the way he did, it must have been to protect you and your mother. I'm sure he would have come back to you if he could."

Luke said something that I didn't catch, and I said, "What, honey?" The word just came out, and I let it stay.

"He sent money," Luke said. "My Dad. Mom told me when she…got sick."

I took this in, and understood. Sometime between leaving his family and dying in an alley, Ned had managed to get cash to Luke's mother. To take care of his wife and son in the only way he could.

"He loved you," I said to Luke. "There must have been something really bad that he wanted to keep his family out of. That has to be why he couldn't come home."

Luke was looking straight ahead. In his profile, reminiscent of Ned's in his second grade photo, I glimpsed his father.

"That's what Mom said." His voice was soft, bruised sounding. "I always thought she was just trying to make me feel better."

"What do you mean, Luke? What did your mother tell you?"

"That he was protecting us. That's why he couldn't come back to Maine."

"Did your mother say who your father was afraid of?"

"She didn't want to talk about it!" This polite boy had snapped at me—a sure sign that the strain was getting to him. "Then she said he killed himself and you say that's not even true."

Before I could respond to that, the boy turned to face me again. His voice was challenging.

"What happened to the guy who did it?"

"The person who killed your father?"

"Yeah," he said. "Him"

I waited a beat, then told him. "He was never caught." I didn't add that when one druggie takes out another and there are no relatives pressing for police action, the case disappears pretty quickly to the bottom of the pile.

I heard a sound I didn't recognize, until I connected it with the flush on Luke's face. My nephew was trying not to cry. The stillness in his look was gone, and his expression was fierce.

"It's not fair," he said. "Somebody just goes and kills him and that's it?" He was looking right at me with that ferocious, pain-filled expression, and his boy's voice cracked as he spoke. "Why didn't you do something?"

"Luke," I said, "I didn't know anything about that kind of life. I called the police a few times but there hadn't any witnesses and it was years ago. I didn't know what else to do…"

"But you do now," he said. "You told me that's what you do. You said you were an investigator."

It was difficult for me to meet Luke's eyes, but I did. Again I remembered being that young, thinking that justice was something that happened if you were a good guy. Just like in Superman, and the Saturday morning cartoons. When does the knowledge come that it's never been that way, and never will be? I said, "Luke, I can't talk about this anymore right now. I know how hard this must be for you, but, honey, he was my brother…"

The passion went out of the boy's eyes. He nodded once, and I saw that the threat of tears had passed. His face looked older as he turned away and said abruptly, "Take me back to school, OK?" I had no choice but to follow his quick pace as he headed back toward the car, and I knew as we passed under the Fall trees that I had seen where it begins—in that look that comes when a child has looked to an adult to make things right, and sees that she can't, or won't.

The drive back to the school took less than ten minutes. Neither Luke nor I spoke. The visitor parking lot had emptied out some, and I found a space close to Luke's dorm. We stood awkwardly at the entrance, me jingling my car keys, until Luke said, "I've got to go. I've got a sh…a lot…of math homework." He blushed, and although I tried not to, I laughed. This kid thought "shitload" would be the kind of language that would shock Aunt Nell. He laughed, too, and I felt ridiculously grateful.

"Luke," I said, " I want to come again. Is that okay?"

"Sure," he said. "Thanks for all the stuff."

"You're welcome," I said, and saw that he had a hand extended for me to shake. I ignored it, and pulled the boy to me. I spoke into his dark hair.

"I'll make a few calls," I said. "Okay? It's been a long time and I can't promise anything, but I'll see what I can do."

He stepped back, gently disengaging himself from my hug. When he looked at me I thought there was a little less of the pained disillusionment I had seen. "Okay," he said. He opened the door and waved to me as he went in. After a minute or so, I turned and walked back to my car.

*O pai*, says Ajax just before his suicide, *genoio patros eutuchesteros*. Oh, child—may you be luckier than your father.

# CHAPTER TWELVE

With the low sun behind me I would be driving into the dark—I felt such longing to be home. I would call Martha, and Sheila. Woody would be happy to see me. I made one quick stop, at the first services area, and called the hospital. Tom was in serious condition. So was I, for that matter, in terms of sheer emotional fatigue. I bought some coffee and walked back to my car, reading the cup as I set it in the cup holder. Red script saluted me as a valued customer and advised that the coffee was hot. As I pulled back out onto the highway I thought of Luke's little room, of the boy's bulletin board with the picture of his father pinned to it, and I knew I had to keep the promise I had made.

The strange day had one more unsettling event waiting for me. I was nearly home, concentrating on nothing more than finding a parking space, when I caught movement off to my left, and a half dozen figures dashed into the street. They did not look human. I seemed to see wings, horns, monster faces, and then it hit me. Tonight was Halloween. These were the children of my city, disguised as the creatures of nightmare. I tooted my horn to let them know they had scared me, and a witch waved her candy bag at me. Just then, I spotted a space and pulled into it before it could disappear. In three minutes I was unlocking my apartment door and greeting Woody as if I had not seen him for months.

"Pretty boy!" I said. "Know what? We're going to call Martha and Sheila and then I'll make eggs for us. How does that sound?"

I got Martha right away, and told her about Tom. I said, "I want to tell you all about Luke—my nephew—but right now I just want to make some dinner and read until I stop seeing the highway lines."

Martha said, "I can't wait to hear about your trip, but I'll let you go now. Oh, there's someone at the door. I get a lot of kids—they like those peanut butter pumpkin cookies I make."

I wanted to say, don't answer the door. The world isn't safe. Some of the monsters are real. But of course I didn't. I said, "Now I'll be craving those cookies all night. Any chance there'll be some left?"

"I put some in the freezer for you," Martha said. "Good night, dear."

Tom's sister answered the phone at Sheila's house. I was relieved. This way I could let Sheila know I was thinking of her, but not have to talk. My energy was entirely spent for the day. Maura said she would tell her mother I had called, and I hung up the phone. Woody and I had our eggs and toast in the living room, while I read aloud from my anthology of short stories. It seemed to me that the American short story was getting shorter all the time, but who was I to complain. My attention span was barely up to a dozen pages tonight. At a little after eight I put the dishes in the sink, gave Woody some of his industrial-strength cat treats, and took myself off to bed.

All Souls Day was milder than the first of November should be, with a brisk wind. It was light out, or at least as light as one could expect, seven weeks before the shortest day of the year. I thought about opening a window but I had so much on my mind that I was afraid I might forget to close it before leaving for work. In Boston, no sane person leaves a window open when she is not at home. My few possessions are insured and replaceable, but Woody... I would never forgive myself if I let anything happen to him.

I showered and poured a fresh cup of coffee, then got out the book I had chosen for Tom. It still seemed like a good choice, even though I had forgotten to have it wrapped. I rummaged in my stationery assortment, looking for something other than a Post-it or a While You Were Out slip. Eventually I found some lined paper that would do for a note, just as soon as I thought of something to say.

My first impulse was to take refuge in a literary allusion, but there were a couple of problems with that. I could write something like *Come live with me and be my love*... but Tom would never live it down if his colleagues got a look at it. The more serious problem was that I didn't want to live with anyone except Woody, who has his own sleeping basket and manages to live a contented life without cable television.

I looked at the clock. I had already called in to my office and recorded a message on the answering machine that I would be arriving late, but there was late and too late. I regarded the lined paper as if my life depended on coming up with the right dozen words or so. Then, not for the first time, Woody came to my rescue. He decided to sit in my lap, which meant he was sitting on the paper. "That's it!" I said, "A note from both of us. Perfect, Woodman."

I teased the clipboard I was using out from under my cat, smoothed the paper, and wrote my greeting in a single flow of words:

*Tom—*
*Get well! Woody and I miss you!*
*Love,*
*Nell*

It wasn't going to walk off with the Pulitzer Prize, but it would suffice. I folded the note and tucked it into the bag with the book. Woody resisted getting down from my lap, but I made my voice into a falsetto and promised him treeeats!, and he raced to the kitchen. That's another thing that makes Woody easy to live with—he's a cinch to bribe.

I took the train into Park Street, which was shrieking, smelly and mobbed, and then got the Red Line over to Charles. At a little after nine on a Monday morning the hospital was bustling. I headed purposefully toward Intensive Care, hoping to walk right past the desk, but no such luck. A man's voice called out to me, "Can I help you?"

"I'm visiting Tom Kramer," I said, holding up my paper book bag as if it were a passport.

"Are you a relative?" the man said. He was bald, with a thick neck and a big mustache, and wore what I thought of as a nurse's smock. Just my luck that I had been spotted by someone paying attention, instead of someone gossiping and having coffee while uncredentialed visitors slipped past.

"Sister," I mumbled. Usually, I would rather cross the Phlegethon barefoot than mumble, but I had to be prepared if challenged to say that I hadn't said "Sister" but "Assistant." No, wait—I could say I *had* said "Sister," but what I meant was that I was a nun. Sister Nell, coming to call on a fellow Christian.

Before I was reduced to such a dismal lie, the phone on the desk rang, and the nurse reached for it. "Fifteen minutes," he said, and I nodded furiously, utterly relieved to have my lie accepted without further complications.

Tom was turned away from the door, and I thought he might be asleep. I said his name quietly, and he shifted in the bed. For a moment I barely recognized him as the man I knew. He was so pale, and looked thin in the ridiculous johnny. I opened my mouth to share the fun about my unlikely alias, then saw how inappropriate that would be. Tom said, "Nell." It was his voice, at least.

"How are you doing?" I asked. "Sheila called me…"

"She told me," he said. "She said you came running."

I didn't know what to say to that. His tone was completely flat. Like hospital visitors everywhere, I took refuge in my gift offering. "I brought you a book," I said. "If you already have it I can get you something else."

"I'm sure it's fine," he said. "Thank you."

"I got your family something to eat," I prattled on. "I called Martha. She sends her love…When might they let you out?"

Tom gave me a look I had never seen from him. The look suggested that I was about as clueless as they come. When he answered me, his tone was bordering on curt.

"I have no idea when I'll get out," he said. "It will probably be a while. Then I get to sit at home in a bathrobe, taking pills and having oatmeal for lunch. Maybe after a few months they'll let me come in for half days and answer the phone at the desk."

"Tom," I said. "Stop it."

He turned away abruptly, and I was reminded of Luke's fierce grief. Tom looked back at me and put out a hand. There was a paper ID bracelet around his freckled wrist. I took his hand, afraid to squeeze too tight.

"Sorry," he said. "I'm not doing too great with this."

There was nothing to say to that, so I remained quiet. After a minute or so Tom smiled at me. It didn't look much like his smile. "So," he said. "What's doing in the wide world of metropolitan crime?"

At that exact moment the nurse stuck his head in. "That's enough time," he said. And to Tom, "Your sister has to go now."

Tom stared from the nurse to me, and finally I saw it—his real, delighted smile. "You know," he said to the nurse, "Ever since we were kids she's been kind of bossy. She used to take my Dick Tracy comics before I ever got to read them."

I let go of Tom's hand and leaned over to kiss him. It wasn't a nun's kiss, but I hoped it was a fair imitation of a sister's kiss. I told him, "Actually I do have something going on, and I don't know where to begin. Are you going to be available for expert consultation?"

"Sure," he said, and I saw a look of interest on his face. Then he added, "Anything for my big sister."

I gave the nurse an outraged look. "He's older than I am," I said. "He just thinks he's funny."

The nurse gave me a no-stalling look that told me that Tom and I had carried off the family carping perfectly. No doubt about it—I was this guy's sister.

# CHAPTER THIRTEEN

I WALKED BACK TO MY OFFICE, stopping for a sandwich-to-go and a diet Pepsi. After the hospital, everyone looked young and healthy, even the ones who were ordering greasy pastrami with extra fries as their breakfast. (I was getting ham and Swiss in a pocket, so my virtue knew no bounds.) As I waited for my order I thought about Tom. He would have plenty of people telling him that the heart attack was a warning, that he needed to slow down and remember that he was no longer young. I stayed away from thinking about sex, at which Tom was quite good. I only had one person with whom to compare him, but still...

I decided then and there that any efforts on my part to keep Tom healthy would not be overt. I had seen the glint of enthusiasm when I had told him I was working a new case and would need his help. Let others count his cholesterol and serve him green salad with phony dressing. My gift to Tom would be letting him know he was needed.

My office was stuffy, a sign that the air conditioning was off for the year and the heat on. My building is old and the windows would open if I put every available ounce of strength into pushing at them, but I am sensitive to street noise and decided to leave them closed. My desk looked messy, and for a moment I wondered if someone had been in my office, but then I remembered—Sheila's call, my switch to automatic pilot, the rush to the hospital and then home, full of worry and remonstrations to Tom for reminding me that trouble likes to strike just when you're least expecting it.

Still, I owed it to my clients to be more careful. The folder on my desk had plenty of private details of the finances and life choices of a bank teller who had gotten pretty confused about whose money he was handling. My clients had a right to expect that the cleaning staff would not be privy to the contents of folders like this one.

I put the folder back where it belonged, locked the file drawer, and checked my phone messages. No new work, but two calls from the dry-cleaning magnate, wanting to know what was up. I thought about this case. True, the guy was a turkey, but he was my turkey, an honest-to-goodness paying client. If I was going to take his money I should be doing what he was paying me to do. I looked at the back of my office door and got an idea. On the hook hung a jacket that some lying three-way mirror had tricked me into buying. It was wool, mouse-gray, with brass buttons and sleeves that I had planned to have shortened but never did. I wore it maybe twice after buying it, then hung it in my office for that emergency when I was underdressed and received a visit from a classy client.

I took the jacket down off the hook and examined it critically. Since it had barely been worn it certainly didn't need to be cleaned, but in my experience cleaners take the customer's word for it that this is one dirty garment. I looked in my street map to confirm the location of the dry-cleaning shop, and dialed the owner's number. Before he could start with me I said, "Mr. Best, I have an idea."

He listened, then grunted. I knew him well enough to interpret this as high praise. We discussed details of time, place and diversionary phone calls, and I set off to have my clean jacket made cleaner still.

B-Clean was in Allston, in a block of low-rent businesses that for the most part paid minimum wage and avoided paying benefits or overtime. Since Workers Compensation insurance is an expensive proposition in Massachusetts, that, too, often went by the board. A little bell jingled as I entered, and in a moment a clerk came out from the back.

"Help you?" she said, as if I might have any number of reasons to be in a dry-cleaning shop, and would have to explain myself. Well, she was right, of course, even if she didn't know it. I held out my ugly jacket and said, "I'd like to get this cleaned."

"Phone?" she said. I used to resist this mercantile trend of insisting on my phone number, but now I just make one up. Someday I'm going to try a Sam Spade type number (Buford 6000 or some such), but this wasn't the time. I gave her a phony number and she looked at my jacket without interest. "Jacket?" she said.

Boy, I had to do everything around here. "Yes," I said, "It's a jacket. In the flesh."

She wrote "ladie's jacket" on the orange tissue slip, separated the copies, and handed one to me. At least I had been taken for a ladie. That was something.

"Saddy OK?" she asked, and just then a phone rang. Because I needed her to go answer the phone, I didn't answer her question about Saturday. In a moment she sighed and went back to where she had emerged from, leaving me standing at the counter. I heard her say, "I'm with a customer," and then, "Oh, Mr. Best! Hi…"

Ron Best had told me that if I ducked around to my left, I would be in the storage area behind the racks of clothing. From there, I would have a view of the employees as they went about their work. Jennifer, whose acquaintance I had just made, would be on until 2, and then Tim would take over. Tim was the employee Ron Best thought was taking home samples of the day's cash.

As quietly as I could I slipped into the back room and picked my hiding place, behind some lengths of thick colored fabrics that mystified me until I recognized that I was looking at somebody's drapes. People had their drapes dry-cleaned? What next. Anyway, these reached to the floor and were just fine for my peeping purposes.

If anyone ever tells me that she wants the glamour of a private detective's life, I'm going to tell her in detail about spending two hours and forty seven minutes on a warm day, without food, water or a bathroom, squeezed inside somebody's loud, heavy drapes. I would never again read about the Trojan Horse without feeling plenty of sympathy for the sweating Greeks crammed inside its belly. In the time I was there, Jennifer talked on a cell-phone, refreshed her makeup, listened to the radio, and read a magazine. When it was completely unavoidable she took money and clothes from customers.

Early in my career I had invested in a glow-in-the-dark watch, but I didn't dare move around enough to glance at it. It seemed that a week must have passed when I heard Jennifer say, "Timmy!" Oh, please, let this be the night-guy, and let him get up to no good as quickly as possible.

"Put the sign up," Tim said. I hoped the sign wasn't stored behind the drapes. Jennifer reached under the counter and crossed to the door, where she hung a sign and drew a mini-blind. Then she crossed back to Timmy, and they greeted like those sailors and nurses in the photos of Armistice Day. I picked up what pointers I could (the lesson lasted a good five minutes) until Tim and Jennifer pulled apart, quite out of breath, and he said, "How'd we do today, baby?"

"Fifty, at least," said Baby. "I've got it right here."

I could not see where "here" was, but I have always had a pretty good imagination. There was some more foreplay, then Jennifer said, "I'll get the sign. We're screwed if Ronnie decides to come by and sees this place closed."

She reversed the process with the sign, and there were loud kissing sounds. She finally left, and twenty minutes later the phone rang in the back and Tim went to answer it. By the time he came back out to talk to the boss while he watched the store, I was halfway down the block, looking for the nearest rest room.

Back at my office, I couldn't wait to get to the phone. It was true that what I had seen and heard would never hold up in a court proceeding, but it should be plenty for Mr. Ronald Best, Jr., to go on. I was going to have a closed case, a satisfied client, and a check. I looked up my client's phone number and sure enough, the phone only rang twice before he picked it up. "Best here," he said.

If that were my name I would have trained myself long ago not to answer the phone in such a leading manner. Given this guy's ego, I suppose it was just as well that his name wasn't Goodenough. I resisted any and all temptation to make wordplays ("The news is Good, Best!") and contented myself with saying, "Mr. Best, it's Nell Prentice. I've just come from your Commonwealth Ave store."

"Did you get him?" he demanded. "Did you nab the bastard?"

In my experience, that particular noun is used to refer to a male, whether he does or doesn't have full knowledge of his parentage. Shakespeare's Edmund calls on God to stand up for them, but for the less articulate it's just a good insult-word, or occasionally an envious epithet (That lucky bastard!). I saw that I needed to be extra clear about what we had here.

"Mr. Best," I said, " I didn't actually see how the cash is being taken, but I did overhear a conversation between…"—here I looked at my notes—"Ms. Jennifer Massey, and Mr. Timothy Bloch."

There was silence. I took that to mean that I should go on with what I had seen and heard. I've trained my memory to the point where I can pretty much quote a conversation word for word. I did so now, adding a description of the amorous activity that had accompanied the incriminating references ("Fifty, at least"). When I had finished my report I waited for an expostulation, congratulations, righteousness…anything. There was only a faint breathing.

"Mr. Best?" I said. "Are you there?" When he said he was, I went on, "Here's my suggestion for you. Why don't you head right over to the store now and confront. Mr. Bloch. Let him know that unless he and Ms. Massey repay what they've stolen, you'll get the police involved."

"I don't know that we need to go that far," he said.

I was completely taken aback by this wimpy remark. I had talked to this guy less than six hours ago, and he had practically been advocating the death penalty for ingrate employees who stole from the till. And now I had handed him the 'bastard' on a silver platter and…

Oh. So that was it.

"Mr. Best," I said, "was it your belief that just one of your employees was involved in the thefts?" He made a grunting sound that I interpreted as a Yes. I went on, "And you thought that person was Mr. Bloch."

At last, he was fired into speech. "Well, of course!" he said. "I never trusted that guy. If I'd known that little Jenny…"

He trailed off, and in my mind I heard warning bells. I had just handed my client an unsatisfactory result, and that meant he would be thinking momentarily about how to screw me out of my fee. He had apparently hired me to get the goods on Tim, and instead I had come back with news he didn't want to hear about little Jenny. I took a minute to think, then made my voice positively hearty.

"Mr. Best," I said, "I think I see the position you're in. If you try to approach Ms. Massey…Jenny… about this, heaven knows what kind of a story she'll come up with. Why, she might even try to accuse you of something improper! So how about this…why don't we get your wife involved? She could have a talk with Ms. Massey and let her know…"

"No!"

I pretended to be so caught up in my bright idea that I had missed his reaction. "That way," I went on, "Ms. Massey wouldn't dare to think there was some reason she could get away with this."

Now it was time for me to fall silent and wait. I did so, actually believing that I could hear my client sweating on the other end of the line. When he finally did speak, he didn't sound like the same slave driver I had been dealing with since our first conversation.

"Ms. Prentice," he said. His voice had grown smooth, even amiable. "You know, it may not be the right thing for me to go with this. I mean, maybe there's some other explanation for what you heard these two kids talking about. It could be anything! So why don't we just let this go for now? I'm not one to make trouble for people." He strove for a bit of humor, which I had never suspected him of possessing. " Maybe these kids had a bet or something. Could be fifty cents, or fifty beans they were talking about!"

"You're sure?" I said. "I mean, it's nice of you to give them another chance, but if you want me to mention this to Mrs. Best, I wouldn't mind doing that for you. All part of the service."

"No need for that!" he said. "Another chance… that's just the right way to put it. I was a kid once myself… no telling what crazy bet those two have. But I sure do appreciate your offer, Ms. Prentice."

"So as far as you're concerned, the job is complete, and I can expect a check from you?"

For just one moment I wondered if he was going to balk. But when he spoke, it was in the smooth tone he had adopted to show his benignity toward the kids, who were so like he once had been. "I'll get it in the mail today," he said. "And rest assured, I've got your card right here, in case I need a good detective some other time."

I thanked him, and reminded him how much he owed me. He enthused over the fairness of the amount, and expressed his overall satisfaction with my professional skills. The minute we hung up I grinned, thinking how in his own office Ronald Best was probably frowning as feelingly as I was smiling.

"Jenny," I said aloud. "You can have him."

# CHAPTER FOURTEEN

THE FOLLOWING DAY I GOT UP early in the still strange morning light but did not go in to my office. I had no appointments until 1 o'clock, and could check any phone messages from home. I needed to think about the promise I had made to Luke. It was obvious to me that if I were serious about finding out who had killed Ned, I couldn't do it from an office in Boston. I would need to go to California, where Ned had died.

I also needed to vote. After all the sideshows about who had done (or not done) what thirty years ago, what people cared about was the economy and the war in Iraq. I thought how Ned had only been two years older than Luke was now when he joined the Marines, with our parents' signature.

I considered all the problems of my being away for as much as several weeks. Mail. Clients. Woody, who was sitting in my lap purring enthusiastically because I was home. Every time I raised an objection to the trip, another part of me saw Luke's face. And Tom's. I put aside my book (I had been browsing in *The Republic*, and reflecting that we were nowhere close to electing a philosopher-king today) and turned on my computer. My address book is truly byte-sized, and Luke's email address popped right up when I hit "L."

*Dear Luke-* I wrote- *It was great meeting you. I want to come again soon and I hope you will come visit me here in Boston.*
*I have been thinking about your father, and have decided to go to California*

*and look into what happened to him. Can you give me some advice on how to get a plane reservation online? Love, Aunt Nell*

Not bad. I hadn't overdone the close-relative pitch, and I had asked for the boy's help. I opened the online edition of the *Boston Herald* (CAN HE TAKE BUSH? blared the headline in the paper's characteristic huge type) and had barely gotten through the weather forecast when an envelope appeared at the corner of my screen. I had mail.

*Hi Aunt Nell-*
*Here is the link to Expedia.*
*Bye from Luke*

My nephew had, indeed, inserted into his note an underlined lavender strip of type promising CheapAirfare along with other enticements. Expedia— what was that supposed to mean? Out of Feet? I opened the link and found some fill-in boxes. I wanted to start in Boston and end up in Los Angeles and I guess I wanted to do it in the morning. Up came my options.

The flight I picked, and booked with my credit card, was the one that had lifted off a runway at Logan Airport three years ago, bound for its terrible rendezvous with the South Tower. It was no longer numbered United Airlines Flight 175, but it was the one.

I knew that Los Angeles was enormous, in terms of land area as well as population, and I would need to be reasonably near the police district in which Ned had died. Luke had helped me with my flight plans, and I'd ask Tom to help me with establishing a rapport with the California police.

I opened the drawer of my desk and lifted out the contents. On the bottom of the pile was the folder that held the few papers I had brought back with me from Los Angeles. The death certificate was there, along with a map of the city, a police report and the business card of the investigating officer, Jon Halloran. The spelling of the first name suggested a younger man, and I hoped he would still be there after eleven years. I left the folder out to bring with me when I visited Tom.

Thinking about it all, I felt a wave of sadness for Ned. Dead at twenty-nine, with a son he had barely gotten to know. I reached for the telephone to call the person who is the closest family I have.

"Martha," I said. "It's Nell. Fine. Everything's fine. I saw Tom. He's better. Physically, I mean. Kind of down, though. Yes, I'm sure he'd love a card…"

We talked for several minutes, then I said, "Martha, I'm planning a trip. Next week. Could I ask you to take Woody?"

Her "Yes!" was so enthusiastic I wondered if I'd get my cat back when I returned. We arranged that I would drive down to Manomet on Friday, with Woody and all his gear, and I would tell her then what this was all about.

It was after eleven by now, so I made some lunch and got ready to go into town. Before walking to the train I stopped at my polling place, where the lines were not bad. In under fifteen minutes I had made my choice for that position which, unaccountably, men fight over.

# —————— CHAPTER FIFTEEN ——————

MY ONE O'CLOCK APPOINTMENT ARRIVED EXACTLY on time and looked like the kind of client an investigator wants but seldom gets. His name was Cecil Brandt and he was probably in his late forties, with silvering black hair. His clothes, haircut and gleaming shoes looked expensive and he had a deep, pleasant voice. I invited him to sit in my client chair and tell me what had brought him to my office.

"I guess you'd call it a domestic situation," he said in his honeyed baritone. "That is, it involves me and my ex-girlfriend. We've been living together for the past couple of years and now she's gone off with some clown and taken Samantha with her."

I sighed inwardly. Custody again. When would I get up the ambition to leave this line of work and start a program of Ancient Greek in the inner city? Something simple. I made a note on my desk pad and asked, "How old is Samantha?"

"Seven," he said. "Almost eight."

I had distinctly heard mention of "a couple of years" of cohabitation. That led me to my next question. "Mr. Brandt, please don't take offense but I need to ask you this. Are you Samantha's father?" I was wondering if I had drawn another Mr. Williams, who had no possible claim to the child he wanted to keep in his life. Maybe I should amend my business card. Specializing in Cohabitation Issues. Mr. Brandt was not offended. In fact, he laughed.

"Laverne could be the mother, I suppose. Samantha's a pug."

I looked up from my notepad. He wasn't kidding. I wrote "dog" under Samantha's name.

"And what would you like to hire me to do?" I asked, although I knew.

"I want you to go over there while Laverne's at work and get Samantha for me. She's really my dog. I picked her out and took her to obedience training and all that stuff. Laverne was too busy sleeping late to even take Sammy for her walks."

"Mr. Brandt," I said, "You appear to be asking me to break into your girlfriend's apartment and steal her...I mean your...dog. That's against the law. I'd lose my license as an investigator." My voice didn't sound too convincing to me. I was thinking of poor Sammy longing for a walk.

"Well, I can't do it myself," he said reasonably. "She had the locks changed, and besides, people in the building would recognize me."

"I'm sorry," I said. "What you're asking isn't possible. But I can suggest something. If you're willing to hire me for, say, forty-eight hours, I'll check into this and make sure Sammy is being treated all right. If she's not, the SPCA would intervene."

He thought about this, then said, "OK. That's better than nothing."

A ringing endorsement. I got out a contract and we agreed on up to four hours work. He told me where Laverne lived, and that she got home from work around six. It would be too dark by then, so I asked about the morning schedule. Laverne usually left the apartment around eight. He described the usual route of Samantha's walk and from his briefcase produced a photo of Laverne, who looked tiresome and sulky.

"I'll go there tomorrow," I said. "I'll figure out a way to talk to her and find out what's going on with the dog. If there's any way I can help you get Sammy—legally—I'll do it."

We shook hands and my new short-term client left. I admired the pale blue check he had given me, then put it in my purse to take to the bank on my way home. After that, I went back to work.

At five, with the sky almost dark, I packed up for the day and headed for the hospital to see Tom. He was sitting up in bed reading the book I had given him. A supper tray was on the bedside table, waiting to be picked up. I kissed Tom and indicated the tray. "Supper at 4:30?" I asked.

"Early, I know," he said. "Makes it even harder to pretend that you're having steak and bourbon instead of broiled fish and cauliflower. The coffee tastes like tap water that's been sitting in the sun."

I laughed, but was stopped by the emptiness in his expression. "Tom," I said, "What do the doctors say?"

"About what you'd expect. Food like this for quite a while. Exercise. No stress. Nell…"—he reached for my hand—"I didn't mean to be the way I was when you were here. It's just that I feel so…useless."

"Well, that's about to change," I said. "I'm going to California on Friday to look into an old murder, and I haven't a clue where to begin."

Tom knew about Ned. He may have guessed that this sudden trip had to do with my brother. He didn't ask. A gleam of interest came into his eyes. He said, "What have you got for names?"

I handed him my folder and watched as he read the report, looked at the map, and studied Jon Halloran's business card. The death certificate was at the bottom of the little pile of papers. He read it, then looked at me. I hoped he would not mention Ned.

"OK," he said. "First thing, of course, is to hope this guy Halloran is still there." He reached for the phone beside his bed and punched in a number.

"Naomi? It's Tom. Fine. I know. It's just a quick thing. Once it's done I'll have less stress. Oh, Naomi, the flowers were beautiful. Did you pick them out?"

I rolled my eyes at these shameless tactics and Tom grinned. He was asking Naomi to have Billy Ryan run that cross-country system that had information on law enforcement operations and personnel.

"H-a-l-l-o-r-a-n," Tom said. "I'll hold." To me, he said, "Billy's the best. Computers dance on their toes when they see him coming."

It was quite an image but evidently not an exaggeration, because after less than five minutes Tom said, "Great! Give me his number…"

Just then, a large dark-skinned nurse came to the doorway. Tom was so engrossed in writing down what Naomi was telling him that he didn't even notice the nurse. She frowned, presumably at the length of my visit, then positively scowled when she saw the folder in Tom's hands.

"Is this man *working*?" she said with disapproval. Tom looked up and I took the folder from him before the nurse could see what was in it.

"No!" I said. "This is just…insurance stuff. I'm no good at it so I was just asking Tom to look it over for me." Inspired, I added, "After all, we want the hospital to get paid."

The nurse looked at me. "Miss," she said. "This man is in serious condition. He doesn't need to be exercising himself over any insurance papers. You just take that stuff on out of here and let him rest."

I straightened my folder and gave her an appeasing look. "Sorry. You're right. I'm just going." I leaned over Tom's bed and kissed him. He whispered to me, "I'll call him and let you know what he says."

The nurse stood in the doorway with her arms folded as I went out. I looked past her at Tom and saw that he was smiling. He had some color in his face, and his eyes were alert and thoughtful. Poring over a pile of insurance papers had been good for him.

# CHAPTER SIXTEEN

IT WAS DARK AND WINDY WHEN I left the hospital and walked back toward the Green Line. It was the reverse of the journey I had made on Friday, and I marveled at how changed my attitude was over those few days. I had been so afraid that Tom was going to die. Now, although the recovery might be long, the likelihood of his surviving and keeping that promise to me about Shakespeare seemed good. I even had a quickie of a case. I looked at my watch. It was almost six. I hoped Sammy was getting to stretch her little bowlegs. If not, help was at hand. "I'm coming, Sammy," I said aloud. No one in the crowd headed toward the T station even glanced at me.

Boston, like all large cities, has a homeless problem. That's what it's called, though I expect it's more a problem for those living on the streets than for the rest of us. The demand for social services increases as the bitter Northeast winter approaches, but some of those living on the street are so far gone in mental and physical illness that they have to be rounded up and dragged out of the freezing weather that will kill them. The inside entrance to the station was not quite blocked by two men on one side and a woman on the other. They all had the damaged appearance of human beings with no place to wash their bodies or their clothes. One man had skin that was almost grape-colored, with painful looking cracks.

I shivered at the sight. What must it be like to have no place of warmth and safety as the night came on? The three shapes in the subway entrance were like ancient sinners, caught halfway between the melee of life and the

The pa

oblivion of death. The place I was heading to, with lights and food and a bed, would be paradise to these souls.

Woody was waiting for me, and I scratched his ears with special affection. Like me, he had a place to be, and someone to love him. When he snuck onto the counter to steal a flake of tuna from the empty can, I gave him a minute to accomplish his theft before saying, "Woody!" He jumped down, swallowing his tuna in mid-leap, and with an innocent look at me settled in to clean his oily paws.

I took my toasted tuna sandwich and bowl of vegetable soup into the living room and ate from a tray while I browsed in the day's half-pound of mail order catalogs. There were few things I couldn't acquire with nothing more than a stamp and my MasterCard. Costly reproductions of museum artifacts. Thousand-dollar toy Rolls Royces. Exotic fruits shipped from a world away. For an extra twenty dollars or so these necessities could be at my door with the speed of Mercury descending from Olympus. I thought again of the subway people in their dirty layers and went for a paper bag in which to bury this slick junk.

I rinsed the dishes, feeding a flake or two of tuna to Woody so it would look as if he were well-trained, then washed my hands and went to my bookcase to decide on my night's reading. I knew what I didn't want, and that was anything to do with brothers, or early death, or the cruel Fates. Surely Herodotus, with his reputation for entertainment over strict accuracy, would have something for me.

I browsed in the first book (too much war) and then the second, and came upon the tale of Hippocleides, who had his future all sewn up and blew it magnificently. Perfect. Hippocleides was the odds-on favorite out of a pack of suitors vying for the hand of a rich man's daughter. But then he had that extra Scotch, and thought he would show off his dancing feet. The rich man didn't think much of this display. And he thought even less of Hippocleides climbing up on a table and finally standing on his head with his legs dancing in the air.

"*Son of Tisander*," the rich man thunders, "*You have danced away your marriage.*"

"*ou phrontis Hippocleidei*," the unrepentant bachelor replies. I could care less.

I laughed aloud. I had read the story before, but it was just the sort of diverting fluff I needed. The Father of Lies Herodotus may have been, but to my mind that just qualified him as the patron saint of private investigators. Woody twitched in my lap when I laughed and I gave him a nudge.

"Come on, Son of Tisander," I said. "Bedtime."

\*　　　\*　　　\*

Everybody, including me, was hoping that this election would not teem with controversy the way the 2000 election had. First thing Wednesday morning I logged on to my computer and clicked on the *Globe* website. The headline read NOT OVER YET. I sighed, and tried the *Herald*. Its front page read, PHOTO FINISH, with a picture of George and Laura Bush. So was it over or wasn't it? I scanned the lead story—apparently Ohio was still counting. I checked my email, deleted the spam, and logged off.

Next, with a mug of coffee in my hand, I set to work putting together a certain look I call Hot to Trot. That's probably not the current phrase, but it gets the idea across.

First came the jeans I had begun popping out of during the last holiday season. I wiggled into them, inhaled, held my breath, and with effort fastened the snap. A bulge of flesh appeared above the waistband, but this was no time for vanity. (No carbs, starting tomorrow). On the floor of my closet, having slithered there under its own power, was a red polyester blouse I had been allowed to keep after helping the police fill out a lineup. The blouse had long, full sleeves and buttoned up the front. I left a third of the top buttons open and pushed the hem of the blouse into the jeans. My breathing grew labored.

If the weather had been warmer I would have tied the tails of the shirt to expose my unappetizing midriff, but the November chill would spare any passersby that blood-freezing sight. Stack-heel boots, an arms-length of cheap bracelets, an imitation leather jacket and there I was—a gal that not even the most desperate would take home to Mother.

By seven o'clock I was sitting on a bench in the tiny park where, according to my client, Sammy was supposed to get her morning walk. It was very cold, and the newspaper I had brought as cover kept rattling and coming apart in the gusts of wind. Seven fifteen came, seven thirty, quarter of eight. Was poor Sammy to have no more than a five-minute promenade before being shut up in the apartment for the day? Just then the door to Number 5 opened and the woman in the photo came out, carrying a pug. She put the dog down on the pavement where it stood shivering. The poor beast needed one of those silly dog sweaters—this was no weather for a bald dog with its eyes pointing in two directions. Laverne nudged Sammy with her foot and the dog started out unhappily for the entrance to the park. I waited until Laverne and the dog were almost up to my bench and then let go of the newspaper in my hand, as if the wind had torn it from me.

"Goddamn!" I said, and then to Laverne, "Oh…sorry. This g.d. wind…" I pretended to spot Sammy for the first time and put on a treacly tone. "Ooooh, what a cute doggie!"

Laverne did not reply to this. She was attempting to step over the blowing newspaper, from which Sammy was shrinking in terror. I jumped up and began gathering up the scattered pages. "Poor sweetie!" I said to Sammy. "What's your name, Sweetie?"

"Say I'm-Mommy's-Pain-in-the-Ass," Laverne instructed the dog. I composed my face in an expression of sympathy. "Oh," I said. "I guess..."

Sammy made a lunge past the newspaper and squatted over a few blades of dead grass. Laverne looked disgusted, as if she had forgotten what the wretched beast was here for, and turned to light a cigarette. When she had it going she held out the pack to me.

"Oh...no thanks," I said. "I'm tryna quit." The correct pronunciation of "trying" strained to force its way between my teeth but I pressed it back. I would read an hour of Emerson for atonement.

Laverne blew out smoke and looked at her watch. "That's right," she said to the shivering dog, "Make me late again. My boyfriend can't stand her," she said, to me. "He wants to get a real dog—a police dog or something. I'd stick my ex with this one but I don't want to give him the satisfaction."

I leaned against the bench, worldly and cynical. "Prob'ly the opposite," I said. "He'd prob'ly be pissed. You and your guy get what you want and he ends up with..." I shrugged, and indicated the sorry specimen that was now yanking at the leash.

"Yeah?" Laverne said. "You think so?"

"I know so," I said, yawning. "I stuck my ex with the kids. See how he likes it."

Laverne was impressed. I was a seriously out-for-number-one girl. She looked at Sammy, who was rooting in the dirt with her squashed nose. "I should do it," she said. "Mitch doesn't deserve to be stuck with this excuse for a dog."

I shrugged, as if I had lost interest in the subject of dogs. "Whatever," I said. "If it was me, I'd tell him he either gets his ass over to pick her up, or she goes to the shelter. Let him worry about it."

Laverne looked at her watch again, then back at me. Her expression was respectful, as if she would like to stay and talk to Hard as Nails Nell if she could. "Thanks," she said. "Come *on*, Sammy." She yanked on the leash and Sammy, feet flailing, reluctantly trotted toward the door they had come out of.

I looked at my own watch. 8:05. In case Laverne was going to call her dog-loving ex as soon as she got to work, I hurried to a payphone to alert my client. I left a detailed voice mail telling him what had taken place and urging him to initially refuse the dog, then act as if Laverne had him over a barrel.

"Make some noise," I counseled, "and then say you'll do it. Get Sammy as soon as you can, before Laverne changes her mind."

As I hung up, shivering like Sammy and eager to find the nearest warm coffee shop, I thought that I no longer had the luxury of doing without a cell phone. I didn't mind the tradeoff of convenience for privacy that using pay phones meant, but I wanted Luke to be able to reach me any time he wanted.

# CHAPTER SEVENTEEN

I was in my office by nine, eager for a day's work. The visit to Tom and the Sammy hostage situation had taken my mind off my forthcoming trip and I wanted to keep it that way. I had two phone messages—a plea for money from a political candidate, and a hang-up. I erased them both, and the phone immediately rang, as if wanting to fill up the empty message tape.

"Prentice Investigations," I said.

"Hold on just a sec," a voice said, then, "Samster?"

There was a shrill yapping in my ear. I thrust the receiver away until a human voice replaced the barking.

"Guess who's home?" said Cecil Brandt. "The minute I got the call I jumped in the car and drove over to get her. The boyfriend let me in. I almost felt sorry for him—I get the dog (*Yes, Sammy!*) and he gets to keep the bitch."

He had worked on that line, and laughed loudly in case I didn't get it. I winced, then said, "I'm glad it worked out, Mr. Brandt. Sammy's a cute dog. She must be happy to be back with you."

"Yeah," he said. "Listen. Want to have a drink with me?"

At 9:12 on a Wednesday morning? He must have realized how his proposal had sounded because he said, "After work, I mean. Five-ish."

Shot in the foot with his own grammatical bullet. I don't drink with people who add "ish" to a word to convey vagueness.

"Thank you," I said. Ordinarily, I would have pointed out that I don't

76

mix work with social life, but I could hardly consider Cecil Brandt to be an ongoing client. How many neurotic pugs would he need to be reunited with? I said, "I'd better not."

My response had been thin, suggesting that I could be talked into accepting the invitation. Probably Mr. Brandt's look at the new boyfriend had set him to thinking about a little action of his own. He said, "It doesn't have to be a big deal. Just a couple of drinks—see if we hit it off. You're not married, are you?"

"No," I said, and for a second heard Luke asking the same question. "I'm not married, but I'm in…"

In what? The preposition hung suspended, waiting for an object to govern. In a relationship? In a serious relationship? Inclining toward intimate involvement?

"I have somebody," I said.

After I hung up the phone (the offer of a drink had not been repeated) I leaned back in my chair and closed my eyes. Whatever had possessed me to say such a thing—and to a client? I felt keenly embarrassed, and strangely brave.

The phone rang. "Prentice Investigations," I said, rigid with professionalism, to make up for my gaffe with the previous call.

"Ms. Prentice? This is Tad Britton at Bromfield Coin. Do you remember me?"

I did. Conventional mnemonic devices seldom work for me, but I had filed away this young man's first name in my mind by turning it into Greek and Latin. *Mikros* and *Parvus*. "Yes," I said. "Of course I remember you. How are you?"

"Good," he said. "That list you gave me of the stolen coins? I think some of them just came in."

He had my complete attention now. I reached for a pen. "We're talking about the list I gave you last year?"

"Yes. It's pretty slow here sometimes and I got in the habit of looking at that list when there wasn't much doing. A guy came in a little while ago and left an album of coins for appraisal." His voice faded a little as he consulted what he had. "There's one of the Temple of Vesta, and one of Otho…"

Nobody but me still cared about this case. The insurance company had paid the owner of the collection, I had been paid, and everybody except maybe the head of the claims department should have been happy. But it rankled with me. I was still sure the owner of the collection had been lying. Maybe it was the fact that the coins were Roman. It galled me (no pun intended) to think of those splendid centurions and emperors being used in an insurance fraud scheme. Like Tad, I had studied the descriptions and photos of the collection long after the other principals had cut a deal.

"Do you have the coins there now?" I asked. "I'd like to have a look."

"Sure. I told the guy I'd need to do a little research and make a few calls. He's supposed to come back in an hour."

It was 9:30. I said, "Good work. I'll be there in fifteen minutes."

I changed my voice-mail message and put on my coat. Before coming to work I had changed out of my Hot to Trot get-up and into tan slacks and a brown blazer. Good thing, because Bromfield Street runs a block down into Washington Street, where the working girls of the Combat Zone would be finishing up for the day.

As I crossed the Common I tried not to feel too optimistic. The coins had disappeared from a Boston suburb, so it would make more sense for them to turn up a long way from here. But it had been a year. Maybe the coins had gone to a distant buyer and had now made their way back here.

I found the tiny shop and opened the door. A bell jingled, and Tad waved from behind the counter. He was just as I remembered him—a pale, friendly kid with stick-up hair and watery blue eyes.

"Thanks for calling me," I said. "Are these the coins?" He nodded, and I picked up the leather folder and opened it. The coins were protected by a clear plastic that had been invented thousands of years after the coins themselves had been cast.

"This one," I said, pointing. My heart started to hurry. "And this one."

Tad nodded vigorously. "And the two right at the bottom," he said. We grinned at each other like co-conspirators. My finger grazed the shiny plastic and I wished I could touch the rough coins themselves.

"Tad," I said. "These are them. Could I use your phone?"

"These are what?" said a voice. Tad looked up, and I turned quickly toward the sound. A bald man in a camel-hair coat stood in the doorway. He was frowning.

Tad looked at me, and I instinctively went on the offensive with the belligerent- looking man. "Did you bring these coins in?" I asked him.

"If it's any of your business—yes. This gentleman is supposed to have been appraising them." He looked at his watch.

"They're stolen," I said, and watched the man's high-colored face. Either his indignation was real, or he was a good actor.

"I bought that collection in good faith from a very reputable dealer in San Francisco," he said. "He had the certificate of ownership for them." He put the briefcase he was carrying on the counter, opened it, and took out several papers. Tad looked at me again, and neither of us took the documents.

"I represent the insurance company that paid the theft claim for this collection," I said. "If you can show that you weren't involved in the fraud, you won't be in any trouble."

"Fraud!" he said. "I haven't done anything. I told you..." I put up a hand to stop him.

"You can talk to the insurance company," I said. "Tad, you gave this gentleman a receipt for...*his*...property?" Tad nodded, and I said, "The insurance company will look into it, and make a determination whether the coins were legitimately sold."

"This is ridiculous," the bald man said angrily. "I'm just going to take these and go...."

"You could do that," I said, "but you'd look pretty suspicious. That security camera"—I pointed to the fluorescent light fixture on the ceiling— "takes pretty good pictures." Tad opened his mouth, then quickly shut it.

"Oh, screw this," the man said, with irritated bravado. "I'm out of here."

He turned and walked quickly from the shop, giving the door a bang behind him. Tad said to me, "We don't have a security camera."

"Thanks for waiting to say that," I said. "I can give a pretty good description of somebody I've looked at for that length of time. He may not have been involved in the theft, but chances are he paid so little for these that he had to know something was fishy. Besides, even if we don't get a line on him, the insurance company will still get to keep the coins as salvage."

"Keep them?" Tad said, startled. "You mean like in somebody's desk?"

"No," I said, laughing. "What I mean is they'll have title to them, unless the owner wants to return the claims payment. Either way, you may be seeing them back here soon, only this time legally."

I used Tad's phone to call the insurance claims person, who said she would arrange for a messenger to pick up the coins. I could expect a small bonus for this outcome, and resolved to send some of it Tad's way.

"Thank you," I said to him as I put on my coat. "It's great when people do the right thing, like you did."

He smiled at me, and traced a finger along the edge of the album. "They're beautiful," he said, sounding wistful.

"Yes," I agreed. I watched Tad's finger moving over the protected coins and thought of Sophocles. He had been dead a few centuries when these troublemakers were cast, but he had had their number.

*"Of all the ills of man—the worst is money."*

I headed back to my office and, as happens to me fairly often, got the latest news from a cell phone owner. As she passed me she was saying, "I can't believe it. Not another four years of him." The woman talking on the phone looked to be in her seventies and had a Kerry-Edwards button pinned to her coat. She was crying.

Back at my desk, I typed up a report and clipped it to the top of the file on the coin case. I left it out, so that I would not forget to remind the insurance company who got back their more modern coin for them. I worked until lunchtime, went across the street for a ham-and-cheese roll-up, and spent the rest of the afternoon organizing my files and making calls. In the same morning I had played savior to a pug and touched—or nearly so—coins that could have been rendered unto Caesar. This was not a dull job.

On the way home, I stopped in to see Tom. "Nell!" he said, and it was still there–enthusiasm that he was needed, that he was not an invalid whose opinion, however worthwhile, would not be asked. I said, "Shhh! If that nurse comes in again I won't be allowed within a mile of my only brother." How strangely that had come out, but Tom was consulting some notes and didn't notice.

"I talked to Jon Halloran," he said. "I told him that you're interested in the case as a relative, but that you're a professional investigator and not out to step on anybody's toes. He's going to look up the file and have it ready for you. He said..." Tom ran his finger along the page, "that you should probably stay at this place called The Bradley Hotel. That way, you'll be close to the station and can take a cab back and forth, if you're not renting a car."

I was a veteran of driving in Boston but I had heard about the Los Angeles freeways. I said, "No–no car. This is perfect, Tom. Thanks so much." He looked really pleased and I said, "I'll bring you a sweatshirt. Do they have sports teams in California?"

Tom laughed out loud. "Yes, Nell. They do. Some of them are quite well-known." Tom had been greatly amused one time when we went to a movie that featured celebrities from the world of sports As Themselves. I didn't know who any of their Selves were.

Tom gave me his notes and we talked for a few minutes about other things. Not for a moment did I consider telling him the spontaneous utterance I had made to Cecil Brandt. His early dinner came, and I kissed him and hurried out. How glad I was to be going home to my own kitchen, to eat whatever I wanted. It wouldn't be Cordon Bleu quality, but neither would it be the anemic chicken leg and pale broccoli I had seen on Tom's plate.

# CHAPTER EIGHTEEN

ON THURSDAY I AGAIN IMMERSED MYSELF in my work, both to get ahead on my cases before my trip and to take my mind off Tom and Ned. There was nothing I could do for Tom except to encourage him and let him know I would be there whether he was sick or well. And there was most certainly nothing I could do for Ned. Some will tell you that the dead want justice, but I'm not so sure. I think that most of them, especially the ones who died the way my brother did, just want peace.

My trip to California was for Luke. To get some answers for him, and just maybe to remove that disillusioned look from those eyes that were just like mine. And if I were to be honest, I would have to admit that the trip was also for me. For seven years I had known how Ned had died, but not why.

I didn't leave the office until almost seven. Visiting hours at the hospital were until eight, and unless Tom seemed not up for visitors I planned to stay until they threw me out. It would be a while before I would be seeing him again. I had the usual visitor's guilt that I wasn't bringing a present, then thought, Never mind. You'll bring him something from California. Something a healthy guy would like.

Is there really anything quite like that heart-stopping moment when you look for a hospital patient and he's not there? Tom's bed in Intensive Care was occupied by a tiny black woman, her eyes closed, with a middle-aged couple sitting next to the bed. The visitors and I stared at each other, just as a nurse walked by.

"Oh, Ms. Kramer," she said, "your brother's been moved to Cardiac Care. Left at the elevators and all the way down."

"Thank you," I said, letting out my breath. I looked at the couple.

"My…brother's…much better. I hope that…" I gestured toward the bed.

The woman smiled at me, "Thank you," she said. "We're all praying. She's surprised us before."

I followed the nurse's directions and found Tom in a room with a young man who didn't look much out of his teens. The boy was lying back staring at the overhead television set, from which a situation comedy blared. I waved at him, getting no response, and crossed to Tom's bed.

"Hi," I said, kissing him. "You've moved!"

"Yeah," he said. "A few more days and I should be out of here. I never realized how bad it is to be in a place where other people tell you what to do and what to eat…you can't walk around…you have to…" He glanced at the shrill television set.

"I can imagine," I said, although I couldn't. I have been blessed with an immune system that I should leave to science. No germ that tries to invade my body lives to tell the tale. "So what have you been doing?"

Tom's face brightened—God, I wanted to see that—and he gestured toward the little rolling table next to his bed. On it was a chess board, with what I supposed was a tricky move set up.

"Ben's chess set!" I said. "Was Martha here?"

Tom shook his head, fingering a knight. "It came Federal Express. I guess she remembered."

Tom and Martha had met in June, just over four months ago, when he accompanied me to her house in Manomet. Martha had mentioned her late husband's chess set, and as Tom said, she had remembered his remark that he played chess. Now she had made him a gift of the chess set, just at a time when he needed to be reminded that his body was having difficulty but his mind was fine.

"I remember Ben playing with these so many nights," I said. "He enjoyed playing both sides. One Christmas I got him an electronic set but their cat Flora chewed through the cord. Ben was happy that Flora was all right, but he was mad because he had been winning. Did Martha tell you that she's taking care of Woody while I'm in California?"

"It's in the note," Tom said. "Are you still nervous about flying?"

"A little," I admitted. "But I'm even more nervous that I might get stuck next to somebody who wants to tell me what Game he's in, or what's wrong with the country."

"Bring a book," Tom suggested. "One of those that looks to the rest of us like it's upside-down."

I laughed, and poked his arm. "That's not a bad idea. Plato is a real conversation- stopper for most people. They're usually sorry they asked what that book is. You know," I said, looking at the elegant chess pieces, " There's a line from the *Phaedrus* that makes me think of Martha." I smiled at Tom. *"Beloved Pan and all the other gods of this place—make me beautiful inside."*

Tom pushed the rolling table to one side and patted the bed next to him. I sat carefully on the edge and reached out my hand. Tom took it.

"I wish I was going with you," he said.

"I wish you were, too," I said. "I've only been to California once. It struck me as a  pretty crazy place. What if they don't let me out when I want to leave?"

Tom laughed. Then he said quietly, "I'd come get you."

I didn't say anything for a minute. Various flip responses had come to me, dealing with how Tom must really like my omelets or my cat or my friend Martha, but I left them unsaid. He was taking a chance with what he had said–maybe it was time I did, too.

"This is part of me," I said. "What happened to Ned. Between him and Michael I didn't know if I could ever love anybody, knowing they could die just like that."

"Nell," Tom said. He slipped his hand out of mine and touched my face. "I'm not going anywhere. OK?"

I let out my breath. "OK. What size sweatshirt should I bring you?"

I felt jittery when I got home, anxious about my impending trip, wondering what I would find. Woody sensed something, and purred loudly as I came in the door of my apartment. I picked him up and talked nonsense to him as he rubbed his head against me. There's a Greek word for it–*microlegomai*–speaking trifles. Letting a warm little cat breathe against you and lighten the weight of the day.

"You're going to visit Martha," I told my cat. "I wish we were both going. I wish I hadn't promised."

But of course I had. I put Woody down and filled his dish, then went looking for something for my own dinner. After the Blizzard of 78 (I had been Luke's age) my mother had always kept lots of canned soup around, and I had continued her prudent habit. I heated up some chicken noodle and crumbled a few crackers into it, then sat at the table reading an anthology of ghost stories as I ate. I wasn't likely to encounter spooky mansions or rattling chains or mysterious cold spots in California, but there was no question–I was going in search of my ghosts.

# ——— CHAPTER NINETEEN ———

IT RAINED HARD THURSDAY NIGHT, AND in the morning the wind rose. Good-sized city trees were swaying in the 50-mile-an-hour gusts. I saw pedestrians trying to stay on their feet, pressing as close as they could to buildings. It made me think of Homer's vivid description of Odysseus's crew opening the bag of winds just as home is in sight. I knew that if I looked up the passage I'd get hooked, so I settled for packing my Oxford Classical Text of the *Odyssey* in my carry-on bag. I hoped no security person would think that Attic Greek was some language spoken in countries that spawn terrorists.

I spread peanut butter on a toasted bagel and ate it as I read my email. That way Woody, who I was going to miss like crazy, could sit in my lap. He smelled faintly of tuna, which I had given him as a special farewell breakfast. As if he wouldn't be spoiled enough during his stay with Martha.

I had packed the night before, careful not to include anything sharp, pointed, jagged or otherwise resembling a weapon. Martha told me that the last time she flew, she had to surrender her knitting needles. Once it would have seemed ludicrous— an 82-year-old lady having her knitting taken away. But that was then—in a world now as distant as Troy.

Woody is usually cooperative and docile about being put in his cat carrier, but not this time. Was some mysterious cat instinct telling him that my plane was going to crash? He cried piteously, then got loose and hid under my desk, but finally I had him in there, with the latch closed. His cries redoubled.

"You're the lucky one," I told him. "You just don't know it. You're staying with Martha—I'm stuck going to L.A."

My complaints cut no ice with Woody. I could hear him through the door as I started downstairs to move the car closer to my building. Maybe he was crying in sympathy for me.

The plan was for me to drive to Manomet and leave Woody off, then Martha and I would have lunch at the Daniel Webster Inn. Michael had loved that place, and I couldn't have stood going there with anybody except Martha. Suddenly I couldn't wait to see her, and I took the steps two at a time as I went back for my disconsolate cat.

Woody quieted down once we were on our way. My little car was shaking in the wind, and he probably thought he should try to escape the notice of whatever was making all this noise. Yellow leaves were being swept down in sheets, and once I had to swerve around a large branch that was right in the middle of the road. I hoped the weather for my flight on Saturday would be better than this.

Martha was starting out the door of her house when we turned in the driveway. I rolled down my window.

"Stay inside! You'll get blown away."

She probably couldn't hear me over the wind but she stepped back and held the door open as I ran for shelter. The carrier bobbed against my chest as I tried to keep it from becoming airborne.

"God," I said, panting from exertion as I set Woody and his plastic housing on Martha's floor. "It's wild out there. Martha…"

She had her arms out for me. I went into them, and everything went calm . The stormy day, my impending trip, Woody's squawking—it all fell away as I let Martha hold me.

"Know what?" I said, pulling back to look at her. "You are one of my favorite people in the world."

"And you are one of mine. And Woody," she leaned down to unlatch the carrier, "is high on my list of good cats."

Woody, hearing this unearned praise, stuck his head out. He saw Martha and began to purr. She lifted him out and settled him under her chin.

"Keep him out of trouble while I get his stuff out of the car," I said, and went back into the wind with a smile on my face.

We got Woody settled with a dish of milk, assorted treats and a new feather toy—only the beginning of his pampered stay, I was sure. I held Martha's arm on the short walk to the car, worried that her slight frame really would get picked up by the gale. Once we were on the road and headed for Sandwich she said, "Nell, how is Tom?"

"Really coming along," I said. "He loves the chess set. It was a wonderful idea to send it. Do you remember the time Flora chewed right through the cord of the electronic set?"

Martha laughed. "I was *winning*." It was a good imitation of Ben's deep voice. Then, "I'm glad to see it get some use. Is Tom all right… emotionally?"

"He could be better," I admitted. "I let him help with planning my trip. Think you could call him a few times while I'm gone?"

"Of course," Martha said. "If you don't mind the competition."

I laughed out loud, as she had intended, and my heart felt lighter. "He can't handle one lady friend at the moment, never mind two. Fetching though we are."

We pulled into the parking lot of the Daniel Webster and ducked more flying leaves as we hurried to the entrance. We were seated in the beautiful conservatory, and I looked at the menu just long enough to verify that it still offered Fruits de Mer, my all-time favorite. Martha and I ordered, and in a few minutes the waiter reappeared with two glasses of Chablis. Martha and I touched them together and sipped.

"Now," she said, "Tell me about Luke."

For the next hour, through salad, seafood, dessert and coffee, I did most of the talking. Now and then Martha asked a question or made an observation (always in my favor) about how I had handled things. When I got to the part about promising my nephew that I would try to find out more about his father's death, Martha said, "He's lucky to have you."

Not "It might be dangerous," or "Do you really have to do this?" Martha understood me. She knew that ever since Michael, because of Michael, I had to try to make things come out right whenever there was a chance that I could.

We drove back to Martha's house, where Woody met us at the door. He gave a plaintive mew and I said, "Did you already lose your nice new toy?"

"It's all right if he did," Martha said. "I bought a whole package of them."

I would have been content to stay much longer, but it was time to head back. I had an early start in the morning. I picked up Woody and held him for a moment, listening to him purr, then set him back down. Martha and I hugged each other.

"Have a good trip," she said. "We'll be right here when you get back."

And I was sure they would. It made up for the lonesome feeling I got as I drove home, knowing that Woody would not be there to greet me and that tomorrow I would travel west, toward Luke's past and mine.

# CHAPTER TWENTY

A DIRECT FLIGHT FROM BOSTON TO Los Angeles takes six and a half hours. Almost half of those hours magically telescope away as the traveler crosses three time zones. I was at the airport early, taking everything in like the infrequent flyer I was. I had heard that security was so tight after 9/11 that I might be asked to take off my shoes to prove I didn't have a bomb in them. Nobody asked me to do that, but I did have to put my purse and Homer in a little basket that passed them under an X-ray which I imagined was taking a close look at Odysseus's great bow, in the moment before he strings it and all Hades breaks loose in the palace of Ithaca's king.

It took a while, but finally, all the boarding and seating and stuffing of carry-on bags was complete, and the pilot's voice came on. We taxied into position, the engines roared with power, and we lifted off. When I opened my eyes, Boston was falling away beneath us and we were pointed into the sky.

Hesiod says that the best time to begin a journey is fifty days after the summer solstice. We humans of the year 2004 had just passed the autumn equinox, so I was a little late, but with Hesiod dead for twenty-seven centuries and my brother gone for eleven years, a season didn't seem to matter all that much. I opened my book and was well into the suitors' taunts to Telemachus (their day would come) when the food carts clattered past and a cunningly packaged breakfast was served. I put Homer aside and proceeded to eat everything that was put in front of me.

Most of the people on the plane settled down for a nap as soon as the breakfast things had been collected, and I decided to try getting a little sleep myself. Jon Halloran had told me that he would be able to see me today, and I wanted to be alert and ready with my questions. I drew the window shade, turned onto my right shoulder and closed my eyes.

What woke me was a feeling of being roughly rocked from side to side. Other people were also sitting up and looking around. The pilot's voice came on.

"Just a little turbulence, folks. We should be through it in ten minutes or so. I'd like all passengers to fasten their seatbelts until we're out of this—the cabin crew will be coming by to help anyone who needs assistance."

I had never taken off my seat belt, so I just sat up and straightened my seat back and folded my hands. For the rest of the flight I looked straight ahead and breathed steady breaths, keeping the plane aloft.

My flight landed in Los Angeles at 11:30, and while the aisles filled with people pulling their carry-on luggage from the overhead bins, I took a moment to set my watch back three hours, and my mental clock back seven years.

The cabbie who drove me to the Bradley Hotel would have inspired a poet. I thought of Horace's *gracilis puer*–the slender youth in a wealth of roses. My driver was probably in his mid-twenties, with dark blonde hair that touched his collar, green eyes and a buff, tanned body in perfectly fitting sport shirt and chinos. He got us out of the airport (I couldn't have driven these mad roads if my life depended on it) and when we were settled in a lane of traffic that seemed to be going a hundred miles an hour, he smiled at me in the rear-view mirror. God, what a smile.

"First time in L.A.?"

"No," I said, dazzled but coherent. "I was here once before." I didn't want him asking what brought me to L.A., so I said, "I suppose you get asked this a lot—but are you in the movies?"

The minute my question was out I felt a) ridiculous, b) middle-aged, and c) like a gaping tourist. My driver didn't seem to mind a bit. He laughed (even better than the smile) and said, "I've done some TV. My agent's lining up a few things for me."

"I don't get to watch much TV," I said, implying that I owned one. "What were you in?"

"*Family Fortunes*," he said, and checked for a reaction. "The soap. I was the cousin who got killed because he looked just like Emmeline's husband."

"Oh," I said, casting about for some credible words of praise. "That must have been interesting."

"It's a start. Also, I did the voice-over for a line-of-credit commercial."

"Imagine that."

We pulled up to the Bradley Hotel, and my driver (Atticus Moore, if his hack license was to be believed) got out to take my luggage from the trunk. At the same moment a bellman came out of the hotel and held out his hand for my bag. I tipped Atticus and wished him well in his career, then followed the bellman past flowers blooming in the November sun and into the hotel.

The Bradley was small, clean and unremarkable. I went up to the desk and gave my name. The clerk, a silver-haired woman who like Atticus was beautiful, said that my room would not be ready until 2, but I could store my luggage until check-in time. I debated for a moment. It was tempting to think of getting lunch in the coffee shop and then relaxing in my room before calling Jon Halloran, but I knew that I might as well get this show on the road. I tipped the bellman for storing my bag (knowing that I'd have to tip him again for carrying it to my room) and asked where the pay phones were. Luke had promised to help me pick out a cell phone, which he assured me would work over very long distances, but I wasn't taking any chances just yet.

Jon Halloran had a nice voice, and I wondered if like everybody I had met so far he was trying to get into the movies. Probably not. He had been a cop for at least eleven years, and that's not a day-job you can forget about while you line up at auditions. He asked whether I had had lunch, and when I said No, he said, "I'll tell you where to have the driver leave you off."

I had always heard that every restaurant in Los Angeles served tofu and kelp and tea made from flowers, but I should have known that a cop is a cop, and most of them know where to get red meat. Jon Halloran was waiting for me at a place called The Big Burger. He waved at me from the corner booth where he'd said he would be—I'd described myself over the phone, right down to the winter-in-Boston pallor. The place was very crowded, so it seemed likely he was a regular who could expect preferential treatment. Or maybe, khakis and sports jacket notwithstanding, it was obvious what he did for a living.

"Ms. Prentice?" he said, standing when he saw me coming toward him. He was a little chunky, with blonde hair cut very short. He had blue eyes— cops' eyes that gave nothing away, even when he smiled.

"Jon Halloran," he said. "I didn't know this place got so noisy. Let's get some lunch, and if we can't talk here, we'll head back to my office afterwards."

We both ordered cheeseburgers, his rare and mine medium, and exchanged brief histories while we waited for the food. Jon said, "I looked up the file on your brother. There wasn't much there. No witnesses, of course. The gun probably in the Bay five minutes after the shooting. Just another dead junkie."

I caught my breath, and Jon Halloran shut his eyes. "Shit. I didn't mean for it to come out that way. I mean, he was your brother and you came all this way to find out what happened—you must think I'm a real S.O.B. to say a thing like that.

"It's just that—you can't let yourself keep caring. Day after day it's the same stuff. Money and drugs and guns, the bad guys and the ones they go after getting younger every day." He looked at me. "The truth is, I didn't remember one single thing about your brother's case until I pulled the file from dead storage."

The waitress came and put our plates in front of us. Jon Halloran tore open his bag of potato chips and ate one. I looked at my cheeseburger, which was running with thin red juice.

"Lieutenant Kramer told you about me. I'm not here to cause any trouble. I have a good reason for wanting to know about my brother—it's a personal reason, and when I've seen what there is to see I'll go home and you can send the case back to dead storage. Will you let me see the file?"

Jon Halloran took a bite of his burger and set it back on the plate. "It isn't pretty."

"I'm sure it isn't. I don't think my brother's life was very pretty. But it's time—time that somebody cared."

We didn't talk much as we ate our lunch, and what we did say had nothing to do with Ned. Wasn't California warm? What was Boston weather like in November? Hey—how about those Sox? (This from him—it took me a minute to remember what they had done, then I made an enthusiastic face and said: Yes! Wasn't that something!) Lest he take this as encouragement to begin discussing players and positions and averages, I quickly found another subject.

"It must get you down—trying to make a dent in the crime statistics. Do you think about getting out—doing something else?"

Jon Halloran put the last bite of his hamburger down and pushed the plate away. He patted his shirt pocket, then quickly put his hand on the table. Right. Quit smoking not too long ago. Momentarily forgot that smoking in a California restaurant is slightly less condoned than parricide.

"Know when it finally got to me?" he said, signaling for the check. I started to open my purse but he said brusquely, "On me."

"Thank you," I said, and waited for his answer to his own question.

"I knew I wasn't ever going to get anywhere when I started busting the kids of the losers I sent away twenty years ago."

The police station was only a few blocks away and the weather perfect, so we walked. The building was stucco, with palm trees outside, but the tropical look did not quite mask an air of defeat. Flaking paint, a thin lawn, people going reluctantly in, or coming out gesturing and arguing. I followed Jon Halloran up the front steps and let him vouch for me to the officer on the front desk, then we walked to his office.

"File's there," he said, pointing to an accordion folder in a chair. "Not a whole lot in it, but you can have a look. I'll be in the break room if you need me."

I thanked him, and he left me standing in the office holding the brown folder. I pulled up a side chair so I could use the corner of Halloran's desk, took a deep breath and opened it.

The first thing I saw was my own name. The document on top of the file was a supplemental report from 1998, stating that Ellen Prentice, sister of Edward Prentice, formerly John Doe # 2122, had come forward to claim the body of said Edward Prentice and cause it to be removed from Burial Site #6, City of Los Angeles.

Under the report was a corrected death certificate, the original death certificate, (both gave the cause of death as Homicide), some typed pages—and photos.

I shut my eyes quickly. The photos were of someone male and young, shot through the right eye. I knew that already, but wasn't about to carry the actual image into my dreams. I turned the photos face down and reached for the reports.

As Jon Halloran had said, there wasn't much. Height, weight, hair and eye color, needle tracks and a small scar over the left eye. Found in an alley on a Sunday morning, with no identification. Interviews over the next few days with the local junkie class, who collectively remembered that the dead guy had not been around very long and was known as Eddie P.

So Ned had finally gotten his friends to use that nickname. Except that they weren't really friends—more like fellow citizens of Hell, wanting only to escape the Devil's notice. Ned had lain unclaimed in a freezer for a month, then been cremated and buried at state expense in the grim spot where I had found him.

I gathered the papers into a pile and slid them back into the folder, the photos still face down. For a minute I just sat quietly, drained, then I got up to find Jon Halloran.

"I appreciate your help," I said to him as he walked me back to the station entrance. "I'm not sure what I'll do next. If you think of anything at all, would you call me at the Bradley?"

"Sure," he said, and seemed to hesitate. "Ms. Prentice—I didn't mean to sound like I did at the restaurant. The job just sucks the life out of you sometimes. I...I hope you find what you came for."

"Thank you," I said. "I hope..." What? That he would wake up tomorrow with the hopes he had had twenty years ago? "I hope that you have something in your life that lets you forget the job."

He smiled then, a boy's sudden smile. "I do," he said. "I just have to remember that."

As I walked back to my hotel I thought about my brother. What a disappearance he had pulled off. Known by a nickname, moving from place to place, no real friends. Had anybody even tried to find out who he was? He must have managed to avoid being arrested, but the Marines would have his fingerprints.

And there was the Why? He must have had a compelling motive to keep his identity a secret from everyone. People he cared about and wanted to protect.

A wife. A son.

In spite of the heat I hurried on my walk back to the Bradley Hotel. It would probably be cool and quiet at this time of day, and I wanted badly to take off my shoes, wash my face in cool water, and call the people I cared about, starting with Martha. I checked in and followed the bellboy (blonde, buff) down the corridor. He inserted the key card—they always balk for me—and a green light blinked. I tipped him for the bags and as soon as he was gone I hurried into the bathroom with my hand already out for a wrapped glass.

"Don't scream."

# CHAPTER TWENTY ONE

SCREAMING IS NOT MY FIRST REACTION to trouble. I wouldn't last long in my profession if I made a practice of sounding like a ninny who's just seen a mouse. Still, the presence of a strange man, albeit well-dressed, in my bathroom did cause me to catch my breath and immediately look for something I could use as a weapon. The man held up both hands in a gesture evidently meant to be reassuring.

"It's OK," he said. "See—nothing to worry about. We just want to talk to you."

I didn't take my eyes off him when he said "we." It could be a trick to make me turn around so he could grab me. I looked in the mirror behind him and saw a second man step from the closet.

"Gypsy," said the first man. "Show her your hands. Like this." His arms were still in the air, and he opened and closed his hands once to demonstrate. Gypsy, with a bored-looking sneer, half raised his arms and showed that his hands were empty.

"See?" the first man said again. "Now Gypsy's going to sit himself down on the bed and I'll come out of here with my arms where you can see them and we'll be ready to have our talk."

He stood still, relaxed and even smiling, as if I were a skittish cat that he didn't want to alarm into flight. Behind me, Gypsy crossed to the bed and sat on the edge with his hands pressed back. He looked impatient and out of sorts, as if this were all a big waste of his time. I took a step back and the guy in my bathroom gave me an encouraging smile. When I was clear of the door he came out slowly and sat on the bed next to Gypsy.

"The chair's all yours," he said to me, pointing to the dainty desk chair pushed in under the phone table. I walked to it and put a hand on the phone.

"Any reason I shouldn't pick this up and report an intruder—two intruders—in my room?'

Gypsy started to get up, but the other man, clearly in charge, put a hand on his arm. "There's a real good reason. Why don't you sit, and we'll tell you what it is?"

He was smiling at me like an invited guest who's all set to enjoy the evening with a friend. "I'm Jory," he said. "And this here personality kid is Gypsy."

By California standards, Jory was an ordinary-looking guy. Dark hair, brown eyes, probably a little under six feet tall. His shoes were shined, and his dark suit fit well and looked expensive. He had good teeth and probably practiced that smile in the mirror.

Gypsy, on the other hand, was a weasel. One of his narrow shoulders was higher than the other, and he had a hollow-looking chest that reminded me of Homer's description of Thersites—"the ugliest man who ever came to Troy." I thought that physical uncomeliness must be a special curse in this land where beauty was the norm.

I pulled the chair out and turned it toward my visitors. "Five minutes," I said. "For you to tell me how you got in here, and what you want."

"Pushy broad, aren't you," Gypsy said, scowling. His voice was high and rasping. I almost began to feel sorry for him.

"Now that's no way to talk," Jory said, frowning. "She's got a right to be asking what gives." He turned the smile back on and directed it at me. "We've got lots of friends. They work here and there in no-money jobs, and if they can help us out now and then and put a little something in their pocket, everybody's happy."

"You bribed someone to let you into my room?"

"Oh, we don't call it that," said Jory, seemingly uninsulted. "You tip, don't you? It's like that—just bigger bills. And of course our friends know we're not going to make any trouble."

I was tired of this. There was an almost flirtatious tone in Jory's voice as he drew out this game of I-know-something-that-you-don't. I said, "What are you here for?"

"Well, why we're here is because of a call from another friend. A good girl, with a kid to support, who knows we'll help her out when she can do something for us."

94

"And what did this good girl do to earn her—tip?"

Jory took his hands off the bed and clasped them loosely over one knee.

"She called our boss. She knew he'd want to know that somebody was taking an interest in the Eddie P. file."

I've had a lot of practice keeping my emotions from showing, and now I concentrated on a neutral expression. Jory was watching my face. I said, "Am I supposed to know who that is?"

"Sure. You got the same last name, don't you? Of course we didn't know that until now. Too bad we didn't get a call when you came here the other time and tidied things up. I have to say—you don't look much like him."

I thought of not responding to that, but these men had the information I had come here to find. "He looked like our mother."

Gypsy gave a mean bark of laughter. "Hey! Eddie-boy had a mother."

Jory turned to him slowly. He didn't say anything—just stared. After a minute Gypsy mumbled, "It's just a joke."

"Mr. Wyman doesn't like jokes like that," Jory said. "This is a lady. She's here to ask about her brother. Mr. Wyman's got a kid sister. How do you think he'd like it if you mouthed off like that to her?"

Gypsy didn't have to think about that very long. His face paled, and he mumbled, "Sorry."

"Say it to her."

"Sorry," Gypsy said, sullen as a teenager. He didn't look at me, but Jory was apparently satisfied that we were back on track. He turned to me with the smooth smile and said, "Mr. Wyman's our friend. He's the one that got the call."

"The call about my brother."

"Right. You and Mr. Wyman have something in common. A mutual interest, I guess you'd call it. You want some answers, and so does he."

I said, "If we have so much in common, why isn't he here?"

Gypsy looked shocked, but Jory laughed. "He's shy. But he definitely wants to meet you. He sent us to invite you"—Jory gave a mock-bow from his position on the bed—"to visit him in his home."

I looked down and saw that I still had a hand on the phone. I took it off and folded my arms. "Does Mr. Wyman live near here?"

"In this neighborhood?" Jory sounded amused. "Mr. Wyman lives in the Hills. He's got movie stars for neighbors."

"Yah," Gypsy said, perking up. "Like that babe on..."

"Shut up," Jory said. "Now."

Gypsy did. Jory said, "So this is your lucky day. You're going to get to see world-famous Beverly Hills, and meet somebody who can be real grateful if he likes you."

"And you'll take me to him?"

Jory did the half-bow again. "Right now."

I made him wait while I unzipped my bag and got out my linen blazer. It was the same one that I had worn to my office the day I made the call to Lee Thomson's office. At home, it would be stored in a garment bag, but here in this land without seasons, it seemed just right. And the chances were good that I was headed somewhere with killer air conditioning. I folded the blazer over my arm and picked up my purse.

"Right. Let's call on your friend, and I'll see whether *I* like *him*."

We took the elevator down to the lobby and Jory pushed the revolving door for me to precede him outside. The heat reminded me that I hadn't had a chance to wash my face or get something to drink. I said, "I need some water. There's a soda machine just back inside…"

Jory touched my arm, lightly but firmly, just as a long white car pulled up in front of the hotel. "Mr. Wyman's anxious to meet you. There's a bar in the car."

The driver of the car, a thin, olive-skinned man wearing a light-colored suit and wrap-around sunglasses, got out and held the back door for me. I slid in, and Jory got in next to me. Gypsy sat in front next to the driver and we pulled out into the street.

"What'll it be?" Jory asked me, opening a built-in cabinet that contained various liquors, wines and soft drinks, and half-bottles of Perrier. "Water, please," I said, and he poured Perrier into a heavy glass and handed it to me.

"While you're out here, you want to try our California wines. Better than that pricey French stuff." Jory's face darkened. "Ungrateful bastards. My old man took shrapnel in the leg in France in '44, and then they turn around and tell us to go to Hell when it's their turn."

I didn't care to discuss the Iraq war with Jory. I sipped my Perrier (which, if I was correct, was imported from France) and didn't answer. After a minute or two Jory put his head back and closed his eyes, and I was able to watch the progress of our journey. We got on the dizzying freeway, then off it, and seemed to be climbing steadily as the real estate grew more and more fabulous, until we were in an area where high gates and electrified fences and guard booths hid the houses from view. The car slowed and came to a stop a few yards from a wrought iron gate that must have been fifteen feet tall. Beside me, Jory sat up straight as the gate opened and we drove through.

"Home sweet home," he said.

It was Tara, transplanted to southern California and without the turnips.

Four stories, with a veranda and columns and lawns greener than money. The driver came to a stop in front of the main entrance and before I could reach for the door handle he was out and around to my side, helping me out of the car. Jory and Gypsy got out and we walked up a wide brick path lined with flowers and up the stone stairs to a front door that could have admitted a three-horse chariot. Gypsy opened the door, and the three of us stepped inside.

The entrance hall was massive—mirrored and waxed, with vases taller than me, holding flowers that seemed to still have dew on them. A man in a white three-piece suit came toward us. "Success," he said to Jory.

"This is our girl," Jory said, then added quickly, "Woman."

Mr. White-Suit smiled at me. "Ms. Prentice. I'm Charles Dunn. Mr. Wyman asked me to bring you to him as soon as you arrived."

Everybody, even Gypsy, looked relaxed and smiling. Mr. Wyman's request had been fulfilled. He would be pleased. I looked at Jory and Charles Dunn with their movie star haircuts and expensive suits, at the luxurious furnishings and the flowers that would be thrown out and replaced tomorrow. And something else altogether came to me.

I thought of Ned's autopsy photos. The ones I had read about, but been unable to turn face-up and look at. I thought of the ugly way his life had ended, in this same city of showy wealth bought with the blood of my brother and so many like him.

"That's why I'm here," I said. "To meet Mr. Wyman."

"At your service."

# —— CHAPTER TWENTY TWO ——

THE MAN WHO HAD ENTERED THE room had the air of someone at home with the things that are his. Jory and Gypsy and even Charles Dunn all seemed to go still for a moment, as if thinking back to what they had been saying when he appeared. Then they all smiled at the same time and Charles Dunn said, "Mr. Wyman. I was just going to bring Ms. Prentice to you."

"No need to stand on ceremony," he said. "Ms. Prentice, I'm Eliot Wyman. Thank you for coming here."

He looked to be in his mid fifties, with a compact, darkly-tanned body and casual clothes that did not quite conceal an air of controlled strength. His eyes were brown, his nose Roman, and he had thick white curly hair. He held out a brown hand to me and I took it.

"Charles," said my host. "May we have coffee? Or…"—to me—" would you prefer a drink?"

"Coffee would be fine," I said, and the room emptied as if by magic. Eliot Wyman and I stood regarding each other, he relaxed and I trying to look as if I were. He said, "Shall we go into the living room? Charles will know to bring our coffee there."

He put an arm out, not quite touching my shoulder, and steered me to the end of the hallway and into a living room that, like his beige shirt and pants, seemed designed to show off his tanned skin and white hair. Everything was in neutral shades, even the clean fireplace, over which hung an enormous oil painting of moonrise over the ocean.

"Please sit down," Wyman said, indicating a pair of chairs upholstered in what appeared to be watered silk. My guess was that no cats lived here, or if they did they were without claws. I took the chair on the left by habit. I'm right-handed, and even when I'm without a weapon I like to keep a possible adversary on my right. Wyman took the other chair and at once Charles Dunn appeared with a tray. The silver coffee service gleamed, and the porcelain cups and pale yellow cookies matched the overall décor. Wyman smiled and said thank you, and we were alone again. He poured coffee and passed a cup to me, offered the cookies (I declined) and sat back with his own cup.

"I can tell that you are Edward's sister," he said.

My hand, just at that moment adjusting to the butterfly weight of the cup Wyman had handed me, tensed, and the cup clinked delicately against its saucer. I steadied my hands and my voice.

"Really? I was just telling your…associates…that he took after our mother. My Dad and I looked alike." I recalled Luke's hazel eyes, so like mine, and pushed the thought away. I didn't want even a mental picture of Ned's son in the same room with this smooth, dangerous man.

Wyman reached for one of the starched, folded napkins on the coffee tray and dabbed at his lips with it. "Not the physical features. Although your eyes are shaped like his. No—it's a kind of *insistent* intelligence that you both have. It was the first thing I noticed about him."

I considered the precise adjective and decided it had been a compliment. Interesting, but even more interesting was the almost caressing tone in which Eliot Wyman was describing my brother. I wondered what their relationship had been.

"It is the nature of my—business—that I am surrounded by fools," Wyman was saying. "Not that I would have it any other way. I need people who can follow simple directions and never try to think for themselves." He stopped speaking and lifted the coffee server, gesturing it toward me. I shook my head. He poured a second cup for himself and regarded me again before sipping at the coffee.

"I didn't realize until I met your brother how much I missed having someone with a good mind around me. And I admit to being intrigued by the puzzle of where he went those times he disappeared for a few days. I could have found out, of course, but I believe we're all entitled to our secrets. I paid him in cash, and he was free to do as he wished with it. He did his job well, and little by little—it pains me to admit this—I became less careful than I usually am where he was concerned."

I concentrated on not crushing my pretty little cup. If it had been Styrofoam, I probably would have had it partly shredded by now. This bastard was toying with me. He must know how I wanted to put on my coldest tone and ask him if he was there in that alley the day Ned died. Did he order the killing? Did he do it himself? But I would play along.

"You got where you are today by being careful?" I asked.

Wyman beamed at me as if I'd just scored 1600 on the SAT. "Now that is exactly what I mean. That's the kind of thing Edward would have said. Getting right to the point. Where I made my mistake with him was in thinking that I could *mold* that intelligence of his. Make it work for me."

"And you couldn't do that?"

He sighed, the disappointed optimist who has tried to do a good deed. "I thought it was working. Of course, I couldn't consider bringing him into my inner circle as long as he was still on drugs. But I have a doctor who is grateful to me, and was most willing to pay a discreet visit here every day. Your brother had his own private Methadone clinic in a considerably more comfortable facility than most addicts make do with.

"When I felt he was ready, I began grooming him. Introducing him to important people, asking his opinion on business matters. There was resentment, of course, but no one was going to complain to my face. Then there was a situation that was right for me to see how far I could trust him."

He set down his cup and folded his hands across his lap. I held my own cup still, not wanting to break the flow of the monologue.

"I had an influential friend. He was...connected, legitimate in a way I knew I was not. He was able to do me a considerable favor. I showed my appreciation in the usual way—in this case an art object I knew he would treasure. Its provenance—" he looked at me to see whether I was impressed, or probably better still unfamiliar with the word—"was not...impeccable... but it would be strictly for his private enjoyment.

"It was essential that my friend and I never be seen together. I had several people who could have made the delivery, but they were known to work for me. Edward was new, and I decided to try him out. I gave him the package and the meeting place, and I stood right in that very door..."—he pointed—"and told him we would have a brandy together when he returned from his errand."

I saw his hands clench in his lap, then loosen. "At first I didn't notice that he was overdue. I made phone calls, a lady came by, and I suddenly realized it was dark. Edward had been gone for hours. I called my friend, and he said the delivery had never arrived."

Wyman looked at me. " Under the circumstances, I don't suppose you'll be able to appreciate the irony of what happened next. I had grown used to Edward's capacity for judgment—I could tell him what needed to be done without having to spell out the details of...execution. I was extremely angry, and just told two of my men to find him.

"When they called and told me he was dead, they expected congratulations."

I made myself look at him. He had just admitted to a part in my brother's death, and knew I couldn't use what he had told me. He was clearly still a very powerful man, and Ned was—what was that summing-up phrase?—a dead junkie.

"Are you telling me you didn't want him dead? For stealing from you?"

"All in good time. Of course I couldn't permit something like that, but I would have liked to hear why he ever thought he could get away with such a thing.

"And I would very much have liked to get my property back."

# — CHAPTER TWENTY THREE —

I LET WHAT HE HAD SAID sink in. "The art work wasn't with him?"

"No. He was questioned rather thoroughly, I gather, and the room they tracked him to was torn apart. It was the kind of neighborhood where no one calls the police when they know they're hearing something they shouldn't be. They just turn their televisions up louder." He looked contemptuous, as if speaking of people far below his own social class.

"What makes you think that the people who killed my brother didn't take what you'd given him to deliver?"

Now the contemptuous look was for me. "Ms. Prentice, I don't think you've been listening to me. Those men would not have *dreamed* of trying a stunt like your brother's. However stupid and greedy they might have been, they knew I would be able to tell if they were lying to me. And I would be very, very angry. No, I have to assume that your brother was able to get my possession someplace where, since I knew so little about his background, I would not be able to follow it."

I had a crucial question. There was something I had to know before I could begin to think what to do with all this.

"What about your men? The ones who killed my brother?"

He made a dismissive gesture—a middle-manager contemplating the high turnover in the fast-crime business. "Dead. One of them overdosed a year or so later, and the other one spent some time in prison until he got into

102

an argument with a fellow inmate who happened to have a shiv in his boot. Their families are taken care of, of course."

The phrase, probably meant to show Wyman in a benevolent light, sounded ominous, and I realized it was essential that Wyman and his "associates" think I was Ned's only family. I said, "Mr. Wyman, I should tell you now—I didn't go looking for my brother until several years after he died. I don't know anything at all about what he took from you."

He smiled at me. "I'm sure you don't. But you may be the key to my getting my property back. A very old, exquisitely beautiful statue of Alexander on a rearing Bucephalus"—he held one hand about a foot above the other to indicate the figure's size—"that was on its way to my good friend, who of course I was compelled to compensate with a second...offering.

"I would like to have back what is mine."

# CHAPTER TWENTY FOUR

I COULDN'T DETECT ANY IRONY IN that last statement. He had as much as told me—that dubious provenance—that the statue was stolen. But he also struck me as a possession-is-nine-tenths-of-the-law type. I said, "Why would I want to help you?"

For the first time his urbane look was replaced by surprise, then he laughed. "Edward's sister, indeed! But perhaps, like him, a little too smart for your own good?"

"Are you threatening me?"

"Ms. Prentice, I don't threaten people. They can, however, find themselves on the wrong side of me, which is unwise. But for those who cooperate with me, the rewards can be substantial."

I opened my mouth to tell him that I didn't need or want the money of a man who had been responsible, however he might deny it, for Ned's death. But it came to me that I wasn't the only one involved here. I had come here for Luke as well as myself, to get answers about his father's killers. Whoever had actually pulled the trigger was gone, but Eliot Wyman was very much still here. If he couldn't get what he wanted from me, he might be inclined to see if Ned had other relatives he didn't know about.

"When I came here before," I said, "the police gave me his things. There was nothing—clothes, shoes, a $10 watch." I remembered holding that cheap watch in my hand, remembering the family heirloom watch my Dad had proudly presented to Ned at his Confirmation. How long ago had it been sold for drugs?

Wyman said, "I believe you, of course. As I mentioned, the men I sent after Edward looked for the statue. It was nowhere to be found. But now I am face to face with someone who knew Edward well—his habits, his—shall we say—haunts."

"But I don't—didn't," I said quickly. I made my voice more casual, fearing that my concern for Ned's son would be apparent to this clever, murderous man. "He left home when he was still a teenager. I didn't know the first thing about his life until I had to go looking for him."

"Still—you grew up in the same house. Presumably knew the places that were special to him...."

Maine. Where Luke lived.

"There was the Cape," I said, after taking a minute to pretend to be thinking back. "My parents took us to Cape Cod every summer. Ned—Edward—loved the beach."

"Ah, see now. It's coming back. Where on the Cape?"

"Hyannis," I said, choosing a town that was, for the Cape, bustling.

"Your parents had a house there?"

"Oh, no—" I took the opportunity to stress that there was no ready money in the Prentice family. "That's for rich people. We'd rent a place. A different one every year."

"I see." He seemed about to say more when a cell phone sounded.

"Excuse me," he said. " Few people have this number, and they know to call only if it's quite important."

He crossed the room and turned away from me, talking quietly into the phone. After a few minutes he folded the phone away and smiled at me.

"Well. I believe you've been all the help to me you can, Ms. Prentice, and I appreciate it. I'm going to give you this number"—he patted the pocket into which he had replaced the phone—"so that you will be able to contact me right away if anything comes to mind about where your brother might have put something so valuable." He looked straight into my eyes. "Or someone he might have given my property to."

"Of course," I said.

"Excellent. Now let me call in my—how did you refer to them, associates—so they can escort you back to your hotel."

Gypsy and Jory must have been very nearby, because they were in the room seconds after Wyman spoke again into his cell phone.

"Gentlemen," he said, "take Ms. Prentice home. She has been very helpful, and has promised"—that look again, full of meaning—"to stay in touch."

# —— CHAPTER TWENTY FIVE ——

Gypsy and Jory fell in on either side of me to escort me from the room and the house. To anyone watching, it would probably have looked as if they were taking special care of a guest who didn't know her way around but I felt their nearness, especially Gypsy's, as faintly menacing. I thought that if I looked to one side or back, I would be physically redirected straight toward the door. The white car was waiting in front, engine purring like a petted cat. Jory held the door for me and got in beside me and Gypsy again got in front. I wondered if I was going to be cross-examined about my conversation with Eliot Wyman, then realized that was unlikely. However strange the circumstances, I had been an invited guest of their boss, whom they clearly feared.

We rode back through the smog in silence except for the driver's humming something I didn't recognize, occasionally singing a phrase or two in Spanish. When we pulled up in front of my hotel Jory got out and went around to open my door, then walked me to the entrance. I didn't feel inclined to shake his hand or thank him for the ride, so I nodded at him and started toward the revolving door.

"Miss Prentice."

I turned back toward him. Jory said, "You seem like a nice girl. Smart, too. But one thing I've noticed – even smart people can be dumb sometimes. What I'm telling you is this. Mr. Wyman is just as smart, but no one's ever called him nice. You don't want to mess with him, OK?"

I widened my eyes a little. Who, me? I said, "I told Mr. Wyman everything

I know, which isn't a whole lot. He asked me to call if I thought of anything that might help him and I said that I would."

Jory smiled then. It almost reached his eyes. "Good," he said, turning back to the car. "See that you do."

I'm not sure why bad guys that keep things on a civil, even urbane level are scarier than the ones who rail and threaten, but they are. Maybe it's because the imagination can always come up with something worse than whatever overt threat has been made. I wanted very much to be in my room with the safety chain on and a familiar voice on the other end of the phone line.

It was a little after four. Seven P.M. on the east coast. Tom would almost surely have after-work visitors—so, much as I would have liked to talk to him I forewent calling the hospital (better in person anyhow) and dialed Martha's number.

"Nell!" came her welcome voice. "Woody is in my lap. Did you know he likes my squash soup?"

I laughed. "He's no fool. It's not soup weather out here—hot and smoggy."

"Have you found out anything?"

That was Martha. Lovely manners but always straight to the point. I said, "A lot, actually. So much so that I'm going to be able to head home tomorrow."

"That's wonderful! Aren't you the clever one."

"A lucky break," I said. It sounded better than telling her I'd been kidnapped and threatened by criminals and was scared silly that they would somehow find out about Luke.

"Nell," Martha said, "this must be difficult for you."

I had lied by omission about my ugly sources, but even if I tried to brush off her comment she would know.

"It is," I said. "But it's always better to know. And of course I'm not doing this just for me."

*Hei aleitheia eleutherosei*, Jesus says. The truth will set you free. I don't know if I'd go that far, but I was keeping my promise, and it felt good. Just as long as I didn't drag Ned's son into just the kind of thing a father wants his child kept out of.

"Where's Woody sleeping?" I asked, to change the subject.

"In my bed. He gets under the quilt so just his nose is showing. For breakfast I give him a little cream with his food."

"I should fly out tonight. Another day or so with you and he'll never come home with me."

We hung up, and I pocketed my key card, picked up my purse and took the stairs to the lobby. I had thought I would have a few days in Los Angeles to find a present for Tom, but the gift shop of the Bradley was going to have to do.

It was like every other traveler's gift shop I've ever been in, adjusted for locale. The ones in Maine have stuffed lobsters and miniature lighthouses and blueberry muffin mix. This one ran to themes of citrus fruit, surfing and the movies. There were a few nice posters—Tom might like the *Casablanca* one—but I remembered my resolve to bring him something suggestive of the active, virile lifestyle that would be his again in no time. Toward the back of the shop were sweatshirts and T-shirts, most of them with eternal sunshine motifs, but I found a handsome yellow sweatshirt in Tom's size that had L.A. Lakers written across the front in white. There was no further information about what the L.A. Lakers did, but I was pretty sure they played a sport. If I were wrong, at least Tom could enjoy how out of it I was. I took the shirt to the register, paid with my credit card and was on my way back to my room when I remembered I wanted to get something for Martha and for Luke. I was going to have to pay closer attention to the fact that my family was growing.

# CHAPTER TWENTY SIX

FOR DINNER I FOUND A PLACE near the hotel that specialized in health food and vegetarian dishes. This was more like the California I had envisioned, and I let the cheerful waitress suggest a kind of goulash that was actually quite tasty. It came with brown bread and a salad, and I ordered herb tea instead of coffee or a drink. Even a few hours of jet lag is more than I'm used to, and I was looking forward to a night's sleep and then my flight, east this time, that would take me home. I walked back to my hotel under a movie-set moon, checked the bathroom to make sure I had no more uninvited guests, and fell into bed without even checking out the wondrously myriad TV channels.

Maybe it was the powerful air conditioning that made me feel enough at home to sleep well on a hot, humid night less than three weeks before Thanksgiving. Tom and I had spent the previous Thanksgiving together, both of us involved in the Andrea Reed case. I always liked to open my email and see that Laura Reed had sent me new pictures of her now three-and-a-half-year-old daughter. I had promised Laura that she would be taking those pictures, but in my heart I had been afraid to believe my own words.

I was up early, eager to be on my way and tempted to skip breakfast, but if my flight were delayed I knew I'd be paying three bucks for a stale muffin at the airport. To my delight I found spread out in the lobby for guests a repast of juice, bagels and coffee. No doubt the cost of this free food was more than built into the room rate I had charged to my credit card, but I fell to as gratefully as any Homeric wanderer who arrives at a host's gate to be welcomed with a lavish feast.

Outside, it was 75 sunny degrees. From my taxi I watched thinly-clad people walk, jog or bicycle on the crowded sidewalks. I knew the majority of Californians were transplants, and wondered if the climate was what lured them and then made them stay. I supposed there could be some appeal to celebrating Christmas with the windows open, but not for me. My heart was in changeable New England, where the people I loved were waiting for me.

Flying east, an hour at a time I lost the three hours gained en route to California. Six P.M. in Boston, the city dark and windy, thick with traffic, sharply cold with a flurry. I was home.

The weight of the past two days—the long trip, the emotions it had stirred up—had completely caught up with me by the time I stepped into my apartment, which seemed profoundly empty without Woody there to greet me. I wanted nothing more than to heat up some soup and fall into my own bed. But it was important to me that I let Luke know right away what I had been able to learn in California. Not all of it, of course—certainly not the part about Wyman's role, deny it though he might, in Ned's death. But enough, I hoped, to bring the boy some consolation at a time he so needed it.

I signed on to my email, clicked DELETE ALL to rid myself of the financial opportunities and prescription drug offers cluttering my spam folder, and typed in LO. Up came my nephew's address. I tabbed to the subject line and watched the cursor blink monotonously as I rejected one Subject after another. Your father? My trip? Bad people I've just met? Finally, before the server could get tired of waiting and shut down as it periodically did, I typed: *I'm home.*

*Dear Luke,*
*I just got back from Los Angeles. I'll tell you about it when I see you. ( I also have a present for you.) I wanted you to know right away that there were two men responsible for what happened to your father, and neither one of them is still alive.*

Again the cursor pulsed as I thought about continuing. Should I assure the boy that I was telling the truth (up to a point) and not just saying what he wanted to hear? I read over what I had written and decided that it sounded right. I tapped Enter and closed with *Love, Aunt Nell.* New as such a phrase was to me, it, too, sounded right.

I sent the note, got out of my travel outfit and into a nightgown, and delved into my supply of chicken noodle soup. Two minutes in the microwave, Parmesan Goldfish for fiber, and I had a meal I wouldn't have traded for the finest cuisine greater Los Angeles had to offer.

# —— CHAPTER TWENTY SEVEN ——

IN THE MORNING I STOPPED BY my office on my way to see Tom. There were a couple of phone messages—I returned the calls and was happy to get answering machines, wanting to see Tom much more than I wanted to be stuck on the phone. My mail could wait, except for a letter I quickly skimmed, from the surprised and grateful insurer of the stolen coin collection. The praise was nice, and the enclosed check nicer still. I folded it into my wallet and thought of the Christmas bonus I'd have for Tad once I'd gotten to the bank.

No one stopped me at the hospital as I hurried down the corridor to Tom's room. The first thing I noticed was that the bed where the teenage boy had been was empty. Tom was sitting by the window reading the *Globe*, the sections he was finished with neatly folded on the rolling bed table. He looked up and grinned when he saw me.

"Tom," I said, and hurried over to hug him. "How are you? What do the doctors say? When might you be going home?"

He set the newspaper aside and got up to move the other chair around for me. "Two days in Los Angeles and you're talking like a prosecutor on *Law and Order*."

I took the chair he was holding. "Sorry—it's just that I'm glad to see you. And you don't get to hear about my trip until you tell me how you are."

"Better." He looked at me. "Really. All the tests look good, and I've decided to stop thinking that a couple of months behind a desk is the end of the world. As for when they're springing me, my insurance company is already acting as if I've been malingering here for a month. So probably tomorrow. There—I've done my part. Now you."

I told him everything. Jory and Gypsy coming for me at the hotel. The scary Eliot Wyman. How Ned had died, and for what. As I spoke, aware of Tom's keen attention, I realized how much I trusted him.

"I'm concerned about Luke," I said. "He was only three when Ned left, but if Ned managed to get the statue back to his wife there's a possibility that Luke knows something about it. Wyman gave me the creeps—I got the very strong feeling that he'd hurt anybody who was in the way of his getting what he wants."

Tom said, "And if your nephew does know where the statue is? What then, Nell? You said yourself it's stolen."

I gave him the most direct look I was capable of. "I don't care about that. I lost Ned—I'm not going to lose his son."

Tom was silent for a moment. A quality of his that I especially loved was his strong ethical sense, his belief that you decide what's right and then do it.

He reached for my hand. "How can I help?"

In the time I had known Tom—a year now—I had been gratified to see how well we could work together. Even after we became lovers, which can wreak havoc with other elements of a relationship. We sat now next to the hospital bed bouncing ideas off each other, coming up with a plan for how I might approach Luke, find out what if anything he knew, and most importantly protect him from Eliot Wyman's men. We were so completely engrossed in our conversation that a volunteer had to call twice from the doorway before we understood that she was delivering a lunch menu for Tom to choose from.

"No rare steak on that, I suppose," I said to him. "Don't worry, though—I'll buy you one when you get out. Which reminds me—I brought you something."

I reached for the bag I had pushed beneath the chair and held it out to him. He took it, reached inside and pulled out the sweatshirt. He looked at it carefully, then at me.

"Wow. This is great, Nell. You know how cold the station gets when the fair city of Newton is scrimping on heat. This will be just the thing…."

I was beaming. "I don't know what sport they play or what lake they're named after, but I thought…."

"A Lakers fan!"

The volunteer who was collecting lunch choices was standing in the doorway. Her tone as she looked at Tom was flirtatious (blue permanent notwithstanding), but I sensed a serious message.

"You're in Boston, Mister. Don't let anybody see you in that! They'll put arsenic in your coffee."

And then it dawned on me. The general term for what I'd gotten Tom was fan gear. There was supposed to be a direct correlation between wearing the shirt and wanting this team—the L.A. Lakers—to roll like a juggernaut over any and all rivals, including the one they no doubt had here in Boston.

Could I have been a bigger idiot?

"Tom," I began. He finished filling out the menu card and handed it to the volunteer.

"Actually," he said—flirting a bit himself, I swear—"my sister's from California. It's a big deal for her to bring me a shirt of *her* favorite team."

The volunteer looked at me. I did my best to appear fit and tanned.

"Oh. Well, that's really sweet then. Just be sure you have her around to explain when you wear it."

She left, and I returned Tom's grin and shook my head. "It's even worse than it looks—I got one for Luke, too."

"Easily fixed," Tom said. "Here's what you do. Take the T to Fenway and follow the signs for souvenirs. Buy Luke a sweatshirt that says Boston Red Sox – 2004 World Champions." I must have looked about to raise some concern because he said, "Don't worry about remembering the year—our parents weren't born the last time it happened. That will leave two of these..."—he held up the Lakers shirt—"...which you and I will wear—"

He did a deft sleight of hand with the shirt, and the logo disappeared.

"Inside out."

# —— CHAPTER TWENTY EIGHT ——

Tom was right—it was a complete no-brainer to find the souvenir shop near Fenway. Once inside, I was confronted with fan gear—for the right team this time—in every conceivable color and style. There were even baby bibs, and caps so small Woody could have worn them. Tom had also been right that I didn't have to concern myself with the year—every item commemorated 2004, in Roman or Arabic numerals.

"Help you?" I turned toward the voice, which belonged to a skinny blonde kid with an earring. His hands were tucked into the back pockets of his jeans.

"Oh—yes. Thank you. I'm looking for a shirt for my nephew. He's fifteen."

Now why had I said that? So this kid would know I wasn't in the market for a bib or pacifier? He turned and walked toward some deep shelves piled with sweatshirts.

"Hoodies," he said, pulling out a black one. In addition to the aforementioned hood the shirt had a capacious pouch in front. "What size?"

The clerk I had consulted with in Los Angeles had recommended an Adult Small, and while Tom had tactfully helped me out of my sports memorabilia gaffe, he hadn't said anything about the size, so I was able to answer the clerk's question with a confidence that belied the fact that I had only been an aunt for a little over a week. He moved to another pile of shirts. "Color?"

I thought of Luke's exotic coloring—half Prentice, half Aquila, which I recalled as the surname of the sister-in-law I would never know. The kid would look good in anything.

"Red," I decided. "An Adult Small red …hoodie."

The clerk slid a shirt out of the pile and led me to a register. I paid with my credit card and took the bag the clerk held out to me. Back in business, for only $29.95.

My car was parked near my office. I could have taken the T into Mass General, but I had driven into the city in the expectation that I would be going straight to the Cape to see Martha and reclaim my cat. The wind had come up, with a dry flurry of snow, but I decided to walk anyway. *Surely you didn't come here on foot*, people say in Homer, but I was in L.L. Bean from head to toe and the November air felt good after the unnatural heat of California. In twenty minutes I was passing the garage where I had expensively stashed my Volkswagen, and five minutes after that I was climbing the stairs to my office.

Martha answered the phone on the third ring. Hearing her voice, I felt even more happy to be home. She said Woody was fine but had missed me (I'll bet) and asked whether I could come for lunch.

"Why don't I take you somewhere?" I said. "Is the Daniel Webster open on Mondays?"

"I think so. But why don't I take you up on your kind offer another time? I'm making bread, and after you called last night I baked a squash so we could have soup."

This meant that lunch would be a fabulous hearty soup that contained, in addition to the squash, corn, rice and kielbasa. Served with Martha's homemade bread.

"If you hear sirens," I said, "it will be the police pursuing me down Route 3 as I drive at ninety miles an hour to your house."

My trip was an unusually quick one, in spite of my staying almost within the speed limit. It was November and a Monday, which meant that the Cape's popularity with visitors was on the wane until warmer weather. Route 3 may as well have been a carriage path compared to the little I had seen of the Los Angeles freeways. For years now there had been talk that the dangerous rotary south of Martha would be somehow modernized, but I doubted that was going to happen in my lifetime, or even Luke's.

There was smoke curling out of Martha's chimney as I parked in her driveway and shut off my engine. The bag from the hotel gift shop was on the seat beside me—had it really only been yesterday that I was on the other side of the country, being obscurely threatened by gangsters, meeting the man who had set in motion my brother's murder? I willed myself to put these thoughts aside, unwilling to bring such events, such people, even mentally into the safe haven that was Martha's home.

"Nell!" She had one hand on the frame of the door she opened to me, and the other supporting Woody. His head was leaning back against Martha's chest, and he looked content as only a feline can.

I wiped my feet on the mat and stepped inside, closing the door Martha had stepped back from. I could smell bread and soup, and a wood fire. Martha put Woody down and came to hug me, down jacket and all. Woody wound around my legs, purring. *Home.*

"I was here on Friday," I said. "But it seems as if I haven't seen you or Pretty Boy here in a much longer time."

"Because of where you went?" Martha asked.

I was startled. Of course she was right. In the few days since I'd been in this house I had journeyed deeply and painfully into my brother's past. But this was not the time to reflect on what I had learned, or what might lie ahead.

Martha exhibited her uncanny skill for seeming to be able to read my thoughts. "I want to hear all about your trip. But why don't we have lunch first—the bread is still warm."

She had made rye bread, with a golden brown crust and a delectable soft center. I accepted the heel Martha cut for me, along with the butter and a deep bowl of soup. I took just a moment to sigh with anticipation before picking up my spoon.

"Oh, Martha—this is amazing. I can taste the real cream. Which I'm sure Mr. Woody got to sample."

"He did, indeed. Just a little, though. I wouldn't want him to get sick in the car."

My hand, reaching for another slice of bread, stopped. I had a sudden, clear image before me of a boy named Monroe Marcus. He and I had had a phone conversation about car sickness, during which conversation I had fibbed a little to console him about his brother Madison's teasing. At the time, I had hoped to bring their mother back to the Marcus boys, but that hadn't happened.

"Nell?"

I put the bread on my plate. "Just wondering how I can keep things I don't want to think about from following me here."

When we had finished our meal Martha made coffee and we sat on the sofa drinking it, with Woody in my lap and my mug held at a careful distance in case he decided to stretch. Outside, the sky was a wintry gray, so unlike the summer afternoon I had brought Tom here.

"I saw Tom this morning," I told Martha. "He seemed a lot better. I just don't know what I'd do…"

"If something happened to him?"

"Yes. Or you. Or Woody." Hearing his name, my cat lifted his head for me to scratch. "It's such a small circle of people…and animals…that mean everything to me…" I trailed off, not sure how to finish my thought.

"Quality over quantity," Martha said. I looked up to see her most mischievous smile.

"Exactly," I agreed, laughing. I reached over to squeeze her hand. "There is nothing I would rather do than spend the whole day here with you, but I probably should go soon if I don't want to be stuck in rush hour traffic with this fellow caterwauling in the back seat."

"One more cup of coffee, then, while you tell me about your trip?"

The version of my trip I gave to Martha bore little resemblance to the detailed account I had given Tom. I told her that Ned had gotten involved with drugs and some bad people, and that his death had been a tragic accident. I made no mention of Jory or Gypsy or Eliot Wyman, or of the missing sculpture. I didn't like being deceptive with her, but these were dangerous people—the less she knew the better.

"It means a lot to me that I'll be able to tell Luke that his father didn't just abandon him."

"When do I get to meet him?" Martha asked. "Why don't you bring him here for Thanksgiving?"

Again I was reminded that for the first time since Michael died I had family—I was Luke's closest relative. When holidays came around I would need to be thinking of him, making sure he had somewhere to go. The realization was not unwelcome.

"And Tom, of course," Martha said. "I'll get a fresh turkey, and maybe Luke will want to mash the potatoes…"

Last Thanksgiving, Tom and I had been in my apartment, having sausage omelets while a snowstorm buried Boston. What a lot had happened in my life in the twelve months since.

"I'll ask them both—thank you. I'd have everybody to my place, but I only have three chairs."

"The right number for society," Martha said, paraphrasing Thoreau. That reminded me of the present I'd brought back from California for her.

"I didn't have much time to find you something," I said as she took *Birds of the Western United States* out of the bag I handed her. "And I know it's not as if you're going to need to identify a California Condor at your feeder, but I thought…"

"It's wonderful, dear. Thank you. I'll get to learn about birds we don't get in the East. And what's more..."

She gave me her widest smile as she looked up from the book.

"...If I get interested enough in these birds, I'll make a trip to see them."

Martha came out to the car with me and opened the passenger door so I could set Woody's carrier on the floor. He began meowing at once—I closed the door firmly and turned to hug Martha.

"Don't stand out here. It's cold."

"Only to those of us who have just come from California."

"Touché." I kissed her cheek. "I'll call you when we get home."

"And you'll let me know about Thanksgiving?"

"I will. Now will you please humor me and go inside?"

She stood watching through the storm door as I backed around and pulled out, waving until I could no longer see the house.

"Lucky you, Woody, "I said. "Getting to spend the whole weekend. But maybe the next time I come here it will be with Luke and Tom."

That prospect was so appealing to me that I emailed Luke as soon as I got home. Woody was exploring the apartment as if he'd been away for a month—for once he didn't even try to get into my lap as I booted up the computer. On the subject line I typed Thanksgiving. I explained about my friend Martha and said we both hoped Luke could come. I decided not to mention Tom, since I hadn't yet invited him. I launched my note into cyberspace, then logged off so I could use the phone, which shares a line with the computer in the best twenty-first century fashion.

"Tom, it's Nell. How are you doing?"

"Good. I'm reading that book you gave me. Poor guy—the brother."

"I know." One of the adventuresome young authors had died in his twenties. "But those kids could sure say they had lived."

We were both silent for a moment. Then I said, "I've just come from Martha's. She'd like you, me and Luke to come for Thanksgiving. Are you free?"

"Damn," Tom said. "If only I'd been able to tell my mother I had an invitation."

"What's wrong with going to your mother's? I won't have a word said against her. Anybody who can cook like that..."

"You're no doubt remembering her roast chicken with cream gravy." Tom sighed. "She tells me that this year, in my honor, we're going to be 'eating healthy'."

"Oh."

" 'Oh' is right. There I'll be with God knows what on my plate while you…"

I laughed. "Better not go there. And you know Sheila is right."

"See if you're still saying that the next time she has you to dinner and there's not a fat or carb for miles in any direction."

It was now mid-afternoon. My building was quiet, and I was still feeling the effects of my trip, so I stretched out on the sofa with a book and my cat, drifting into a pleasant nap that lasted until the sound of doors opening and closing signaled that my fellow tenants were arriving home. I turned on the computer and saw that I had mail from Luke.

*Hi Aunt Nell-*
*I can come for Thanksgiving. Some of the guys invited me home with them,*
*but I told them I'd probably be with you. I think it was really their mothers*
*who made them ask me.*
*Luke*

I read this message several times, taking in the implications. No doubt Luke was right—the mothers of his classmates had probably leaned on their sons to bring home this boy who had nobody.

*But he does have somebody*, I thought. I answered Luke's note and traded computer for phone to give Martha the news.

Because I hadn't known how long I'd be away I had emptied the refrigerator of all perishables. That meant soup and crackers again tonight, black coffee in the morning, and then a raid on the supermarket. I fed Woody, listening to him purr, and realized that I felt every bit as content as he sounded.

—— CHAPTER TWENTY NINE ——

Tom was released from the hospital on Tuesday. His brother was picking him up, and other family members would be coming by as soon as he was home, so it would be a few days before I would be seeing him without any other people around. I was just as happy to have the time to think through what Tom's changed physical condition might mean for him, and for me. Our relationship had begun with a shared desire to solve a case, after which we had discovered that, while I was clueless about sports and he was equally so about the classics, we always had lots to talk about. I genuinely liked him before we ever spent a night together, which I happen to think is the best way to go about such things.

And the sex was well worth the wait.

I'm one of those people who's never ill, so it's often hard for me to really understand how this kind of scare must affect people. Back in June I had told Tom I was ready to come back to life. But my hurt had been emotional—a deep fear that if I loved somebody the way I loved Michael, that person could be snatched from me just as Michael had been.

When I saw Tom in the hospital, I didn't have a moment's regret. If a few months were all we were going to have together, that would still be infinitely better than years of the isolation into which I had retreated when Michael died. I intended now to make the most of every minute I could spend with Tom.

But his injury was physical. His heart, that miraculous organ most of us take for granted, had stopped doing its job. I wondered if it might be a long time before he felt ready to do anything that might tax his heart.

I decided to call him and see how he was, then suggest that I come by his place Saturday night with a DVD and a pizza. I had my hand on the phone when I rethought that last part. Make that a DVD and a broiled chicken.

"It's the weirdest thing," Tom said when I asked what he was doing. "I never thought I'd be lying on the sofa at three in the afternoon reading every word of the newspaper twice and forcing myself not to turn on the boob tube. The only reason I can restrain myself is imagining your expression if you found out I'd been watching *Judge Judy*."

"It's only for a little while," I said. "Before you know it you'll be leaping tall buildings again. But for now—how about if I bring a movie and dinner to your place this Saturday?"

"A movie and dinner sound great. But by Saturday I'll have had five days of staring at these walls. Let me take you out."

I opened my mouth to ask whether he was sure he was up to it. Then, just like in Homer, no words passed the barrier of my teeth. Finally I said, "You're on. What movie do you want to see?"

"*Troy*."

As the week passed I thought often of my trip to California. It was strange and disquieting to have stood right next to the man who had been the catalyst for my brother's death. But Ned was beyond my help. It was Luke I had to think of now.

Tom and I had decided on Legal Sea Foods for an early dinner on Saturday—the movie was said to be nearly as long as the actual war. As I dressed for my evening out I was filled with a sense of gratitude. A week ago I had thought I might lose Tom, just as I had feared. But Atropos was snipping somebody else's life-thread. It felt like a second chance, one I would make the most of.

Even at 5 P.M. there was a wait at Legal Sea Foods. We sat near the entrance with our drinks (Should he be having wine? I absolutely had to stop this) and waited for our table to be ready. It was too noisy to talk much, but I was perfectly content to sit holding Tom's hand and watching the people. A group with a baby told the receptionist there were six and a half in their party, and Tom and I smiled at each other at this coy nonsense.

"Kramer," the amplified voice said. "Kramer for two."

Everything smelled wonderful—I scanned the menu in an agony of indecision. "What are you thinking of getting?" I asked Tom.

"Broiled scrod and a tossed salad."

"Oh." Reluctantly I drew my eyes away from the deep-fried offerings. "Well, that *does* sound good. Maybe I'll…"

"Nell."

"What?"

"Get the fried clams. It's fine, really."

I looked at him, at his smile. "You are a wonderful human being. In addition to being a mind-reader."

I wonder what the people close to us in the movie theater thought of my reactions for the nearly three hours I sat watching *Troy*. I did my best to suppress my shock as liberty after liberty was taken with the divine Homer. Since Tom would occasionally laugh and squeeze my hand when I inadvertently gasped, I suppose I was not wholly successful in keeping my outrage to myself.

"Paris!" I said to Tom in the car. "Paris was the *hero*. Patroclus and Achilles were *cousins*. Achilles liked girls!"

"Can you stay?"

I stopped in mid-rant. "What?"

"I've missed you so badly. I want you to stay with me tonight."

I had one fleeting thought about his health. I had virtually no thought of Woody, whose food and water dishes were full. I didn't have a nightgown, but we could turn up the heat.

"I thought you'd never ask."

I was up before Tom the following morning. He stirred when I got out of bed as quietly as I could, then pulled the blanket up over his head and went back to sleep. I felt touched by the trust implied in his lack of alertness—I knew how quick his reflexes were in any situation in which there might be danger. I tiptoed from the room and put yesterday's clothes back on. In the kitchen—spare and tidy—I found a jar of instant coffee and heated water in the saucepan that apparently did duty as a kettle. I sat at the counter sipping the coffee, not turning on any lights or feeling the need for a book. After a half hour or so I heard Tom moving about in the bedroom. I filled the saucepan and turned on the flame under it. Tom came into the kitchen in a bathrobe and looked from the stove to me.

"I'm a virtual goddess of domesticity," I told him. "I ground the beans, refined the sugar and fashioned the cup on my potter's wheel."

Tom found a brown mug in the sink and mixed water and instant coffee in it. "Let's go in the living room."

We sat on the sofa with our coffee, each thinking our thoughts. The day was slow in coming, but I was in no hurry. Finally, as winter light filled the room, I said, "I could sit here all day, but I suppose I should be heading home. Is there anything you need? Some way I could make myself useful?"

Tom put down his cup and wrapped his arms around me. "Oh, don't worry. You've certainly done that."

# CHAPTER THIRTY

WOODY WAS DELIGHTED TO SEE BOTH me and the guilt-trip can of tuna I'd picked up at a 7-11. My guilt was not for leaving Woody alone overnight, but for scarcely giving him a thought in my relief and pleasure at having Tom back. I spooned some of the fish into his bowl and smiled at his audible enjoyment of it as I headed for the shower. I microwaved some banana bread oatmeal and booted up my computer. I had mail from Luke.

*Dear Aunt Nell-*
*My friend Nick is going to be in Hyanis for Thanksgiving. His Dad is taking some guys to a hockey game. They asked me to go. Is it OK if I say yes?*
*Luke*

A sense of unease took precedence over my wanting to immediately correct Luke's creative spelling of Hyannis. The very place where I had claimed my family vacationed, in order to steer Eliot Wyman and his thugs away from what was now left of my family—Ned's son. I thought of making some excuse why it wasn't a good idea for Luke to accept his friend's invitation. But in truth I had been wondering about what I would do with him for four days in my cable-free, computer-game-lacking apartment. He wasn't likely to want to sit around reading Cicero, and I wasn't sure what was open over the holiday. I hit Reply.

*Dear Luke,*

*That's really nice of your friend. Of course you may go. Please ask his mother
if I can drive you to Hyannis* (I was tempted to boldface the word, then
thought, oh, please) *late Thursday afternoon after we leave my friend
Martha's.*
*Love,*
*Aunt Nell*

It felt distinctly odd after forty-two years to be *in loco parentis*. The more
I thought about that, the more I realized that there was something I should
be talking to Lee Thomson about. I needed to ask him how I could go about
applying for guardianship of this boy I had known exactly two weeks.

The next day, I began that process by emailing Luke to ask him if he had
any objection to my becoming his legal guardian. His reply was waiting when
I got home: *OK*. A man of few words, like his father. I felt a by now familiar
pang that Ned's life choices had deprived him of the opportunity to see his
son growing into a man.

Lee Thomson told me that there would be paperwork galore and a
thorough investigation of my background and character, but I was "the
natural choice" as long as Luke agreed. "Don't take this the wrong way," the
attorney said, "but it's actually a plus that there's not a lot of money involved.
Lucas is on scholarship, and his mother had life insurance but not a whole
lot. The house in Maine is paid for, and the life insurance will cover most
expenses until Lucas turns eighteen."

Oh, yes—the house in Maine. The place Ned had lived for a short time,
and where his son had grown up. I said, "Is your firm involved with the
property?"

"No. Everything is so recent. We were all glad to find that the boy had a
relative. If he hadn't, eventually one of us would probably have been appointed
guardian and arranged for the sale of the house."

I could see that would make sense. A boy of fifteen could hardly live alone
in rural Maine, and I was not in a position to move there from Boston and
take cases involving stolen lobster traps. I saw that I was getting way ahead
of myself.

"Could you begin drawing up the papers? I know these things take
time, but I'll feel better if I know I have legal standing if anything should
happen…"

I couldn't help but think that the chances of something bad happening to
Luke had been smaller before he met me and I began to look for answers about
his father's death. But there was no turning back now—I had promised.

"Certainly," Lee Thomson said. "I should have something out to you
in a few days. Call me if you have any other questions, and a very happy
Thanksgiving to you and your family."

# —— CHAPTER THIRTY ONE ——

I KEPT BUSY THE LAST FULL week before Thanksgiving. A number of clients who would be traveling checked in with me for a status on their cases, which necessitated reading files, making calls, and writing reports that would allow me to keep my billing straight. A day care center I had done some work for called to have me do a couple of background checks. And exactly a week before the nation's big family holiday, I found out what had happened to Faith Howe.

Faith's sister Irma was the person who had hired me. There was an inheritance at stake, and Irma Harrington made no attempt to hide her exasperation that I hadn't been immediately able to determine her sister's fate. But now one of my many inquiries had brought results. On my desk was a death certificate, dated September 5, 2001, issued by a doctor at a Chicago hospital.

Faith Judith Howe. Caucasian, age 27. Five feet seven inches, one hundred and two pounds. Cause of death: Accidental overdose of heroin and other narcotics.

Looking at the single sheet of paper I felt a mix of emotions. Even though the chances of my finding this girl alive had been slim, I had not entirely given up hope until now. And of course the parallels with my brother's death were inescapable. ( *Just another dead junkie*, I seemed to hear Jon Halloran saying, before he remembered who he was talking to and apologized.) Had Faith's death really been an accident? One thing was certain—Irma, whose bitterness about her sister's reckless life was so evident, would have no interest in taking this any further. I had found the answer she needed, and was sure she would want only to put the entire sad situation in the past. Well, who could blame her?

I needed to let Irma know, but wasn't up for more of that bitterness, more of the assertion that Faith had ruined several lives and deserved whatever she got. Maybe so, but when somebody dies that young, after such a life, it seems that somebody should care.

Knowing Irma must be at work, I dialed her home number so I could leave a message on her answering machine. The phone rang three times, and a voice answered. It didn't sound like that of my client.

"I'm sorry—I may have dialed the wrong number. I'm trying to reach Irma Harrington."

"This is she."

Now I realized that it was her voice, though sounding stuffed up. Since I thought I'd be talking to a machine (*I have some information—please call me.*) I hadn't planned what to say. To stall, I said, "It's Nell Prentice, Mrs. Harrington. I thought you'd be at work."

"I've had a bad cold. I was going to go in today, but it's so raw out that I thought I'd give it one more day."

"Oh. Well, it's good you're feeling better..." I drew in a breath. "Mrs. Harrington, I've received some...documentation...on your sister."

Documentation. Great—makes it sound as if her passport came through. Next stop Hell. Before I could begin again my client asked, "Is Faith dead?"

Her voice, even with the lingering congestion, was flat. I said. "Yes. I'm sorry—she is."

"Where did she die?"

"In Chicago. A hospital in Chicago."

"I wonder how she ended up there. New York I could have understood. She loved it the time our parents took us there."

I sensed that she needed to keep speaking. She went on, "Faith was about five, and I was nine. It was Easter vacation. I remember I made my neck sore trying to see the tops of buildings. Faith was doing it, too—we were making each other laugh. Then I heard my mother calling, all panicky. Faith had been right there, a few steps behind me, and suddenly my mother couldn't see her. I should have stayed right where I was, but in the confusion—people were stopping to see what had happened—I got past the crowd and ran back to where Faith had pointed out a puppy to me. And there she was, down on the sidewalk petting that dog on its leash. I went running back to my mother and said, "It's all right—I found her.""

*Don't do this to yourself,* I wanted to say, and maybe I would have, but

Irma's voice changed, back under tight control. "Thank you for letting me know, Ms. Prentice. You'll send me the paperwork and your bill? I'll see that it's paid promptly."

I was sure that she would. The paperwork filed with the court, the check written to the investigator and Irma Harrington could go about the business of forgetting the sister who had once wandered off in a dangerous city, but that time had been saved.

The Monday before Thanksgiving was the forty-first anniversary of the assassination of President John Kennedy. I hadn't even been two years old, so of course had no memory of that day, but when I got older my mother would talk at this time of year about the young President as if he had been a beloved family member. Watching the news footage this year, I could see the appeal—a youthful, charismatic man taking over from a bald and affable General who must have seemed to many to embody the past.

I had spoken with Luke on the phone about what time I would be picking him up, and knew that classes on Wednesday morning ended at ten. I found I was looking forward to the drive back with both of us in the car and maybe a chance to find out a little more about this boy who shared my name and my genes but about whom I knew very little. I left Boston in a light snow, driving under the speed limit most of the way, and reached Ashfield a little before eleven. The first thing I saw as I drove up the long driveway to the parking lot was a half-dozen boys, their coats in a heap on the ground, having a snowball fight. As I watched, Luke, in a checked shirt, made a dead-accurate hit on the back of a boy's neck and a minute later went down laughing under the retaliatory onslaught of the boy and his friends.

I drove on up to the dormitory, knowing that my nephew would probably have been discomfited if I'd stopped, but glad I hadn't missed the sight of his face glowing with cold and exertion, just the way his father's had when our Dad would take Ned and me sledding.

Luke didn't have a lot he was bringing for the Thanksgiving break—a duffel of laundry, a few clothes, a laptop. Seeing the clothes I remembered the sweatshirt I'd bought for him.

"This is for you," I said, handing him the bag. "It's sort of a souvenir of my trip, but you'll be able to tell I didn't get it in California."

"All right!" my nephew said, holding up the shirt as I sent off special blessings to Tom for saving me from a major act of cluelessness. "Can I wear it?"

"Of course. I'm glad you like it."

He pulled the shirt over his head, flipped up the hood and tucked his hands in the front pouch. I had been right—the bright red color looked great on him. I amused myself for a moment by imagining his horror if I said so.

"Thanks, Aunt Nell."

"You're very welcome. Ready to go?"

There were several sign-out checkpoints, so it was noon before we were headed back down the driveway toward the road. The snow had stopped, after leaving a picturesque coating on the trees.

"We'll stop for lunch at Sturbridge," I said. "Is that okay?"

"Sure."

I decided not to press for conversation. We'd be spending the next couple of days together, and chances were that even if he continued to be reticent with me, he'd probably be more open with Martha. Most people were. There was one thing, though, that had been so much on my mind that I wasn't going to be able to put off asking about it.

"Luke, there's something I want to ask you. About what you said the last time I was here. If you could just answer this one question for me, then we could change the subject…"

He was looking wary. Well, who wouldn't? I decided to stop beating around the bush and just come out with it. "You told me you thought your father had committed suicide. I wondered where you got that idea."

He didn't answer right away. When he did speak it was in a low voice.

"My mother. That's what she said happened."

Now I was even more mystified. Why would a woman tell her child such a thing, when it wasn't true?

"Can you remember exactly what she said?"

This time he nodded, and I realized that hearing of his father's death would be something a boy would be likely to remember, word for word.

"She was sort of mad at me. And I was mad, too, so I told her I was going to run away and find him. Then she yelled at me that he wasn't coming back ever—that he'd killed himself with drugs."

Languages are one of the things I live for—that unique experience of determining what a word or phrase really means. Seldom do I think of how easily confusion can arise in the English language—especially when the hearer is a child.

"I can see why you took that the way you did. I probably would have done the same."

Of course I wanted to ask him if people used drugs at his school, if he did. But I'd promised him just one question this time, and had no idea what I'd say if I heard something not to my liking. This business of being an aunt wasn't all buying presents and watching snowball fights.

"Want the radio on?" I asked, and was so relieved when he said okay that I didn't say one word about the noisy rubbish on the station he tuned in.

There were several Ashfield boys with their families at the Sturbridge rest stop. We adults ended up letting the kids get a table together, while we took our burgers and salads to the far side of the room where it was a lot quieter. I was relieved that no one gave me the third degree after hearing my basic explanation that I was Luke's paternal aunt and was taking him to the Cape for Thanksgiving. That started a conversation about the Native American protests that for several years had been complicating the Thanksgiving festivities in Plymouth, and then someone mentioned the cost of college and I was able to relax and listen to the expert views of people who had been doing this for at least fifteen years instead of a few weeks.

Luke fell asleep in the car when we were just past Worcester and slept the rest of the way to Boston while I, having turned off the radio, drank in the silence and privacy that until very recently I had taken completely for granted. I parked a block from my building and touched the bright red sleeve of his sweatshirt.

"Luke? We're home."

# ——— CHAPTER THIRTY TWO ———

HE OPENED HIS EYES, BLINKED AND shook his head, then stretched as lithely as any cat. Lately I had noticed that my own cat, at nine years old, was getting up a little more slowly, jumping a little less high. How affecting it was to see this young person whose every limb and muscle was so supple. *Like a young tree I reared him*, says Achilles' mother, and now I could see how apt the simile was. Then I thought of the photo of Faith Howe at this same age, and gave my head a slight shake to make the image of the doomed runaway girl disappear.

Luke was looking up the street and I said, pointing, "That's my apartment up there. Let's bring your things up and you can meet Woody."

He unbuckled his seatbelt and got out of the car, reaching into the back for his bags and computer. I unlocked the front door and collected my mail, then led the way upstairs.

"My cat loves company," I told my nephew. "Just let me get hold of him before we open the door all the way."

Sure enough, a nose poked out at the level of our ankles as soon as I pushed the door open a few inches. I inserted my purse in the space and used it to nudge Woody back into the room as Luke edged in behind me.

"There," I said, picking up Woody as Luke, with both hands full, closed the door with his foot. He did it exactly the way I performed that maneuver myself—was this another thing that was in the genes?

Luke dropped his bags to the floor and set his computer on top of them. "Can I hold him?"

"He'd love it."

I passed Woody into Luke's outstretched hands. The boy turned Woody expertly into a secure position and my cat leaned back, purring like an outboard motor.

"He likes you. He's going to want to sleep with you for sure."

"That'd be okay."

This brief reply gave me a tremor of hostess anxiety. I'd never had a teenager under my roof. When Martha stayed here we could talk for hours, or just sit quietly. She would often have some sewing with her, and would ask me to read aloud while she worked. We were currently about halfway through *Pride and Prejudice*. And when Tom stayed here—well, let's just say we could always find something to do.

"Would you like something to drink?" I asked Luke.

"Sure."

I checked the refrigerator, which I had carefully stocked. "Coke or ginger ale?"

"Coke, please."

We sat on the sofa with our drinks (in glasses—it was up to Aunt Nell to set a good example). Woody lazed between us, no doubt the only one of us completely at ease. As I got up to put the glasses in the sink my eye fell on Luke's laundry bag.

"I know," I said. "Let's do this. The washing machine's down in the basement—let's throw in your stuff and then we can go into Boston. Have you ever been to the Quincy Market?"

He shook his head. I said, "It's a great place. Do you like pizza?"

This time he nodded. I said enthusiastically, "We'll go to Pizzeria Regina. How does that sound?"

"Okay."

Okay it is. And your Aunt Nell will have a nice glass of red wine with her pizza. Maybe two.

When I started to pick up the laundry bag to take to the basement Luke said he could do it, so I gave him a handful of quarters and the detergent and off he went, down the stairs at a run, probably as relieved as I was to have a few minutes free from the need for conversation.

"Well, Woody," I said as he curled around my ankles, "this is going to be interesting."

Luke seemed to enjoy the subway ride into Boston, reading the posters and looking out at the tunnel walls and clutching the seat arm with a big grin when the car lurched as it came into a station. I found myself looking forward to showing my brother's son some of the sights he would be seeing for the first time. We got off at Haymarket and walked through the early dark toward the lights of Faneuil Hall. Inside the market, we strolled with the crowds past stalls offering gadgets for left-handed people, baby items, stuffed toys and sports memorabilia. At a stand featuring Red Sox items I gestured to the pins, hats, photos and pennants and asked Luke, "Want a souvenir?"

"I have my shirt," he said. "Aunt Nell…"

"Yes?"

"You don't have to get me stuff."

I was not at all sure how to take this statement. Was my nephew a polite, unacquisitive boy who saw no reason he should be showered with gifts, or was I seen as trying to get too close, too fast? Either way, it was time to back off.

"Okay," I said, and like my nephew left it at that.

At Pizzeria Regina we ordered a large meatball, with mushrooms on my half and extra cheese on his. I'd have to avoid places like this for a while when I was with Tom, so was making the most of dining out with a healthy fifteen-year-old. The paper plates we crumbled for the trash contained nothing but crumbs, and very few of those.

Back at my apartment, I fed Woody while Luke went downstairs to put his clothes in the dryer. Since I couldn't imagine our sitting in silence—or worse, in awkward, forced conversation—in my living room, I unfolded the sofa bed and gathered up my own reading to take into my room.

"Luke," I said when he'd returned from the basement, "Did you bring a book?"

He looked as startled as if I'd asked him to name the nine Muses. After a moment he said, "I've got homework and stuff, but I wasn't going to do it tonight."

I laughed at that. "No, I wouldn't think so." I saw that the look he was giving his computer was one of longing. Before he could even ask, I walked to my bookcase and pulled out a paperback from between Roth and Sarton, holding it up for Luke to see.

"*Catcher in the Rye.* Have you read it?"

He shook his head. I tossed him the paperback, which he caught. "See what you think."

I left the door to my room open and sat reading for an hour. When I went back out into the living room Luke was flopped on his stomach on the sofa bed with Woody beside him and the book open.

"Luke? I'll go down and get your laundry."

He looked up at me. "Thanks." Then immediately his eyes dropped back to the book. "This is good."

I suppressed an impulse to cheer as for a gladiator. Was I witnessing the birth of a reader? I made my voice as off-handed as I possibly could.

"I thought so, too."

He was still reading when I returned with the bag of warm laundry, which I dropped next to the sofa bed. Luke said, "Thanks," then laughed.

"What's funny?"

"This kid—Holden—he just says whatever he's thinking. Like right here—" Luke turned back from the page he was on— "He just comes right out and tells you that he lies all the time."

I remembered that now, from my own reading of the book when I was Luke's age. It had probably struck me funny, too, at the time, though a quarter century later I was less charmed, making my living as I do trying to sift truth from lies. Holden Caulfield—he'd be on Medicare by now, probably still out of step. I decided I'd try rereading the book after Luke was finished with it.

"I'm going in my room now. Do you know where everything is?"

"Mmm-hmm."

"Just look in the refrigerator if you get hungry or thirsty. The blue towels in the bathroom are for you."

He was looking at me with those familiar hazel eyes. Well, he had managed for fifteen years without my hovering—probably he could do it one more night.

"Right. Well, good night. I'll see you in the morning."

"G' night."

Woody followed me with his eyes as I crossed the living room to my bedroom. A strip of light showed around the frame after I closed the door, and I found myself looking up from time to time from Anne Tyler's latest to see if Luke was still up. Around midnight, I put my book down and went to the door, opening it quietly.

Luke was sprawled on his back, arms flung out, still in his clothes. The Salinger paperback had slipped to the floor. Woody, curled against the boy's leg, gave a small mew at the sight of me. Luke stirred and opened his eyes.

"Hi," I said, and added unnecessarily, "You fell asleep."

He raised himself on an elbow, then put his feet on the floor. I pointed to the duffel. "Your stuff's right there."

"Okay," he said, his voice muffled with sleep. He picked up the bag and took it into the bathroom. In two minutes he was back in the living room, wearing striped pajama bottoms. Surely he hadn't been in there long enough to brush his teeth...

As Luke got into bed and pulled the sheet over him, Woody crawled under the lifted sheet. I watched the shape of my cat moving along the shape of the boy and thought that once again Woody had the right idea. Go with the flow.

"Goodnight, guys," I said. Luke mumbled something, and I reached across to turn out the lamp, resisting the impulse to touch the boy's thick curls. In the shadowy dark I went back into my room, put my own book aside, and turned out the last light in the house.

# ── CHAPTER THIRTY THREE ──

I WOKE EARLY ON THANKSGIVING DAY, listening in the dark for any sounds of wintry weather. The forecast had been for "possible flurries"—a far cry from the fierce snowstorm that had buried Boston on this day a year earlier. Tom had come here—I remembered serving sausage omelets, and thought now of his rueful comment that this year's holiday meal at his mother's would be more in keeping with his new dietary routine. It was for the best, of course—both Sheila and I wanted him around for a long time to come.

I got up and put on my robe, opening the door quietly and tiptoeing through the living room where Luke lay sleeping, only a few curls showing over the top of the blanket. I started the coffee and fed Woody, then, deciding that the sound of running water probably wouldn't disturb someone who lived in a boys' dormitory, I ran a quick shower and washed my hair. When I passed through the living room again on my way to get coffee Luke didn't seem to have stirred. I left my bedroom door slightly open for Woody, and had only had my first sip of coffee when he slipped in and joined me. He purred beside me while I read my book and finished the carafe of coffee, then I lifted him from the bed so I could tidy it before getting dressed. I had decided to wear my favorite navy skirt, with a bright paisley blouse. Martha's a good influence on me—she was sure to be wearing something pretty herself, and would be lavish in her compliments on my outfit.

It was after nine by now, and I could hear Luke moving about in the other room. Woody poked the door open wider to greet our guest, and I followed him. Luke was sitting on the edge of the rumpled sofa bed.

"Good morning, Luke."

"Morning."

"I hope you slept well. Did you want to shower before breakfast?"

"Okay."

He got up and, as he had done the night before, took his duffle bag into the bathroom. I set out cereal, milk and juice and put four slices of whole wheat bread into the toaster. The shower stopped running, and in another five minutes Luke came out, wet-haired and barefoot, dressed in chinos and a bright blue shirt.

"You look nice," I said, and then wondered why I had made such a remark. Had I feared that he might adopt the Compleat Goth look the minute he got off school grounds? And what could I have done about it if he had?

"Why don't you start?" I said. "I'll just wait for the toast to come up."

He pulled out a chair and put his napkin in his lap. Whatever that school cost it was worth every penny. Or maybe his mother had been the one to insist on good manners. In two swallows he drained the glass of orange juice I had set at his place, then filled a bowl with cereal and added milk nearly to the top. I brought the toast to the table and put down two slices for each of us. We ate in silence, Luke finishing everything and saying No, thank you when I asked if he'd like more toast. He carried his dishes to the sink.

"Okay," I said. "I guess we may as well go. It's about an hour to Martha's house, but there'll probably be traffic."

"Can I bring this?"

He was holding up *Catcher in the Rye*. I started to say that of course he could, then reconsidered.

"Actually, Luke, I'd rather you left it here. There's something I need to talk to you about."

We made our way out of the city in traffic that was heavy but not impossible. The holiday absence of the otherwise unending construction helped. Luke sat silent, watching the other cars and occasionally turning to see something we had just passed. I knew so little about him. What were his interests—what was he good at? What did he really think about his father's leaving him.

When we were on Route 3 and moving along steadily under the gray sky I said, "Luke, you know that I talked to people in California about your father."

"You said they were dead. The guys who killed him."

"Yes." I was momentarily stopped by his bluntness, before realizing that it must be a defense mechanism. "Yes. That's right—they're both dead. But there are still some—I guess you could say loose ends."

He didn't say anything, but I could tell he was listening intently. I went on, "Your father had something with him just before he died. Something that wasn't his. It wasn't very big, so it would have been easy to hide. Luke, can you think of any place your mother might have kept something like that, if he sent it to her?"

"My Mom didn't steal."

Oh, God. "No, of course not. I just thought she could have been keeping this package for him until he could...give it back."

I was making a mess of this. Luke said, "What was in it?"

"A statue. Alexander the Great on his horse. About this high." I duplicated the gesture Eliot Wyman had made, keeping one hand on the steering wheel and raising the other above my lap.

"She never said anything."

"Did she have any place where she kept valuables?"

He thought about that. "She had a box for papers. Once..."

I waited, then said, "Once what, Luke?"

"She forgot to lock it and I looked at the stuff inside."

"What were you trying to find?"

"Stuff about my Dad." He spoke in the direction of the window. "She'd never tell me anything when I asked."

I sensed that he had told me as much as he knew. After a moment I said, "Would you like to go back there?"

"To Farmer's Grange?"

I had learned from Luke's records that this was the name of the tiny town in Maine where the Edward Prentice family, first three of them, then two, had lived for most of Luke's childhood.

"Yes. Maybe over Christmas vacation. You could show me around, and get anything you might want from the house."

"Could I see my friends?"

"Yes, of course," I said, touched and saddened at the thought of his many losses. What would a visit to his home be like for him, with both parents gone?

"Zach is my best friend."

"We'll visit him first then. Can you let him know as soon as you're back to school?"

"I can send him a note from Nick's. They're wireless."

"Oh...fine," I said, and after that we rode in silence for the fifteen minutes it took to reach Martha's house. I pulled into the driveway and saw her waiting in the doorway and had that ridiculous, welcome thought which the sight of her often brings. Everything was going to work out.

I got the apple pie I had picked up at the bakery out of the back seat and closed my car door. Luke was getting out on the other side. Martha came to me and put her arms around me and we stood there without saying anything until she kissed me and said, "I'm so glad to see you both."

That reminded me of my manners and I said, "Martha, this is Luke Prentice. Luke, I'd like you to meet my friend Martha Hayes."

"Hello, Mrs. Hayes," he said, and walked around to shake hands. I wondered if Martha was going to try to hug him, but her instincts were fine-tuned as always—she settled for shaking hands and saying, "I'm very pleased to meet you, Luke. Come inside—both of you."

Martha's dining room table was set for three, and the smell of roasting turkey filled the house. "We are *very* traditional this year," Martha said as we settled ourselves with cold drinks. "Turkey and dressing, mashed potatoes and gravy, and green bean casserole." She turned toward Luke. "That's a special holiday recipe, Luke—you put onion rings on top and then bake it in the oven."

"My mother knew how to make that."

Martha blinked, and I saw her swallow. Her eyes were wet and I said quickly, "I for one am starving. Is there anything I can do?"

"No thank you, dear." Martha got up and started for the kitchen. "Unless you want to show Luke the yard. I had juncos out there this morning—there was plenty of bread left over from the stuffing."

Luke followed me into Martha's yard, where I made small talk about how far from the Cape we were and how warm the ocean got in summertime, compared to Maine. When we went back inside the turkey was sitting on the counter, golden brown, and Martha was mashing the potatoes. I made a reasonably good job of wielding the carving knife, and in just a few minutes we were all sitting at the table ready to begin the meal. I suddenly wondered whether in Luke's family grace was said at the table. I looked across at Martha, who not for the first time read my mind.

"Thank you for my guests," she said. "Luke, the gravy boat is quite full—may I pour you some?"

Everything was, of course, delicious. Only once, helping myself to more creamy potatoes and adding real butter to them, did I think guiltily of Tom. I'd just have to downplay the richness of the food, or better still not mention it at all.

Luke and I cleared the table while Martha put on coffee and heated the pie I had brought. She carried it whole to the table and said, "Could you cut the pie, please, Nell? And who would like ice cream?"

I held up my hand. "That's two, then," Martha said. "Luke?"

He was silent. I said, "Luke, do you want vanilla ice cream on your pie? It comes from a place just down…"

To my astonishment he stood abruptly and flung down the fresh napkin Martha had given him. Making a choking sound he ran toward the living room, where I could see him by the front door, his shoulders heaving. "Luke!" I said, starting to get up.

"Let me, dear," Martha said. She got up from the table and went to my nephew.

"Luke?" I heard her say. "I'm sorry something upset you. Can you tell me what it was?"

I thought he wasn't going to answer. Then he said in muffled voice, "Nobody knows me anymore. Nobody knows what I like. When you put ice cream on pie it melts too fast. My Mom knew that. She wouldn't even have asked me."

Adolescent, irrational—and utterly heartbreaking. I tried to think of the right thing to say, and while I was doing so Martha did the right thing. She took Luke in her arms. He was taller than she was, and I saw her familiar hand reach up to touch the back of his head. They stood together by the door, the boy weeping and the woman making wordless sounds of comfort.

I had a sense of intruding on a deeply private moment, and looked away, down at the hand-embroidered holiday cloth that covered the table. Out of the corner of my eye I saw Luke take a step back and Martha's hand drop to let him go. He swiped at his eyes with the back of his hand and bit his lip—his father's gesture of bravado. I sent Martha a helpless look: now what?

"Luke," Martha said. "Do you like animals?"

There was a silence. I made myself keep quiet. Finally, Luke nodded.

"I had a cat," Martha continued. "Quite a few cats, actually, over the years. But this was the one I had when I first knew your Aunt Nell. Flora."

No response, but I could see that he was listening.

"Flora lived a good long life for a cat. Sixteen years. After she died I said I wasn't going to get another cat, but that's what I say every time."

"Older than me," Luke said, his voice husky. Martha and I exchanged a look as if we were hearing the horses of Achilles miraculously speak, then we both laughed.

"So it is," Martha agreed. "In any case, I'm rethinking my resolution. And I was wondering, Luke—the next time you come, do you think you could go to the shelter with me and help me choose a cat?"

My breathing sounded to me faintly shallow, but Martha's voice was calm and certain. Of course there would be a next time. Luke's voice, when it came, was a little less throaty. "I guess so."

"Good," Martha said. "Now that we've settled that, why don't we have our dessert. Is that knife sharp enough, Nell?"

I cut three generous slices as Martha went to the freezer and returned with a quart of ice cream and a serving spoon. I watched in admiration as she ladled a scoop of ice cream next to my piece of pie, not touching, then did the same with her own portion. "Luke?" she said.

The boy slid back into his chair, looking not at us but at our dessert plates.

"Yes, please," he said.

# —— CHAPTER THIRTY FOUR ——

I HAD TOLD LOIS PATTERSON, MOTHER of Luke's friend Nick, that I would be dropping off my nephew in Hyannis before dinnertime—homemade pizza, she had told me, so I understood why Luke wanted to be there for that. Luke and I helped Martha clear the table and rinse the dishes, after which Martha and I had coffee. Luke was quiet except for polite responses when asked a question, but Martha and I had as always a steady supply of things to talk about. I would have loved to be staying the night, but it was growing dark and Woody would be waiting to be fed. I put down my coffee cup and said, "What a lovely afternoon, Martha."

"Don't leave before I wrap up some leftovers for Woody."

"What will you call your new cat?"

It was Luke. Martha and I turned to him. "Why, I don't know," Martha said. "First we'll have to find the right cat, then you can help me choose a name."

"What if he already has a name?"

I could see, plain as day, Martha listening for the question behind the question. She said, "That would be different. We wouldn't want to take anything away that he came with. If he already had a name then of course he—or she—could keep it." I saw that her blue eyes were sparkling in a way I recognized and loved. "Even if his name was...Murgatroyd."

Luke looked startled, then he grinned. "That's such a dumb name. He'd *want* us to find him a better one."

"Oh, those are Nell's genes," Martha said, and before Luke could react she had wrapped him in a hug that he, grinning with pleasure, didn't seem to mind in the least. When Martha finally let him go she held out her arms for me.

The early evening was quite dark, with a few snow flurries, as I drove south toward the Cape. I was concentrating on my driving and quite comfortable with the silence in my car. Once we were over the Sagamore Bridge and had passed the Sandwich exits I said to Luke, "Does Nick have brothers and sisters?"

"He has a sister. When I stayed there one other time she kept following me around. I told my Mom and she said I should let her because I was their guest and someday I wouldn't mind." He snorted at this impossibility, and again I felt a sense of loss that I had never known Ned's wife.

"Aunt Nell?"

"Yes, Luke?" I looked over at him.

"Could you not say anything about my mother?"

I couldn't tell whether he was referring to the emotional scene at Martha's, or was speaking more generally. "They're your friends, Luke. I'll do whatever you want."

"It's just that everybody looks at me like—it's him—the kid whose mother died."

"I think I see."

"Anyway—" He rubbed at the condensation on his side window and sketched a face that began disappearing even as he drew it. "They'll see that you're with me."

The Pattersons' beach cottage was larger than many primary homes, a shingled behemoth with decks on three levels, smoke coming out of the chimney, and the sound of the Atlantic very near. Lois Patterson answered the door in slim black velvet slacks and a yellow satin top cut to show the top of her breasts. Either she'd had Nick when she was in the third grade, or she was that modern phenomenon, the trophy wife—a term that has taken on new meaning since Homer used it.

"Hi," she said, looking me up and down in the way some women do whenever they meet another female. She appeared satisfied that I was in no way competition, and turned her head toward Luke. I saw her eyes widen.

"Lukie! Haven't you turned into the handsome devil!"

*Lukie? Handsome devil?* She was flirting with my nephew! Luke realized it, too—he was blushing, which only improved his good looks. I opened my mouth to say, "He's fifteen," then closed it as I realized she had been, too, a couple of election cycles ago.

"Lois—tell Luke to come up."

We all looked toward the stairs. A disembodied voice, in the process of changing, had issued the order. Lois gave Luke a distinctly regretful look, then said, "The prince has spoken. Go on up, Luke."

Luke started to run toward the curving staircase, then stopped and turned to me. "Thanks, Aunt Nell. For bringing me and all."

Before I could reply, Lois called up the stairs as a parting shot, "*Somebody* has manners." I managed to get in "You're welcome," as Luke took the stairs two at a time and managed to stop just short of colliding with a balding, heavy-set man who had appeared at the top landing and was beaming down at us. He was wearing corduroy pants, a cardigan and bedroom slippers, and looked to be in his late fifties.

"Sweet pea," he called out, "Why didn't you say we had company? And here's Luke! Boys' day out, tomorrow, right, Luke?" My nephew murmured something and managed to escape past Nick's father with nothing more than a manly squeeze of his shoulder. Mr. Patterson hurried the rest of the way down the stairs and flung an arm around his wife.

"Introduce me, love bug. Then who's for a drink?"

Lois sprawled languidly on a beige crushed-velvet sofa as her husband hurried to a fully-stocked wet bar and filled our requests (more a petulant demand on Lois's part) for white wine, then poured several fingers of Scotch over ice for himself. His wife's posture revealed even more of what was on offer under the skimpy top, and I saw him swallow before he noticed that I was still standing.

"Good heavens—sit down, sit down!" He fussed with ushering me to a loveseat before taking a seat—timidly, it seemed to me—beside his bored-looking wife. As if trying to make up for her lack of affect, he said in an eager tone, "Angel, what say I have Nancy bring in some nibbles?"

For the first time since I'd arrived she looked directly at him, lowering her eyes to his abdomen, then bringing them back up to his face with a look that was openly contemptuous.

"After that meal?"

He blinked, then in a show of good-sport behavior patted his large stomach. "New Year's resolution!" he said to me. "Take a few pounds off—get in shape. Have to keep up with these young fellows…"

For a moment I wondered if he'd just confessed his age-difference anxieties to me, but then he said, "Luke's a fine boy, a fine boy. We were all mighty glad he could spend a little time chez Patterson." He gestured to include Lois, who didn't seem to be listening. "Truth is, we feel your boy is a good influence. We wouldn't mind one bit if our young fellow would apply himself half as much at that school we're paying for, would we, lovey?"

I saw it register with Lois that I might actually think she was Nick's mother. She gave her husband a cold stare.

"Jesus Christ, *lovey*—what do you expect? The kid got Carla's brains."

I had to admire what happened next. Joel Patterson went white, and seemed about to speak. Then he appeared to remember that he had a guest in his house. *Somebody has manners*, I thought, as he smiled at me and said with remarkable composure, "We didn't realize Luke had an aunt."

I took the opening quickly. "There's a reason for that. Up until a month ago, I didn't know I had a nephew." Even Lois momentarily lost her bored expression as I faltered on, "One of those family situations, you know..."

Lois drained her wine and looked at the glass as if it had made the comment. "Do we ever know. Joel!"

He jumped, just perceptibly. His wife was holding out her empty glass.

"Do you think you could get everybody another round, if it's not too much trouble?"

"Not for me, please," I said. "I'm driving...", but Joel was seizing my glass and speed-walking to the bar. "Right you are, pet! No reason to be sitting around without a drink..."

He was back in less than a minute with refills all around, gamely trying to save the very awkward situation. I could tell that neither of them would notice if I had only a token sip of my drink. Joel said, "Well! What shall we drink to?"

One of Anacreon's lusty imperatives came unbidden into my head. *Bring me a bowl, that I may drink without stopping for breath.* Joel Patterson was clutching his Scotch as if that was precisely what he had in mind—and who could blame him? I lifted my glass. "Family."

"To family!" Joel echoed with maximum enthusiasm. He was sweating, his face damp and shiny, though it could have been the Scotch. Lois looked from one to the other of us with a suspicious expression—could Luke's doddering aunt be putting them on?—before raising her glass a fraction of an inch.

"Family," she said. "Let's hear it."

Now that I'd met the Pattersons, it came as no surprise that "our Nancy" ("Just like one of the family," Joel assured me) was the person who would be whipping up the homemade pizza. Joel's invitation for me to stay and join them was so hopeful that I almost took pity on him, especially since I doubted Lois would be joining her husband, two teenage boys, and an uninteresting guest in the consumption of carbs. But in the end I wriggled out of the uncomfortable situation by invoking, not for the first time, Woody.

"That's so nice of you," I told Joel. "But I have a cat at home waiting for his dinner. And I should probably get to bed early if I want to hit those Black Friday sales."

This last was such an atrocious lie that I nearly looked up to see if Zeus's thunderbolt was about to strike. I loathe sales. I would pay full price and ten per cent over before I'd join the hordes lined up in the winter dark for the start of the Christmas shopping madness. My least favorite phrase in the world is that slogan *Don't you just love a bargain?*

The boys were called downstairs—Nick, Joel's stocky lookalike, to be introduced, and Luke to say goodbye. Under cover of their lively noise I managed to make my escape. Joel and Lois stood in their grand front doorway, he waving as if his favorite sister was off for two years in Borneo, she shrugging off the arm he tried to put around her shoulders. The perfect white Christmas lights lit their faces as I drove past the house and out the semi-circular driveway. When I looked in the mirror before pulling into the street only Joel was still there.

The traffic was light as I drove toward Boston, passing one commercial establishment after another tricked out in lights, hoping to suggest to the seasonal consumer that Christmas was just around the corner. My street was quiet and I had a choice of parking spaces—apparently a number of my neighbors were spending Thanksgiving somewhere other than at home. I locked the car and climbed the stairs, anticipating the sight of two bright eyes that would be staring at me when I got the door open.

"Sweetie!" I said to my cat. "Lovebug! Who's for a move to Ultima Thule?"

# CHAPTER THIRTY FIVE

"How was Thanksgiving?" I asked Tom.

It was Friday morning, and I had reached him at work. Although it was after nine, I was still in bed with my second cup of coffee and Woody stretched out behind me in the frosted window. I had no appointments scheduled at my office, and didn't think it was a likely destination for the Black Friday crowd.

"Good. My mother hovered a little, and everybody had to suffer along with me with no butter or salt on the table, but it was nice to see everybody. Maura's pregnant again, so that was one of the things my mother was happy about."

"What were the others?"

"You and me."

I stared at the phone. "Tom, you didn't…"

"No, of course not. She has radar. She's been that way ever since I was a kid." Tom paused, possibly just to make me ask, if I didn't want to expire from curiosity.

"What did she say?"

"She said, 'Don't let this one get away'."

Now I had nothing to say. This was clearly a very good time to choose my words carefully. In the silence I could hear phones ringing in the Newton police station. Finally I said, "So it's not just Woody?"

Hearing his name, my cat swung his head toward me, then back to the wintry view. No help from him.

"No, Nell. It is definitely not just Woody."

I was glad that Tom was at work—this conversation was headed like a runaway chariot toward the subject of *us*. I said brightly, "Martha asked about you. She was really happy that you're feeling better."

The sound that came through the receiver was definitely a sigh. "How is she?"

"Wonderful!" I bubbled, my head out from under the guillotine blade of Relationship Talk. "She's such a good cook and I took my nephew and then I got to meet one of his friends from school…"

I chattered on, careful to omit details about the rich food and the even richer Pattersons ("They seemed *very* nice," I blatantly overdid it), and ended by telling Tom that I would be taking Luke to Maine during his Christmas break.

"He doesn't know anything about the…missing object…" I said carefully. (Were calls to police stations recorded? Was Naomi, who had transferred me to Tom's line, listening in?) "But I need to resolve this, for his safety. If I can find out what Ned did with…the package…there won't be any reason for… the people involved…to take an interest in Luke."

If the call were being recorded, all those lacunae would sound pretty suspicious. Tom said, "Those aren't people to fool around with. What if they decided to come looking for you, and you had the boy with you?"

"Do you think I'd ever put him in danger?"

"I'm thinking of myself, sitting here worrying. Why don't you humor me and let me come along?"

The quandary this put me in reinforced how much things had changed. A month ago, I would have been quick to remind Tom that I didn't need or want a babysitter, and could certainly look out for myself and my clients (of which Luke, as far as this trip was concerned, was one), but with Tom's health crisis I was conscious of needing to tread more carefully. The last thing I wanted was for him to feel he was useless—or even a liability.

"We'd be staying at Luke's house…"

"I'll get a motel room."

"Can you get the time off?"

On the other end of the line Tom breathed in, then out. His voice when he spoke sounded very controlled.

"Nell. I will drive up separately from you. I'll book a motel online, the way any twelve-year-old knows how to do. I'll behave around your nephew as if you and I are just friends who have done some work together. I won't use the circumstances to strong arm you into anything you're not ready for. Just answer me yes or no—do you want me to come with you?"

"Yes," I said, before I could analyze this situation into an early grave. "I want you to meet Luke, and... I'd just feel better if I knew you were there if there was any trouble."

"I'll put in for the time right away. See you this weekend?"

"For sure. Maybe a DVD and dinner at my place? Away from the crowds?" I stopped short of uttering some cover language about how Woody wanted to see him. *I* wanted to see him.

"Sounds good. Will you trust me to pick out a DVD?"

I laughed. "You're getting pretty good at knowing what I like." Did that sound like a double entendre? What if Naomi *was* listening in? Suddenly, happy at what I had and aware of how close I had come to losing it, I didn't care. "Bring a change of clothes if you're on duty Monday. And while you're here maybe you can give me some ideas about what Luke might like for Christmas. You were a fifteen-year-old boy once."

Tom said, "I'll ask Maura—Timmy just turned fourteen. When I was that age, I probably wanted a Beatles album. But who knows—maybe the kid inherited his aunt's taste for things that don't go out of style."

Tom arrived on Saturday night with the DVD of *A Hard Day's Night* and a CARE package for Woody from Sheila's kitchen. "See what I mean?" Tom said. " I didn't have to tell her I'd be seeing you."

Maybe there was something after all to Sheila's sixth sense. Tom had his cell phone, but it didn't ring once. Sunday morning we were drinking coffee (decaffeinated) and he got a few drops on his bright blue shirt, so I kept it to add to the wash after he left. Woody lay on it when I left it folded on my dresser, so I ended up hanging it in my closet.

My Monday email had a note from Luke. He was back at school, thanked me again for taking him to Martha's, said he'd had a good time with Nick, and concluded, *Our team lost.* It was probably a safe bet that he thought I knew who "our team" was—thanks to Tom I had been able to put off breaking it to my nephew that my knowledge of sports pretty much ended with the funeral games for Anchises—but that didn't mean I couldn't seize an opening when it was right in front of me. I typed, *I enjoyed seeing you and am looking forward to our trip. My friend Tom will be meeting us there—he is a sports fan, so the two of you will have something to talk about,* and felt qualified for a high level position in diplomacy as I hit Send.

# CHAPTER THIRTY SIX

BUSY AS I WAS AND SMOOTHLY as the newer parts of my life seemed to be going, I spent an inordinate part of the time between Thanksgiving and Christmas fretting. My mind went round and round with the unsavory people I had met in California, Tom's health, Luke's future. Then on a gusty Saturday morning as I was reading in bed, Woody gathered himself for his spring into my lap and missed. His claws caught in the side of the mattress and he scrambled the last few inches. Of course it didn't bother him in the least—he wanted to be on my bed, and now he was—but as I scratched his extended throat I felt that special poignancy that comes with seeing that a creature you love is no longer young. I did a quick calculation—nine in cat years, wasn't that forty-five in human years? That really wasn't bad—but Martha was eighty-two...

I flung back the bright quilt Martha had sewn for me. "Come on, you," I said to Woody. "Let's celebrate your relative youth with some tuna."

Maybe because I was dwelling way too much on what Virgil calls the rolling years, I attached some extra significance to the call I received a few days later from Marcie Breen. The voice on the phone in my office sounded very young.

"I was calling to talk to Miss Prentice."

"This is she."

"You're the investigator?"

"Yes." I hoped this wasn't going to be one of those calls that ended abruptly when the prospective client found out there was no Mr. Prentice.

"I looked in the Yellow Pages. The others were all men. I thought a woman might understand better."

I pulled a calendar toward me. "I prefer to meet clients in person. Would you like to make an appointment?"

"Yes, I mean, I'd like to…but I sort of need to know how much it costs…"

Judging from the voice, I wondered briefly if she was going to be dipping into her allowance. I said, "I don't charge anything for a consultation. If I think I can help you, then we can discuss my fee. Can you come in tomorrow?"

"I work in Boston—I get off at three."

"Four o'clock, then? I'm right downtown."

"Could we say three-thirty? I need to be home by six…"

I supposed I would be finding out why that was important. I said, "Three-thirty it is. You said your name was Breen?"

"Yes. Mrs. Marcie Breen."

Marcie Breen—Mrs. Breen—didn't look quite as young as she had sounded on the phone, but I figured if she had voted in the recent election she had been just about eligible. She had a plump face pink from the cold, curly brown hair and large brown eyes. When I took her coat I saw that she was wearing a snowman sweater. I hung up the coat, offered her coffee which she politely declined, and went back around to my desk chair.

"How may I help you?"

She looked down, then up at me. Her dark brown eyes were her best feature. "It's my husband," she said.

I suppressed a sigh. Of course it was. But there I was—racking up extra credit in Getting Ahead of Myself. "What about your husband?" I prompted.

She fingered a shiny ring on her left hand. "His name is Jerry. We've been married almost a year."

"And has something happened?"

She looked up in alarm, as if I knew something I wasn't telling her. "Like what?"

"Mrs. Breen," I said patiently, and saw that she liked hearing her married name, "I need to know why you're here."

She stopped touching the ring and put her hands in her lap. "I thought you'd be able to find out what's going on with Jerry. So I could stop worrying."

A lot of the time, people who come to me decide too late that they would have rather kept worrying than go looking for answers. I hoped more than I usually do that this wouldn't be one of those times. I said, "Tell me why you're worried."

"My husband works as an orderly. At Boston City. He goes in later than I do, and gets home at six."

I made a note. "Has he been coming home late?"

"No. But then after supper he goes out again."

I looked at her. "And you don't know where?"

"No. I asked him, but all he would say is that it's business. Something going on at the hospital. He says it's temporary—just for a few weeks."

"How long is he gone?"

"Until pretty late. I looked at the clock last night when he came in and it was after midnight. I pretended I was asleep, but I'm not sleeping very good wondering if he's in some kind of trouble."

I closed my notebook and laid the pen next to it. "So you want me to find out where he goes?"

She started to nod, then said, "I was telling you on the phone—I need to know what it will cost. I'm sure you'd be worth it—it's not that—but I have to be sure I can afford it..."

I looked at her childish face, then at the sweater. The snowmen were dancing with their broomstick arms out at their sides. T.J. Maxx was my guess—thirty per cent off while supplies last. Her wedding band looked like silver, with no gem stone.

"Let's do this. If you haven't said anything to...Jerry... he should be easy to follow. I'll see where he goes, and if he meets anybody. Fifty dollars should cover it."

Normally, I have a five hundred dollar minimum before I'll consider taking a case. But I was still thinking that Jerry's "business" was probably of the funny variety, and if I was right I would at least be able to break it to her gently.

She already had her purse open. "I went to the ATM." She produced a white envelope which she held out to me. "I didn't really have any idea, but that's how much I took out. Fifty dollars."

Even if I was going to be tailing an unsuspecting person I would need to keep out of sight, so I asked Marcie Breen if she had a photo of her husband. She got out her wallet and handed me a wedding picture. Jerry Breen, smiling next to his bride, had an open, friendly looking face made studious by glasses. The two of them looked as if they should be at the prom.

"I'll be sure you get this back," I said. "With my report."

The next night, I was parked just down the street from the address Marcie had given me. I had arrived a little after six, and didn't even have to wait an hour before the man in the photo came out of the house and got into a car that, under a streetlight, looked at least half the age of its driver. I started my own car—no Spring chicken itself—and followed Jerry Breen down a street of rental duplexes and onto the highway. There was quite a bit of traffic, but Jerry's Honda stayed in the right lane, leading me to guess that we would be getting off after a few exits. When the sign for the local mall appeared, Jerry put on his blinker. I followed him down the ramp and into the mall parking lot and found a space not far from the one he pulled into, near the entrance to Sears.

Most of my tracking jobs involve a quarry with some reason to be paranoid—parents ducking out on child support, bogus disability claimants, runaway teenagers. It was gratifyingly easy to tail a man who had no reason to be suspicious. Jerry Breen locked his car and walked at a leisurely pace toward Sears, where he held the door for a woman and a child before following them inside. I waited another full minute, then went inside myself, pretending to study a shopping list (Jerry's wedding photo) while keeping Jerry himself in sight. He crossed the store to the back and walked through an archway over which a sign read EMPLOYEES ONLY.

I hadn't been expecting this. Not having the option of following my target into a restricted area, I browsed nearby in Housewares until, after five minutes, Jerry came back out wearing a blue smock and a name badge. With me behind him he moved through the crowds of shoppers into the toy department, where he spoke to a man in an identical smock behind the cash register enclosure, then changed places with him.

I began to feel a little better about this assignment. I stayed close by as Jerry waited on customers for twenty minutes or so, at which time an announcement came over the loudspeakers. Santa was back from his dinner break, and would be available for pictures in the bicycle area. (No fool Santa, and Sears.) A wave of parents and children moved quickly in that direction as I took the opportunity to stroll over to Jerry's now quiet counter.

He greeted me with a smile as I said, "You must be the man of the hour, working in the toy department right before Christmas."

He looked a little flustered by my comment. "I'm new at this. But the kids all seem to know what they want. Running out of the stuff they see on TV is the only problem."

"Yes. Well, I'll bet you're just the person to help me. I need help picking out some Christmas toys."

"For a boy or a girl?"

"Boy," I said without hesitation.

"What age?"

As I started to reply, I realized that the only boy I would be buying for this year had left Tonka trucks behind a decade ago. I said, "Five," then knew immediately where that had come from.

"Two boys, actually," I said. "Twins. They're five and a half."

Jerry pondered this detail. He seemed genuinely interested in coming up with a good recommendation. He said, "Chances are their parents will get them the stuff that's hot this year—the things we run out of. Do you know if they have a train set?"

I pictured the Marcus twins' room, and the rest of the small house in Riverton which I had explored so thoroughly. "No, they don't. I bet they'd love one, though."

Jerry came out from behind his counter and led me to a train setup near the wall. He picked up a remote from a shelf above the train and pointed it. Lights flashed, a whistle sounded, and the train began circling past trees and houses and cows.

"Oh!" I said. "It's perfect. Do you have it in stock?"

"I'm sure we do. And if not, I can let you take the floor model. Just let me get somebody to take over the register so I can go check the stockroom."

He went back to the desk and used the phone. We talked for a few minutes about the upcoming holiday, until a young woman appeared, smiled at me and spoke to Jerry, then went to stand behind the register. While Jerry was gone I picked out a number of accessories. The whole setup would take up most of the floor space in the boys' room, but I couldn't imagine that they or their father would mind. I added two engineers' caps to my pile of clear plastic boxes and carried everything to the register just as Jerry reappeared.

"Thanks, Alice," he said to the young woman, who gave us both a wave as she left the area. To me he said, "We have it. It comes in two boxes—they're kind of bulky, so I had them sent to the pickup area. You'll be able to drive right up in your car."

"Terrific," I said. "Thank you. You've been such a help. Nobody would ever guess you hadn't been doing this for a long time."

He looked pleased. "It's just until Christmas. My wife"—he looked down, a proud, slightly bashful bridegroom. "This will be our first Christmas, and our anniversary's the same week. I have my eye on something special for her, so this is for the extra cash I need to surprise her."

I had my MasterCard out, and laid it on top of a plastic box containing a Railway Crossing sign. "Nothing like a nice surprise," I told him.

Marcie Breen had told me she'd be waiting by the phone to hear what I'd found out, so I called her as soon as I got home. She listened in silence as I told her where her husband had been spending his evenings, and gasped when I quoted his description of planning "something special" for her.

"I feel awful!" Marcie said. "To think of him doing this, and all I could do is act suspicious. Ms. Prentice—this is the most wonderful news. I can't wait for Jerry to get home so I can tell him how I'll never again..."

"Mrs. Breen," I said. I waited until I was sure she was listening. "One of the things my clients get—at no extra charge—is the benefit of my experience. Here is my advice for you. Don't tell him."

"But..."

"If you say anything you'll spoil the surprise. But more importantly, you'll be letting him know that you didn't trust him."

There was silence on the line, then she said, "Are you saying I should *never* tell him?"

I thought carefully before answering her—about the fragile nature of trust, the difficult task of repairing it once it has been shattered.

"On your anniversary," I told Marcie Breen. "The fiftieth one. Not a day sooner."

After we hung up I looked at the clock. It was not too late to make one more call, to a number I didn't have to look up.

"Harry," I said when he answered, "It's Nell Prentice. Fine—things are going well. What about you? I think of you and the guys a lot."

Harry said that things were improving, day by day. The boys missed their mother, but they were seeing a lot of their grandparents and would be spending Christmas with them.

"Well, that's the thing," I said. "Would there be a good time for me to come by between now and Christmas? I'd love to see you guys—and I have a present for the boys."

# —— CHAPTER THIRTY SEVEN ——

On Saturday it was snowing lightly. I made several trips to my car with the train set for the Marcus boys, both for the much-needed exercise and to keep one hand free for the icy outdoor banister. When I had everything securely stowed in my hatchback, I made a last climb to my second floor apartment to say goodbye to Woody and snap all three of my door locks. Gray slush sluiced from under my tires as I pulled away from the curb and headed toward Riverton.

I had been telling Harry the truth when I said I often thought of him and his twin boys. A lot had happened to me since the sad ending to my search for Kristen Marcus, but I never thought back on the case without a futile wish that I could have called Harry with good news about his missing wife. He had said on the phone that the family was doing okay, but I wanted to see for myself. I slowed and put on my blinker, and turned down the short street the Marcuses lived on.

There was a Christmas tree in the window of what I knew was the living room, and a wreath on the front door. As I pulled into the driveway and shut off my engine, the side door opened and a boy in a red sweater stepped outside, waving. I waved back and could feel that I had a big smile on my face.

"Monroe! Do you remember me? We..." The boy was grinning at me, and I suddenly realized why.

"Madison?" Even as I said his name in astonishment the boy I remembered as small and very shy grinned even more widely. "Did you *grow*?"

"I guess!"

But it was something else. The little boy who hadn't been able to meet my eyes now had an open, confident expression I had previously seen only in a photograph. I stepped from my car and held out my arms.

"Just tell me you haven't gotten too big for a hug."

Madison led me by the hand into the house, where Harry and Monroe were waiting in the kitchen. I hugged each of them, and Harry said, "Let me take your coat."

"I need it another minute," I said. "I have something in my car for these guys."

Monroe opened the door to precede me outside, with Madison right behind. Harry said, "Coats."

"*Daddy...*" It was both twins.

"Daddy nothing. No coats, no going outside."

The boys turned and ran down the hall toward their room as I grinned at Harry. "Ogre."

He looked abashed. "It's just me, deciding what's best for them. I probably overdo it—they're really good boys."

I looked at him, and saw the sadness in his eyes. This would be the family's first Christmas without Kris. I said softly, "They're lucky kids, Harry."

Madison and Monroe returned in corduroy coats, unbuttoned, and in five minutes we had the packages out of my car and stacked next to the tree. I had put everything in plastic bags to keep the snow off the toys—the boys regarded the bags eagerly.

"Can we open them, Daddy?" Monroe asked. Madison nodded in agreement with this idea, and Harry looked at me.

"If it's okay with Miss Prentice—sure."

"Of course," I said. "Otherwise, how will I know if you like what I picked out?"

Monroe pulled the plastic tie sealing the largest bag and reached in. His hand came out holding a lumber car.

"Oh, *cool*," Madison said, reaching for the other bag. Harry said, "Boys."

His sons paused, looking momentarily baffled. Then Monroe said, "*Thank you*, Mrs. Prentice."

"Thanks!" Madison said. Looking at their bright faces, I felt an ache that their mother wasn't here. Not for this moment, or for all the ones to come. I said, "You're welcome—I was pretty sure this place needed a train. Do you suppose we should start by putting the tracks together?"

Harry went to make coffee while the boys and I figured out how to snap the sections of track together. Their small hands proved more dexterous than mine at the task, and after a few minutes I was able to leave them to it and join Harry in the kitchen.

"How have you been?" I asked my former client as I sipped the coffee he'd set down in front of me. It was the same question I'd asked him on the phone, but here in his house, watching him, I felt that I could get a better sense of how he was really doing.

"Pretty well," he said after a moment. "I miss her, of course. I'd give anything if it hadn't happened. If she'd just thought she could talk to me…" He was quiet for a minute, then he said, "There's only one thing I wouldn't give—the boys. They're everything to me. All I want is for them to be happy."

"They seem great," I told him. "Both of them—but Madison was the real surprise for me. I thought he was Monroe."

A look of such pride and love came into Harry's eyes that my heart caught. He said, "It's because of the singing."

"The singing?" I asked. "Madison sings?"

Harry nodded. "The kindergarten teacher was putting on a Christmas play"—he caught himself—"a *seasonal* play, and she called me at home to say she wanted Madison to do a solo. I started to tell her how shy he was, and she said she thought he had perfect pitch."

Harry was not a handsome man by the world's standards, but as he talked about his child there was a wonderful glow in his face. He even seemed to forget that he'd always had a hard time using my first name.

"You should have seen him, Nell. The other kids were in a kind of ring behind him and he was standing up so straight the way the singing teacher taught him and when those first notes came out, just the way he'd practiced them…" Harry gulped, and swabbed at his eyes. "Sorry."

"Harry," I said, "It's a good thing I wasn't there. They would have had to carry me out."

We both knew we'd better get off this subject and the image it evoked. Harry said, "I worry about Monroe, though. He still doesn't ever want to talk about Kris. I keep thinking maybe I should be finding him someone to talk to…"

I nodded sympathetically. "The important thing, Harry, is that you're there for them—watching them and listening to them, wanting the best for them. And I'm sure their teachers are keeping an eye out. Monroe may just need more time."

Harry was looking at me as if I were a fount of child-rearing wisdom, and I said, "Listen to me—since when am I an expert?" I took a breath and said, "Although I may be getting some practice. It seems that I have a nephew, who just turned up in my life. He's fifteen—both his parents are dead. With his mother it's very recent, and I guess he's a little like Monroe—he seems to be holding most of it inside."

Harry said, " I think all we can do is try our best and let them know we love them."

Before I could reply to that the boys came bursting into the kitchen. "Daddy!" Madison said. "We put the tracks together. Will you come and make the train run?"

"Please don't interrupt," Harry said, but he was smiling. This he could do. He couldn't bring their mother back, or shield them from all the dangers and disappointments they would face when beyond his protection, but right now, in this little house, he could make the train run.

Harry let Madison pull him by the hand into the other room, and I saw that Monroe wasn't following them. I smiled at him, and he said, "I heard Daddy telling you about Madison singing at school. I was in the show, too, but I didn't sing. I was a reindeer."

I thought fast. "I interrupted your Daddy, so he didn't get a chance to tell me how good you were. And, Monroe, I don't sing, either. But I can do other things. Pretty soon you'll start to find out all the things you're good at."

"Like what?" He sounded skeptical.

"Oh, I don't know…skiing, swimming, playing the piano…" Inspiration struck. "Maybe you'll pitch for the Red Sox!"

Monroe looked delighted. "Like Wakefield!"

The only Wakefield I ever heard of had a vicar. What was it with that sport—did every male no matter what age have a passion for it? I said, "Right. And I'll expect a free ticket." I put on a ditzy, confidential voice, as if I were being interviewed. "Oh, yes—I know Monroe Marcus *personally*. From long before he… won all those games."

Monroe took my hand and turned toward the living room, where excited voices suggested that the train was about to make its maiden run. "Mrs. Prentice?"

"Yes, honey?"

"Did you buy Madison and me a train because you don't have a little boy?"

I squeezed his hand, and spoke past the catch in my throat. "Actually, Monroe, I do have a boy. He's just not little."

# —— CHAPTER THIRTY EIGHT ——

CHRISTMAS THIS YEAR INVOLVED A CONSIDERABLE amount of planning and cross-communication. In past years I had always received invitations and had only to accept, purchase a bottle of good wine and maybe a plant, and present myself, suitably attired, at a bedecked door. This year I needed to work out logistics involving Tom, Luke, Martha and Woody, and found myself enjoying the challenge. I'd bought presents for everybody (Woody was getting cat grass and toys) and packed and repacked my hatchback so there would be room for Luke's things and Woody's carrier. On Wednesday morning, in a dry snow flurry that was just beginning to stick to the ground, I set out for Ashfield.

Luke was expecting me at his school at noon—we would drive back through Boston, stopping by my apartment to pick up Woody. From there it was on to Martha's for dinner (she had promised us homemade chicken pie) and an overnight stay. On Thursday we would make the drive, which I calculated at five hours or so, to Farmer's Grange, the place that Ned had for a few years called home.

The road got more and more slippery the further west I drove, with several fender benders tying up traffic. It was 12:30 by the time I signaled my turn into the school grounds, passed the administration building, and pulled up in front of Luke's dormitory. He was waiting under the portico, and as soon as he saw me picked up his pack and duffel and came running for my car, heedless of the ice underfoot.

"I'm sorry I'm late," I told him. "There were quite a few accidents on the road—we'll probably need to take it slow going back."

He shook his head at the notion that my time of arrival was a problem. "My friend Dennis just got picked up. We were goofing around in the snow." He had on jeans and the red sweatshirt I'd given him, with a black vest over it and no hat or gloves. *You look wonderful*, I thought, and of course did not say.

"We'll get lunch before we get on the highway," I called to him as he opened the hatch and flung his bags in. There wasn't going to be much room for Woody and *his* gear, but maybe he could ride up front with us—a feline GPS pointing us toward Martha's house. I smiled at the thought as Luke banged the hatch closed and ran around to get in beside me. "Want to go to that place we went to last time I was here?"

He yanked on his seatbelt and snapped the buckle. "They're closed this week—nobody's around. But if we go that way"—he pointed—"there's a Burger King."

*Oh blood of my blood and flesh of my flesh*

"You, sir, have a deal."

A little over three hours later we were cruising in the snow near my apartment looking for a parking space. I said to Luke, "Why don't we do this. Ordinarily I'd double- park and run up, but I don't want to take the chance of being towed with all our stuff in the car and Mrs. Hayes expecting us for her justly famous chicken pie. If I give you my keys, could you put Woody in his carrier—it's on the kitchen table—and bring him down here? And lock up everything after you?"

"Sure!" he said, as if I'd given him some exciting, even perilous, assignment. He was still so much a boy, inside that gangly body. He looked suddenly solemn. "Aunt Nell—I forgot something."

"Not a problem. If it's something you have to have, we can probably stop somewhere and replace it." The minute the words were out I hoped the item left behind wasn't some expensive piece of electronics.

"When you said Mrs. Hayes—I forgot to get her a present."

I looked at him. His father had been just such a worrier about small oversights. I said, "Honey, don't give that another thought. I put both our names on the packages for her."

He was out of my car in an agile bound, clutching my keys as he sprinted toward my front door. I watched him work the outer lock and disappear inside and thought, *Honey, you don't need to be a grownup just yet. I can do that part.*

Luke held the cat carrier in his lap with the wire door facing me, so Woody could talk to me for a few minutes before settling in to sleep. I refrained from asking Luke whether he was *sure* he had locked up securely. My computer was insured and its contents backed up, my books would only interest a burglar who read Plato, and what was important and irreplaceable was right beside me.

"Nell!" Martha called from her lighted doorway. "Luke!" She started carefully down the walk toward us and I said to Luke, "Could you jump out and take her arm? She forgets she's not your age." He opened his door and was quickly at her side, letting her hug him and then keeping one arm around her as he turned toward me. Woody, sensing that activities of a social nature were going on without him, began to mew on the seat beside me. I opened my door and reached for the carrier.

"Come on, Mr. Gregarious. It wouldn't be a party without you."

Martha had set the table with her best china and cloth napkins. A centerpiece of evergreens held red and green candles. Since it was just the three of us, Woody could stay under the table, with all of us knowing to be careful with our chair legs. As Martha cut the chicken pie, she waved a piece of meat on a fork to cool it, then slipped it under the table.

"Watch your fingers," I told her. "He's likely to take them off snatching at something that smells that good."

She smiled at me. "Woody is a perfect gentleman." So, I noticed with pleasure, was Luke. As Martha scooped large slices of golden crust filled with chicken and vegetables and gravy onto our plates, he sat opposite me with his napkin in his lap until Martha had filled her own plate and said, "Please start." Clearly we Prentices were not about to be outdone in the manners department by a cat.

"Presents!" Martha said, when there was nothing left of the main course or the chocolate sorbet that had been dessert, and the dishes were soaking in the sink. She led the way to the glowing tree, and I saw how she had made things just right. At the back of the tree was a pile of packages no doubt from or for Martha's many friends. At the front, carefully arranged, were the presents for the three of us who were starting our Christmas celebration a few days early.

"Luke," Martha said, "would you like to hand things out?"

"No thank you, Mrs. Hayes."

I wondered what the previous Christmas had been like for him. Probably he had been in Maine, with his mother and maybe his friend Zach he had spoken of. Martha said, "I shall, then. But be forewarned—the two of you

162

are certainly going to have to help me up once I've gotten down under this tree."

Luke was sitting cross-legged on the rug, and I didn't want to be the only one of us needing a chair. I sat on the floor opposite my nephew and hoped it wasn't going to be up to him to lift both Martha and me back onto our feet. Martha reached for the first package.

"It's for me!" she said. "From Nell and Luke." She gave it a shake. "It feels like a book…"

Martha's gifts to Luke and me included a hand-knit sweater for him in the color Homer calls *poryphoros*—sea blue, and for me a scarf and mittens in a rainbow of bright colors. ("I used up all my yarn ends," she told me.) Also books—the new Jumpha Lahiri for me, and *Huckleberry Finn* for Luke. As he thanked her Martha said, "Before I wrapped it I reread parts of it. As you will see, Luke, it contains some rather unfortunate language—words we would *never* use today. I'll be interested to know what you think."

I hid a very broad smile by pretending to examine the stitching in my new mittens. Luke looked as if he wanted nothing more than to go off somewhere private and begin looking for the words in question. But then the next present was from me—an iPod. Even before he said, "Oh, great!" I could tell from his expression that Tom's sister's suggestion had been an excellent one. I had thought about adding a subscription to *National Geographic*—Ned had loved that magazine—but had realized again that I knew virtually nothing about the boy's interests and had no business trying to turn him into his father. Instead, I had chosen a book on the Hubble space telescope and a copy of *The Count of Monte Cristo*. How thrilled I had been at his age by that adventure story—I had a moment's thought that I definitely must not try turning Luke into me.

Martha had made a pillow for Woody. "I was going to get him a basket for when he stays here," she explained, "but he sleeps on my bed."

"Martha," I said, "Is that *velvet*?"

"Velveteen. I'll put it in the wing chair he likes, right next to the window."

By now we were surrounded by wrappings and ribbons, and only one box remained under the tree. "To Aunt Nell from Luke," Martha read. "What can this be?"

I took the package she was holding out to me. Luke was looking down, very self-conscious, and I vowed that even if he'd bought me the Cliff Notes to Homer I'd say it was just what I'd always wanted.

"Mr. Kensington helped me pick it out," Luke mumbled. "He's the Latin teacher. If you don't like it you can take it back."

I opened the package with special care. It had been professionally wrapped, with narrow gold ribbon and the gold seal of a bookstore in Ashfield. Inside was a boxed two-volume set of Graves' *The Greek Myths.*

"Oh, Luke," I said.

"You probably already have it."

"No, I don't have it." I slid the first volume out of the orange case. On the cover, an onyx-black Zeus grasped in one hand—the other was stretched toward his heaven—a white swan. "Luke, this is the most amazing..."

He was crimson. "It didn't cost much. Mr. Kensington said if you had it he'd go back with me to get something else."

"I wouldn't give this up for ten million dollars." I swallowed. "Thank you."

"It's OK," he said, and under the blush I saw relief and pleasure. I got up (thankfully, without assistance) and went to hug him. Martha said, "May I see, Nell?" and I went to give her a hand up. We resettled on the sofa and turned the pages of the book together—Hermes, Pan, Orpheus—while Luke examined his iPod and affected nonchalance toward our exclamations. "Luke!" Martha said suddenly, and he looked up.

"I just *know* the name for that cat we're going to get is in this book."

By nine, Luke was settled on the sofa bed reading and Martha and I were upstairs in the guest room, talking quietly. I was on the bed, sitting against the headboard, and Martha was in the rocking chair, with Woody on her lap. She told me how much she was enjoying getting to know Luke, then said, "It's a big responsibility."

"Tell me about it," I said. "Sometimes I'm almost in a panic thinking about how little I know about how to do this. If Michael and I..."

There was no sound in the room but our breathing, the click of the rocking chair, and Woody's purr. Then Martha said, "How do you think it will be for you—visiting the place where your brother lived?"

I thought about her question. "I'm curious. Apprehensive. Really angry at him that he never got in touch."

"I know," Martha said. It would be unlike her to point out the futility of being wrathful toward the dead. She sighed now. "The past. You and Luke will be making a trip not everyone cares to take."

"I promised him," I said, and with those words realized that the trip Ned's son and I would be taking wouldn't change the past, but just might make a difference in the future of one boy.

# CHAPTER THIRTY NINE

FOR BREAKFAST MARTHA CUT THICK SLICES of homemade banana bread and arranged them on a large platter of eggs and sausages. Luke finished two slices of the bread, a plate of food, and milk and orange juice before Martha and I were ready for our second cups of coffee. "More, Luke?" Martha asked him.

"No thank you. It was really good."

"I'll pack up the rest of the banana bread for you to take in the car. Now where's Woody? He always likes a little bit of scrambled egg…"

I stowed the presents in the back of my car while Luke stood saying goodbye to Martha. I heard her say to him, "Remember about that book you gave your Aunt Nell. I know we said we'd see what a cat was like before we named him—or her—but I'm positive the right name is in there."

"OK," Luke said. She hugged him again and I said as he came toward me, "Could you get in the car, please, honey? I just need a minute with Mrs. Hayes."

She and I both smiled at the energetic bang of my car's passenger door closing. Martha said, "I'm so glad you brought him, Nell. Having someone that young around always raises my spirits."

"As you do mine," I said, drawing her to me. "And I appreciate your keeping Woody. I trust he'll still be invited to visit after you get that new cat you and Luke are planning on?"

"Are you serious? Woody is a Prentice, and Prentices of any age are my family."

She stood waving after us as I pulled out of her driveway. Luke was holding his iPod, but had explained to me that it would not be operational until its owner completed a registration process. A sort of *tabula rasa*, I supposed, and was grateful for that unlooked-for boon. I was hoping Luke and I could talk some on the drive, which would not be possible if one participant in the conversation was wired.

"Aunt Nell?"

I had been musing on likely conversation-openers, and was slightly startled to have the matter taken out of my hands. "Yes, Luke."

"This guy who's going to be there—is he your boyfriend?"

Was Tom Kramer my boyfriend. Good question. I said, "Lieutenant Kramer is a very good friend of mine. He's helped me a lot, and we can talk, and best of all he likes Woody."

I mentally braced for some knowledgeable question about sex—I hadn't thought to prepare a response if that came up. But Luke said, "Do you think he'll like me?"

Another echo of his father. Ned had never, to my knowledge, expressed such reservations about how he might appear to others, but he had often been shy and awkward when meeting new people.

"I'm sure he will," I told Luke. "He likes people who are smart and nice, and that's you. And here's something else—he's going to want you to like him, too."

He appeared to be thinking about what I had said, and I felt a brief puff of hubris that I really wasn't half bad at this. When he said my name again I waited to hear whether he had taken in my words of wisdom.

"Would it be OK if I had another piece of the banana bread?"

By noon we were at Portsmouth, and a half hour later pulling into the Kennebunk rest area, where both Luke and I were unaccountably ready for lunch. We walked across the sanded parking lot in a light snow, checking out the parked flatbed trucks carrying lumber and Christmas trees. Should I try to get a tree when we reached Luke's house? No, not a good idea. I needed to take things one small step at a time. I put my arm across Luke's shoulders.

"Burger King, my man? I hear that in Maine they make the burgers out of moose meat."

"Gross!" Luke said, grinning, and I felt like the most successful comedian since Aristophanes.

Between Kennebunk and Portland Luke fell asleep, and in the quiet I let my thoughts drift to the last time I had been in Maine. It was now almost a year since Daniel Reed and I had traveled to Sanford in the southern part of the state to rescue his daughter Andrea, whose abduction had been the last desperate step in a scheme to cover up fraud and lies with more lies. The important thing, the only thing that mattered, was that in the playing out of all this greed and folly we had been able to save a two-year-old girl. Sometimes, I can even close my eyes and see Andrea's sweet face, instead of that other baby—the one in Michael's arms in the last seconds of his life.

The signs for Route One took us through Brunswick, where I slowed, then stopped, for a traffic light. Luke opened his eyes, blinked several times, and sat up in his seat. I said, "About another hour, I'd guess."

He didn't respond, and again I found myself wondering what was going on inside his head. At the end of the street we turned left, and in twenty minutes were crossing the bridge at Bath. Luke stared out the side window, the set of his shoulders looking tense to me, but I felt it best to leave him to his silence. There would be time for questions once we reached Farmer's Grange.

"This is it," Luke said.

I had almost forgotten he was there. "That's the road," he said, pointing.

I signaled for the right turn. "Thank you, Luke." The road we were on ran along a river, past fields and apple orchards and, unexpectedly, a driving range. We passed a blue and white sign for a Baptist church and Luke said, "That's the house."

It was white with green shutters, two stories, set back in an open field. The porch light was on and the driveway plowed, just as Miles Abbott, father of Luke's friend Zach, had promised when I spoke with him on the phone.

"I've been keeping an eye on the place," Miles had said. "You won't need a key—there's one around someplace, but nobody locks their doors around here."

The compacted snow in the driveway squeaked under my tires. I turned off the engine and heard it ticking in the stillness. Luke unsnapped his seat belt and got out of the car, making his way to a side door, where he stopped to wait for me. I got out on my side and walked the few yards to join him.

My first thought as I stepped inside the house in which Luke had grown up was how thoroughly it was a home. We entered through a yellow kitchen, with worn appliances and photos on the refrigerator. A hallway led past stairs to the upper floor—Luke stopped at the bottom of the stairs while I looked into the living room. In addition to chairs and a sofa I could see more photos, books, pillows, and some kind of sports equipment under a coffee table. Luke, his hand on the staircase rail, seemed to be avoiding looking directly at what must be very familiar surroundings.

"So." I said. "Do you want to get anything from your room before I take you to your friend Zach's?"

His breath came out as if he had been holding it. He used his hand on the banister to propel himself up the stairs, turning right at the top and pushing open a door. I stayed where I was, and after five minutes the door opened and Luke came out carrying some tapes and a pair of boots. Perhaps his mother had planned to bring the boots on a visit to Ashfield once winter set in. As he came down the stairs I said, "All set? Do you need a hand with anything?"

He shook his head and crossed the kitchen to the back door. Without turning to face me he said, "Aunt Nell…when you come back here afterwards… could you stay in my room?"

*And not in my mother's,* I heard as clearly as if he had said the words. I smiled, even though he couldn't see my expression.

"That's just what I'll do," I said. "It's nice of you to offer."

Tilda and Miles Abbott spoke with a distinctive local accent that bore no resemblance to the corny drawl affected by comics and storytellers imitating Mainers. Their son Zach was tall and skinny, with a buzz cut and glasses. The first thing Tilda did after hugging Luke and shaking my hand was invite me to stay at her house.

"The boys'll be bunking in Zach's room, so the sofa's free. We've known Luke his whole life—I don't like to think of his family staying in the house all alone."

"Oh, I'll be fine," I said. "I'm used to being on my own. And then tomorrow a friend of mine is driving up…"

The interested look she gave me made me certain she could tell, without benefit of Latin case endings, that my friend was male. I went on, "I know him from work. Originally. He had a heart attack a couple of months ago and it's been difficult for him, so when he said he wanted to come along and look out for Luke and me I said yes…"

Could this possibly be me going on about such personal matters with someone I just met? Tilda regarded me with very blue eyes, then pointed at a clock behind her on the wall.

"We eat at five Christmas Day. You bring him."

# CHAPTER FORTY

TILDA HAD WANTED ME TO STAY for supper, but I was able to say truthfully that, after Martha's lumberjack breakfast followed by a burger and fries in Kennebunk, I was for once not hungry. She then went to her refrigerator and, taking out a casserole dish, spooned its contents into a plastic container. "Rice pilaf and chicken," she said, holding the container out to me. "I've got pork chops for the boys—Luke loves them."

Yet another fact about my nephew that was news to me. I said, "Thank you—this is so kind of you. Rice and chicken is one of my favorites, and now I won't have to stop at the store."

Tilda was writing the reheating instructions on a large Post-it. "Probably just as well," she said. "We don't have a store."

The house looked very deserted when I pulled back into the driveway and saw it for the first time by myself. As I pushed open the unlocked door I felt for the light switch, a little uneasy at the thought of entering a dark house. As soon as I'd hung my coat on a hook in the kitchen and put Tilda's dish on the counter, I went through the downstairs turning on more lights. What had Ned's life been like in these rooms? Had he gone to California in search of easy money that would buy his family a fancier place, never realizing that his life would matter more to them than anything money could buy?

The living room shelves held a few books—Ned had never been a reader— and at least a dozen framed photographs. I studied each of these carefully.

My brother in yellow coveralls and waders, holding up a lobster. A pretty, dark-haired woman who had to be Luke's mother, Doris. The two of them arm-in arm in front of a garden fence. Luke as baby, child, and embarrassed-looking middle school graduate. My assumption had been right—he'd been adorable.

After I'd seen everything in the living room I went back into the kitchen to look at the items fastened with magnets to the refrigerator door. Luke, in an obviously recent school photo. Luke with skinny Zach. A dog-and-cat cartoon that I didn't get. A clipping from the local paper about well testing. I straightened the photo of the two boys then picked up the Tupperware container Tilda had given me and read her simple instructions.

While my meal heated in a pie plate I'd found in the cabinets I went back into the living room in search of a book. If I am by myself, with no Woody, I always have something to read in the hand that's not holding my fork. One of the higher shelves held field guides and paperback fiction mixed together in no apparent order, a hardcover *Best Loved Poems of the American People* inscribed: Jane Mary from Granny. Christmas, 1940. And—my hand reached for it—a paperback of *2001: A Space Odyssey*. I opened the book to the copyright page—1968. When 2001 finally arrived decades later, it would be remembered not for some imagination-stirring mission to outer space, but for a transforming act of evil. I thought the book must belong to Luke, but on the next page was Ned's name, in the barely legible handwriting that had caused him trouble in school.

Carrying the book, I went back into the kitchen and was just about to reach into the oven for the pie plate when I remembered this wasn't a microwave and a potholder might be a good idea. I found one with roosters on it near the sink, and safely transferred my dinner onto a waiting plate. I tried the food before carrying the plate to the kitchen table. Tilda's leftovers were delicious—just the kind of home-cooked repast that spoiled me for my own brand of cooking, which usually consisted of two minutes and fifteen seconds on HIGH.

The book had black and white photos from the movie, so I looked at those before turning back to the Foreword.

*Behind every man alive stand thirty ghosts...*

I read for an hour at the table, then rinsed my dishes and Tilda's container in the sink. My mother had taught me that such a container should never be returned empty, which meant that tomorrow when I went into the big city—Rockland, Maine—to meet Tom, I would want to buy some gourmet treat for the Abbotts.

I carried my suitcase and the book up to Luke's room and set them both on his bed. There were posters on the wall of sports teams and rock bands—only by the evidence of uniforms and haircuts could I hazard a guess as to which were which. In the bathroom across the hall I changed into my nightgown, brushed my teeth, and then instead of returning to Luke's room I passed his door and tried the door of the room next to his. It opened, and I stepped inside. I'd promised my nephew that I wouldn't sleep in his mother's room—I didn't say I wouldn't have a look.

The room that had been Doris Aquila's (the name she had gone by) was quite unfussy. Green curtains, white bedspread, prints of flowers on the wall. There was dust under the bed and on the dresser—Lee Thomson had told me that in the final weeks before her death from breast cancer, Luke's mother had slept on the first floor in a hospital bed. "Church ladies" had come to clean out her clothes and personal items, saving her few pieces of jewelry for Luke's benefit. Lee Thomson said the rings and pearls were probably of negligible cash value, but he had sounded impressed at the honesty of Doris's friends. I had told him that at some point we might want to ask Luke if he wanted the neighbors who had cared for Doris to have the jewelry as mementos.

There was a single photograph in the room, framed, on top of the dusty dresser. I crossed the room and picked it up, holding it to the light. It was of Doris and Luke, standing in a meadow next to a cairn of what looked like blocks of granite. Luke looked to be about two years old—he was holding his mother's hand and beaming at whoever was taking the picture. Ned, proud of his beautiful family? Mother and son were dressed for summer, and Luke was barefoot.

I looked for a long time at the captured moment, then set the frame back exactly as I had found it and turned out the light.

# CHAPTER FORTY ONE

ON THE MORNING OF THE TWENTY-FOURTH, I woke to the sound of wind. Everything else was quiet, and I lay in Luke's bed for at least ten minutes before hearing any sound of human activity—an approaching vehicle. There was a hiss of air brakes—a trucker, then, putting on some miles before the sun was even up. I listened to the sound grow louder, then recede, before swinging my feet onto the floor. I hadn't thought to bring slippers, but Luke's dresser had plenty of socks, and I had borrowed the thickest pair I could find to wear to bed in the chilly house.

Tilda had said that even with the refrigerator defrosted, there should be a good supply of non-perishables from which I could scrounge breakfast. Cereal without milk didn't appeal, and besides, it seemed that this family favored the healthy kind of cereal that's loaded with anti-oxidants and tastes like a calendar. There was rice and beans and soup, the first choices too much trouble and the last requiring a can opener, which I hadn't spotted. Ah—I opened a cabinet above the counter and saw a jar of instant coffee and one of peanut butter, the smooth kind. I'm a fan of the crunchy variety, and made a mental note to stock both kinds for when Luke came to visit. A tin made to look old-fashioned held graham crackers with which, as I waited for water to boil, I made a half dozen peanut butter sandwiches. When the kettle whistled I fixed a mug of coffee to have at the table with my breakfast and another chapter of my book. The Hal 9000 was telling Poole that he was sorry to interrupt his birthday celebration seven hundred million miles from Earth, but there was a problem. I took a second cup of coffee into the living room, where I stretched out on the sofa in my flannel nightgown and Luke's socks and let Arthur C. Clarke's genius carry me beyond the stars.

Sunlight was coming through the streaked windows, and I felt none of the unease I had experienced the night before. I rinsed my breakfast dishes and repacked my overnight case, including Tilda's container and my book, and added Luke's socks for my next load of laundry. When I took the socks off, the bathroom floor felt icy—if I was going to be spending much time in Maine I was going to need some heavy socks of my own. After putting my bag in the car I walked to the end of the driveway so I could see what the house looked like in daylight, then got behind the wheel and headed north.

Friends familiar with mid-coast Maine had told me that while I was up this way I should try to visit Camden. A half-hour drive along Route One took me to a stop sign, beyond which was a tidy commercial section. I drove down a long block then up another, passing shops and churches and bed-and-breakfasts, and parked next to a handsome brick library, closed for the holiday. Just beyond the town was a magnificent mountainside, topped with snow. I walked back the way I had come and was pleased to find several open bookstores. The friendly people working in them seemed just as happy to welcome browsers like me as legitimate last minute shoppers, and to direct me to their competition. At the last place, a block behind the main street, an obliging young woman in a denim jumper recommended a store that sold gourmet chocolates, the perfect comestible with which to fill Tilda's dish. Just a few doors down on the same side was a deli, where I had soup and oyster crackers while watching a man-made waterfall sluice into a picturesque harbor.

Tom had made plans to stay at a motel in Rockland. It was four o'clock when I drove back through that unassuming city and made the right turn that Miles Abbott said would take me back around the block and onto a one-way street. The motel parking lot was nearly empty. I parked right next to the entrance, got my bag out, and—urban habit—locked the car before going inside.

"Evening," the man at the desk said. He was a big fellow, with thinning hair and a chipped front tooth that showed as he smiled at me. The counter he stood behind filled half the tiny lobby, with the rest of the space taken up by a table with coffee and hot water carafes on it, and a rack of souvenirs and postcards. "Help you?"

"I…"—I was unsure how to phrase my request in a place that looked as if it would still have a rotary phone—"Is there a way to call up to somebody's room?"

173

The clerk consulted a register that lay open on the desk. "You don't look much like one of them terrorists. Just go ahead and give me the name."

"Kramer," I said. "Thomas Kramer."

"Oh, sure—he came in right around lunch time. Room 304. Elevators are that way, and you're going to want to turn left when you get off."

"Thank you," I said, moving toward the short passageway he had indicated.

"You have a nice night now, Mrs. Kramer."

Room 304 was near the end of a carpeted corridor, a good distance from the elevators and ice machine. Unless Christmas revelers were going to be arriving later, it looked as if Tom had found us a quiet place to spend the night. I set my bag down in front of 304 and knocked.

Tom opened the door wearing a dark green sweater and jeans. He was grinning, and I got that amazing feeling that comes when you see in a person's eyes how happy he is to see you. Maybe almost as happy as I was to see him.

"Hey, you," I said. "What are you doing meeting women in motel rooms?"

"Nothing yet," he said. "But later will be another story." I closed the door behind me and we kissed. He had his hand behind my neck, and it took me a moment to catch my breath when we finally stepped apart.

"If that's a preview of 'later,'" I said, "I can hardly wait. Luckily, the clerk thought I was your wife."

"There are worse fates," Tom said. "And worse assumptions he could have made."

I hadn't thought about how we'd get dinner with everything closing early, but Tom had eaten lunch in a nearby sub shop that would be open until six. "What do you say?" he asked me. "A pizza and a bottle of red wine, and then whatever ideas we can come up with for celebrating."

He wasn't supposed to have pizza. Or wine. I wasn't supposed to feel like a giddy teenager. I said, "No double cheese, and with a salad. I need to start eating right to stay in shape for my good-looking man."

I've spent Christmas Eves in different places, with different people. This year, it was a deluxe pizza with wine drunk from plastic glasses, that Jimmy Stewart chestnut on cable, and Tom. Caesar's legions could have galloped down the corridor all night and I wouldn't have heard a thing.

# ———— CHAPTER FORTY TWO ————

I OPENED MY EYES ON CHRISTMAS Day unsure for a second where I was. Then it all came back—Maine, a motel. The aftertaste of one glass too many of Rite Aid red wine. Tom. I turned in the king sized bed and found no one else in it.

"Good morning."

I flailed to sit up, all too conscious of what my face and hair and precaffeine squint must look like. My flannel nightgown, which at some point I must have put back on, was bunched up and cutting into my throat as I turned my head toward Tom's voice. He was sitting in the room's one low armchair, wearing a robe, reading *USA TODAY*, and drinking coffee. I reached up to feel my hair—it was so much worse than I'd imagined.

"Where'd that come from?" I managed to croak from my dry, constricted throat. No more red wine for me, or at least none from the cellars of a chain drugstore.

"This?" He held up the coffee. "They have it downstairs. Want me to bring you some?"

In the time I had known Tom I had seen many stellar qualities in him, but none to compare with this. He had just offered to bring me a draft of the nectar that would restore me to life.

"…would be wonderful," I mumbled, from behind the sleeve I had raised to shield my face.

As soon as the door closed behind Tom I shot out of bed and in three seconds had cold water gushing from the bathroom faucet. Face, teeth, hair (Oh, God—somebody smash that mirror—how had I ever let him see me like this?) As I smoothed my nightgown, demanding of myself why I had shopped at the Vermont Country Store instead of Victoria's Secret (at least I wasn't wearing my nephew's socks) I heard the door to the room open. Thank God—who could have blamed Tom if he'd jumped in his rental car and floored the accelerator?

"Hi!" I said. "I mean, good morning." He was carrying a cardboard holder with three coffee cups in it. I stared at them like one of those wandering Trojans, who's in such desperate need of sustenance that he's eating his table.

"I've already had a cup," Tom said. "So two of these are for you. If you want to get back in bed"—he smiled, no doubt noticing the results of my frenzied makeover in the short time he'd been gone—"you can start on the first one and I won't say a word until you're ready for the second one."

I stared at him, my open mouth contributing, I'm sure, to my matutinal loveliness. I crossed to the bed and arranged the pillows against the headboard before climbing back in. As Tom handed me my coffee and turned to go back to the chair where he'd been reading the newspaper I said, "If word ever gets out about you there'll be women lined up from here to Portland. But they'll not have you."

We had our second cups of coffee sitting side by side in bed, our shoulders touching. His warm skin had come to be familiar in its own way, freckled where Michael's had been white, brushed with a light fuzz of red hair. I reminded myself that I was supposed to be looking out for his health and had better be getting out of bed before I started having ideas.

"I'm going to shower, OK?" I said. "Unless you wanted..." I had been going to say, "Unless you wanted to go first," but Tom's grin told me he was finishing my sentence in a quite different way. Apparently I wasn't the only one with ideas.

"Or I suppose we could share the shower," I said. "Later."

The clerk on the desk told us that we could get lunch (it was almost noon when we finally made our way down in the elevator, holding hands) in the motel coffee shop. We lingered over sandwiches and more coffee, then returned to our room and bundled up for a walk. The day was cold and overcast, but windless. Across from the motel entrance the harbor looked wintry with shrink-wrapped boats drawn up in the yard. We walked down the one-way street past shops and restaurants and a museum—nothing was open, and there were few other people about. At the end of the street was a traffic light, and across from that a huge Christmas tree made from lobster traps. We crossed to the other side of the street we'd come down and walked to the motel, stopping at the entrance to take in the ferry dock and bus terminal opposite. I imagined them bustling with activity in the summer months, and thought how nice it might be to come back here in warmer weather. I squeezed Tom's hand. "I'm glad you came."

"Me, too." He looked at me. "Back when…I didn't know what was going to happen, whether I was going to die, what kept coming back to me was that it had taken me all this time to find you and now maybe a few months were all we were going to get."

His ears were red and his breath was steaming in the cold air. I said, "Whatever we get, Tom, let's make it count. Every day of it." I laughed then, a little embarrassed. "Listen to me—your own personal post-Socratic philosopher."

He leaned in to kiss me, unhurriedly, and I stopped talking. After a long moment he drew back and smiled at me.

"Ready to go in? I have something for you."

The dilemma of what to get Tom for Christmas had occupied my mind for weeks. To Luke's generation we must appear as creaking elders who should be way past any interest in the opposite sex, but to me at least Tom and I were still in that exploratory stage in which the choice of a gift was fraught with underlying meanings. In the end, I'd selected a Just Good Friends present— Sandburg's biography of Lincoln—and a dove-gray cashmere pullover that I hoped would announce You Are The Guy For Me.

What, I had to wonder, would the present he had chosen for me have to say for itself?

The box Tom produced from his suitcase was very small. No more than four inches square and maybe an inch high. It was unlikely to contain the new translation of Herodotus the classical world was buzzing about. I took the package from him and turned it in my hands, then asked, "Do you think you could open yours first?"

He opened the sweater first, lifting it out of its tissue wrappings and saying as he held it up in front of him that it was beautiful and the exact color he would have chosen for himself. Nothing about his interpreting the subliminal message the sweater was telegraphing. But then he opened the set of books and hugged me to him and said that he was so lucky that his woman (*his woman!*) knew him well enough to get him the perfect present. Is there anyone on this earth who understands men?

"What pretty paper," I said. Wrapping paper, pretty or not, is not an enthusiasm of mine, but I was buying a few extra seconds. I removed the gold bow and slid a fingernail under the tape that sealed the shiny silver paper.

Inside, a white box, and inside that a layer of cotton. I lifted the cotton out and saw a pendant.

The chain, like the wrapping paper, was silver. From it hung a silver oval incised with the image of a woman, helmeted and holding a spear.

"It's Athena," I said.

Tom sounded pleased. "I told the guy in the shop you'd know right away. I got it at that place in Cambridge that has Greek jewelry. I told the guy about you and he said this was the one to get. He said Athena was the smart one."

I held the pendant out to him and, turning, bent my head. "Will you put it on me?"

He brought the necklace ends together and fastened the clasp. "Let's see," he said, and I turned around. "Yes—that's what I thought it would look like."

I went to the mirror. For our walk I'd put on the inside-out yellow Lakers sweatshirt I had misguidedly purchased for Luke. Against its fuzz, the pendant gleamed as bright as the goddess's shield would have on the battle ground.

"I won't wear this every day," I told Tom. "It's too special. But every time I put it on I'll remember this moment, being with you, today. Thank you, Tom."

"You're pretty special yourself. You're welcome."

Tilda had assured me that the opening of presents at the Abbotts always took place on Christmas morning, and that this year Luke had not been forgotten, so I felt at ease arriving at their house bearing only Tom and the Tupperware container of gourmet chocolates. There was wine and cheese set out (I planned to go easy on any alcoholic beverages after last night), with cider for the boys. After a half hour of the adults getting to know each other—the boys had been introduced to Tom, then allowed to take their food and drink back to Zach's room—Tilda returned from checking the oven and said that dinner was ready. She had made roast beef, with potatoes and carrots crisply glazed from baking in the meat juice. She and Miles sat at either end of the dining room table, with Tom and me across from the boys. At Tilda's request we all joined hands while Zach said grace, then Miles picked up a carving knife and asked who wanted an end slice.

A half hour later, accepting everyone's heartfelt compliments on the meal, Tilda said, "There's apple pie and coffee, and those beautiful chocolates Nell brought, but why don't we wait a bit? Zach, would you and Luke please clear the table?"

At once the boys were up and vying to see who could carry the tallest stack of dishes. Tilda seemed unperturbed by any potential for catastrophe as she and Miles collected the serving dishes and followed the boys into the kitchen. Tom and I, who had been told we were guests and should just sit, smiled at each other. "Nice people," Tom said.

"Aren't they? I'm so glad Luke is getting to spend today with people who knew his parents."

My nephew came back into the dining room, followed by all three Abbotts. Zach said, "Mom, can we watch TV?"

"*May* we. Did you ask your guest if that's what he wants to do?"

Zach looked at Luke, who nodded vigorously. Miles said, "All agreed, then. Tom, Nell—want to join us?"

Now Tom looked at me. It wasn't a please-rescue-me look. I said, "You guys go ahead. I'll help Tilda finish cleaning up."

As Miles let Tom and the boys go ahead of him he said, "So who does everybody like for the Rose Bowl?" Tom's reply sounded very knowledgeable, and the boys' excited answers no less so.

"Football," Tilda said, seeing my expression. "Come talk to me about anything in the world except sports while I load the dishwasher. More wine?"

The dishwasher was a noisy older model that actually enhanced our conversation by overriding the sound of the television. Tilda asked me about my work—I was sparing as always with details—before telling me how she and Miles had met in high school and married when they were eighteen.

"We thought we'd have a big family," she said, trailing a finger down her wineglass. "Miles is one of six, and I've got three brothers. But it turned out to be just Zachie, so of course we loved having Doris and Ned as neighbors, with Luke just our boy's age."

"Was Ned happy here?" I asked. Tilda looked at me with those striking blue eyes.

"You bet. He told me he loved the way people accepted Doris—didn't care that she was dark and had an accent. You know that they met when he was in the Marines in Puerto Rico?"

"No," I said, and unbidden came the thought, *Damn you, Ned. I would have accepted her. Our mother would have accepted your wife and child. She would have loved them.* Aloud, I said, "Maybe you're wondering—the fact is that Luke's existence came as a complete surprise to me."

Tilda didn't seem much taken aback by such a situation, and I reminded myself that she had known my brother and no doubt seen what it did to his family when Ned left that last time and never came back. She said, "Ned thought the sun rose in Luke. Doris said he'd spoil him, but I don't think you can love a kid too much, as long as you remember he's going to need to break free some day."

"Then why?" I said.

"Why did he leave? I wish I had an answer for that. All Doris would say was that he was making good money on the Coast and sending most of it back."

I remembered Lee Thomson saying there was money in trust for Luke. I drew in a breath and said, "Luke thought his father committed suicide."

Tilda's blue eyes widened and she put a hand to her mouth. "Oh, no. The poor kid…"

"It was a misunderstanding," I said. "He knows now that's not what happened." Wanting to change the subject I said, "So—you and my brother's family were really close."

"Oh, Lord, yes. Doris and I were thick as thieves, and the boys—well, Luke was like the brother Miles and I had wanted to give Zach. They'd fight sometimes of course, but an hour later we'd hear them laughing together. I always told Doris…"

She stopped speaking—I sensed she was about to say something serious and important to her.

"Nell, I want to tell you something. Please don't take it the wrong way."

Never an easy pledge to make when you don't know what's coming, but I nodded.

Tilda stood and carried our empty wine glasses to the sink, then came back to sit opposite me at the table. She clasped her hands together on a Christmas placemat.

"Luke was three the last time he saw his father. When we had a party for his fourth birthday, he said he wanted to wait for his Daddy before he blew out the candles. Doris and I went upstairs so we wouldn't spoil the party with crying. That's when I asked her why she wasn't getting somebody—the police, or somebody like you—I told her Miles and I would help pay—to look for Ned. She got really overwrought and said that was the one thing he said she should never do. He told her the people he worked with were"— she closed her eyes for a moment, evidently searching for Ned's exact words—"nobody to mess with. He said that no matter what, she had to promise him, for Luke's sake, not to try to find him if he didn't come back or get in touch."

Tilda drew a breath and looked straight at me. "You knew about your brother's problems with drugs?"

I nodded. "It started when he was in the Marines. Our parents made him get help and he'd be all right for a while, then he'd relapse. A psychiatrist told my parents that the biggest problem was that Ned was very high-functioning—he could do hard drugs and still lead a pretty normal life in other areas." I met Tilda's unflinching look. "The psychiatrist said it could only end one of two ways—rock bottom so he'd have to stop, or dead."

And now we both knew which it was. Tilda said, "Never here. Doris told him if he used drugs around Luke she'd leave him and take Luke with her. Doris was no fool—he might be clean here, but she could see that extra jazz in him when he'd come back from his trips with his pockets stuffed with cash.

"Luke was the reason for all of it. Ned loved that kid so much. Doris thought that it was still possible—that there would finally be enough money and Ned would be back to stay. But of course that never happened. Luke asked questions for a while, then he either forgot about his father or didn't want to talk about him. When he was thirteen, he got into a big argument with Doris over his wanting a dirt bike, and he said he was going to run away and find his father. That's when Doris told him his father was dead. I don't think she planned to do it, but once she had, she added in the part about drugs. There was a big story going around about a kid who'd brought drugs into the middle school, so Doris told Luke that's how it happened—to keep him clear of that kind of trouble. I can't believe he came up with suicide from what she told him..."

In a way, of course, it *had* been suicide. The minute my brother ran afoul of Eliot Wyman and his murderous thugs, he had effectively signed his own death warrant.

"Tilda," I said, "Did Doris ever say anything about Ned sending more than just money?"

She shook her head. "He'd bring things with him when he came—big presents for her and Luke. That's what made Luke's birthday that year really hard—Ned had been hinting around like a kid himself that somebody was getting a bike. The party just brought it all home for Doris, and she couldn't stop crying. Then she started talking about what would happen to Luke if she died."

I said, "Did she have some health problem?"

Tilda shook her head. "No—her diagnosis came maybe six months later. She wasn't even thirty." She looked at me, that direct look again, but almost pleading this time.

"I told her to set her mind at rest on that score. It wasn't going to come to that, but if it ever did, Luke's home was right here with us. I know the legal rights are on your side..." Her eyes widened again and her face colored. "Oh, that came out completely wrong! You're wonderful with him—I was so happy when that lawyer called and said Luke had family..."

"Tilda," I said. "You've been honest—now it's my turn. I've spoken with the lawyer and I feel reasonably competent about assuming guardianship of Luke. I should be able to sign his school reports and take him edifying places when he'd rather be at a baseball game and maybe even lay down the law if he starts wearing his pants so his underwear shows..." We both laughed.

"But the thought of sharing my apartment and the kind of life I live with an adolescent boy, well, that's got me worried."

Tilda was silent. I wondered if she thought the feelings I had just expressed were selfish. I supposed they were. She said, "Would you consider letting him live here?" I must have stared at her, because she said, "You must think I have some nerve. It's just that all of us think of Luke as family and if you'd let him come to us summers I'd feel like what I promised Doris…" She trailed off, lifting her chin, as if expecting me to be confrontational.

"Have you spoken to your husband about this?" I asked.

"Yes. He's all for it. Not Zach yet, of course, but I've seen how he is ever since that scholarship came through for Luke."

"Tilda," I said, and she looked at me with what I thought was a little hope. "It's very important to me that Luke know I want him. If he wants to live with me, then we'll work it out. But I have an unusual job and strange hours and what I care about is that he be with the person or people who can give him the best life. What do you say I lay all that out for him, then ask him if he wants to live here until he's out of school? To have two families."

"Thank you," Tilda said.

"I'm the one to be saying thank you. You and Miles would have to agree to accept financial help—it's Luke's money, not mine. I've only known the kid a few months but take it from me—he'll eat you out of house and home."

Tilda laughed. "That's what teenaged boys are supposed to do. Speaking of which, they're probably ready for dessert. Could you go see who wants pie while I put on some coffee?"

Tilda had closed the kitchen door when we began talking about my brother's family, and as I opened it I heard the television and men's voices, then a boy's laugh. Luke's—he sounded like Ned.

Tom and I arrived back at the motel at nine-thirty. The temperature had fallen, and a few hazy stars shone beyond the streetlights. As we were riding up in the elevator I asked Tom, "What did you guys find to talk about?"

"The Bowl games," he said with enthusiasm. "Miles thinks that with Vince Young quarterbacking, the Longhorns might actually take it. Especially when you look at the defense lineup…"

The elevator pinged, and the door opened on our floor. Taking hold of his arm as we stepped out I said, "Tom?"

He looked at me. "You are a wonderful man. I love you. But could we pretend I never asked?"

He looked startled, and I wondered if my declaration, which I had neither planned nor expected to make, had discomfited him. Then he grinned.

"Done. And I love you, too."

# —— CHAPTER FORTY THREE ——

ONE THING I'M GOOD AT IS learning from experience. True, Tom had seen me newly wakened after an eventful night and hadn't been turned to stone, but I wasn't taking any chances on a repeat sighting. He was still asleep on the day after Christmas when I slid ever so carefully out of bed and began tiptoeing towards the bathroom.

"Nell?"

I turned toward his voice. "I didn't mean to wake you."

"Just as well. I'm due back at work tomorrow—it's probably high time I started breaking myself of the habit of staying in bed with a beautiful woman."

I looked him over. His eyes were barely open, but he looked fine. It wasn't fair.

"For that chivalric comment, sir, I shall save you *gallons* of hot water."

I was in the shower maybe ten minutes, keeping my promise by turning off the water while I washed my hair, then toweled it off and wrapped the towel around me. When I stepped into the room it felt cold after the hot steam I had been standing in.

"Tom!"

He was sitting back against the headboard of the bed, staring. His face was white. Oh, God—I knew it. It was his heart. The phone—where was the phone...

"Nell," he said, and pointed. At the television I had heard faintly through the bathroom door when I turned off the shower. I moved around to where I could see the screen.

True poets understand that the more momentous an occurrence, the simpler the words needed to describe it. Virgil uses *aquae mons* to let his readers see for themselves the mountain of water Juno raises to swamp Aeneas's fleet. On the television, a wave that looked as tall as a skyscraper was towering over whatever lunatic with a camera was filming it. People were running—they looked as tiny as the people who came with the train set I'd bought. Trees were coming down, walls, houses.

Tom put out a hand for me and I grasped it. "What in God's name…"

"It's a tsunami."

I sat on the bed, squeezing Tom's hand bloodless, all sight and sound reduced to the horror we were seeing. On the screen, the same gargantuan wave would crest and break, then re-form like an image from a nightmare. A voiceover was putting words to the pictures—Indonesia. Thousands. Tens of thousands. Human toll. And that exotic word that we'd probably all once learned in fifth-grade geography and would now never forget. Tsunami.

I relaxed the grip I had on Tom's hand, and saw that it was white where I'd been pressing it. The next hours were sure to bring details of how such a thing could have happened and what was being done to rescue survivors, but for now it was just the same pictures, over and over and over. The mountain of water.

"I have to call Tilda," I said to Tom.

Tilda told me the boys had come downstairs early to try out the video games they'd gotten for Christmas. They had turned on the TV and seen the same sight Tom and I had just been watching. Tilda said, "I made them turn it off. Zachie had nightmares after 9/11—who didn't?—but I'm in charge here and I'm not having those pictures bombarded at the boys non-stop."

I could hear that she'd been crying. Would I have let Luke keep watching? There were so many answers I didn't have, and I found myself hoping that Luke would decide to make it easier for both of us by letting Tilda, with her common sense and years of experience, help raise him. I said, "May I come over? There's something I need to talk to Luke about while I'm still here."

"Coffee's on. I'll get out a cup for you."

Tom said he'd stay at the motel to pack and have breakfast, then come by the Abbotts before he left. Holding him, both of us quiet, I thought how trite it is to say that one never knows if a goodbye is going to be the last one, but there on the other side of the world thousands of people had seen the trite become true.

"Aunt Nell," Luke said, before I'd even closed the door behind me, "There was this humungous wave in India. It just came up out of the ocean and drowned all these people on the beach..." Beside him, Zach was nodding excitedly.

"I know, honey. It's terrible. I'm glad Mrs. Abbott made you turn off the TV. I don't want you being scared by seeing something like that."

He looked stunned, then his face colored with what I could tell was anger. Well, what did I expect—I'd just treated him like a three-year-old in front of his friend.

"Sorry," I said, and borrowed from Tilda. "That came out all wrong. I'm very upset at the thought of all those people." He shrugged, probably the only sign I was going to get that he had accepted my apology. "Anyway, I'm going to have a cup of coffee with Mrs. Abbott and then I need to ask you something."

Tilda and I sat at the kitchen table with coffee and English muffins. Neither of us said much—conscious, perhaps, that we were warm and safe in coastal Maine even as another ocean drowned everything in its path. When Tilda got up to put our plates in the dishwasher she said, "Shall I get Luke for you?"

"Thank you. Thank you for everything, Tilda."

She went out, and in a minute Luke came into the kitchen, looking apprehensive. I said, "Hey, it's not all that bad," and then felt shallow and insensitive, given the suffering the television pictures had just shown us. I said, "Luke, the thing I want to talk to you about is sort of private. Could you close the door?"

He did as I asked, then appeared to be planning to lean against it for our talk. I said, "Come and sit down," and he did, sighing. We would have been roughly at eye level if he hadn't been slouching and looking at the floor.

"Luke," I said, "Do you remember when we were driving to Mrs. Hayes' house for Thanksgiving and I asked you whether your mother had any place she might have put something valuable?"

Nod.

"And you said there was a box for papers but you couldn't think of anything else?"

Nod.

"Well, now that you're actually back here and have been in your house, I wondered if anything else occurred to you—any place your mother might have put a package to keep people from finding it."

"I already told you..."

He stopped. I saw something come into his eyes.

"Luke, this is very important. Please tell me what you just thought of."

"It's stupid."

"*What* is stupid? It's just us having this conversation. Please, Luke."

He directed his voice toward his shoes. "When I was *really* little my Mom would take me to leave stuff on this pile of rocks out behind the house. I couldn't go by myself because she said there was an old well under there and I could get hurt."

The photo in Doris's room. She and Luke next to what I had thought of as a cairn. I said, "But you'd go there with your mother."

He nodded. "If we had bread or crackers or stuff we'd put them out there and then see what animals would come. She said it must be like…magic…for them to come and find somebody'd left them food. She said they must think it was their treasure rock."

I sat in silence for a moment, picturing the young mother teaching her child to feel for other living things. Then I said, "Thank you, Luke. Nobody except you could have told me that."

"Can I go now?"

"In a minute," I said, striving to keep the exasperation out of my voice. That barefoot toddler in the photo was gone forever, replaced by this child-man hell-bent on disavowing his younger self. On the short drive here I'd rehearsed how to broach the subject I needed to raise. "Luke, Mrs. Abbott wants you to come here for February vacation. Not as a houseguest"—I remembered his observation that such invitations were probably coming from his friends' mothers—"but more like…"

I had been about to use Tilda's word. A brother. The brother she and Miles had wanted to give Zach. The part of my brain charged with choosing the right word, now newly attuned to the critical ear of a fifteen-year-old, turned a thumbs-down.

"…more like Zach's best friend. It's your choice, Luke. I'd drive you, of course, and if you wanted to stay with me instead that would be great."

No response. How did parents do this, day after bloody day? I put a smile on my face and said, "You don't have to decide now. Just think about it, OK?"

"OK," he said, and got up from his chair. I watched him go, quickly, as if fearing I was going to call him back. Then I took out the cell phone he had helped me choose—it placed and received calls and sent and received text messages and took pictures and did pretty much everything except keep me from hating it. The number I needed was in my purse. On the second try at pressing the tiny numbers I connected with the motel and asked for Room 304.

"Tom," I said. "I need you to meet me at the house."

# ———— CHAPTER FORTY FOUR ————

I WAITED FOR TOM IN THE driveway of my brother's house, watching in the rearview mirror for his car. When he pulled in, I got out of my own car and took his hand. "Thanks for coming. Let's go inside."

The house was chilly—I hadn't expected to be back here and had lowered the heat. Tom and I kept our coats on as we sat on the sofa and I told him about the photo in Doris's room and Luke's description of the 'treasure rock'. "You can see it from the kitchen window," I said, getting up to show him. There was a light crust of snow on the stones, but they were clearly the ones in the photograph.

Tom said, "And you think she might have put the statue there?"

"It would make sense. Luke wasn't allowed to play around it by himself, so there wasn't much chance he'd come across something he wasn't supposed to see."

Tom looked down at my winter running shoes. "Do you have boots? That snow might not hold us."

"It doesn't matter. This feels right to me, Tom. Let's go see."

There were bird and animal tracks everywhere on the frozen snow, and then human tracks as Tom and I set to work. As we lifted the granite blocks, we laid them out in a runic pattern that would allow us to put them back the same way. After a few minutes we were left with a half dozen blocks pressed into the earth around an iron cover.

"Be careful," Tom said as I ran my hand over the rusted surface. "Here—take my gloves."

I put the right glove, heavy leather, on my hand and prodded the cover. There was nothing to grab onto, but I managed to get my now protected hand under an edge, and with Tom's help moved the cumbersome disk and turned it over.

"It's upside down," I said, pointing. "There's the handle—somebody tied that rope to it and then put it back the wrong way." I looked down into the hole the cover had hidden. "There's something down there."

The rope was a heavy nylon, knotted securely to the pull ring. Tom stood on the cover to keep it steady while I drew up the rope. I had three feet of it coiled beside me when a black rubber bag, the size of an old-fashioned doctor's bag, slid to the surface.

Tom and I looked at each other. I reached out to touch the knots that held the drawstring bag, and was visited by a momentary vision of that long-gone toddler falling here, down and down. I shivered, and it was not from my soaked and frozen feet.

"Let's put everything back," I said to Tom. "Then we can have a look."

We opened the bag on the kitchen table, with a sense on my part of a somber ceremony. On top was a layer of flannel, thickly folded. Beneath that, bubble wrap. I pictured Doris wrapping the package with such care, thinking Ned would be coming back for it. I had no doubt what was going to be in the final layer of cotton.

The statue, small, as Eliot Wyman had indicated with his manicured hands, was exquisite. The artist had sculpted Alexander and Bucephalus with such skill that I half expected the horse to whinny, the boy-king to sound his battle cry. And then I thought that it was for this, this lovely, inanimate thing, that my brother's life had ended at twenty-nine. And a line from Dickinson came: *I died for beauty.*

"What will you do?" It was Tom—I'd forgotten him as I gazed at the—Luke's word—treasure. The black horse and rider glittered in a fall of winter sunlight.

"I know what I *should* do," I told Tom, not taking my eyes off the statue. "Turn it over to the Los Angeles police, and tell them where it came from. Let them look into what museum or private collection is missing this. Stir up as much trouble as I possibly can for Mr. Eliot Wyman and his...associates. And if it weren't for Luke, that's exactly what I'd do."

"You're going to give it back," Tom said.

"Yes." Now I looked at him, at his good, intelligent face. "I try to be a person who does the right thing. It sickens me—the idea of this man who had a part in Ned's death, getting to enjoy his money and his pretty things. But I want…" I drew in a breath, and let it out. "I want it to end here."

Tom said, "What will you tell him?"

"Wyman? That he's welcome to it, just as long as I never have to hear his name again."

"I meant your nephew."

Tom was right, of course. I wasn't going to ask Luke's opinion of what I'd decided to do, but he was the one who had set all this in motion. He had a right to know. I picked up the statue and began repacking it in the shiny black bag.

"I'll play it by ear. He already knows I was looking for this. I'll just have to take the chance that he won't say anything if I tell him how important it is."

"Want me to come along?"

I smiled at him. "Thank you, but I'd feel better if I knew you were on the road. It's supposed to snow some more. Tom, I appreciate…everything. Your coming here, being with me, not judging me for this."

Tom reached over and covered the hand I was resting on the package. "You judge yourself enough," he said. "I hope there are things you need me for, but that's not one of them."

Luke listened in silence as I told him that I'd looked where he suggested and found the missing statue. We were sitting in my car—Zach had looked way too curious as I left the last time, and I could hardly tell Luke's friend that he couldn't eavesdrop in his own house. "Luke," I said, "I'm going to take it back."

"No way!" He was outraged, then looked furious because his voice had cracked.

"Luke," I said. I wanted to touch his shoulder but knew I mustn't. "This man in California—he didn't kill your father, but if it weren't for him your father might still be alive. All I can hope is that the law will catch up with him for other things. But, Luke, I know what your father would have wanted." He started to speak, and I said, "Let me finish. He wanted to keep you safe. And to do that for him, since he can't do it himself, I have to get rid of what's putting you in danger."

Now was his chance to argue with me, maybe even to voice childhood's impotent cry: It isn't fair. But he didn't. Instead, he looked at me with the expression of a protected boy who had just had a man's glimpse into how the world works.

"Let him have it," he said, " I hope it brings him all the bad luck there is."

# ———— CHAPTER FORTY FIVE ————

Eliot Wyman answered the door himself. When I called, I had used non-specific language ("I want to see you. I have something for you"), but of course he understood. He'd offered to send a car to the airport for me, but I declined, setting a condition that he would meet with me alone. Wyman's manner was every bit as polished as I remembered, but his eyes went eagerly to the package I was carrying before he began offering me refreshments, and a more comfortable place to talk than the foyer we were standing in.

"I told the cab to wait," I said. "I'm flying right back out. What you're after is in that package—I'd appreciate it if you'd wait until I'm gone before you open it." I set the package down on a narrow marble table, to avoid having our hands touch.

"Of course. But I shall regret it if I don't take this opportunity to ask you one more time if you would consider coming to work for me. You have Edward's intensity, but apparently not his recklessness."

"No," I said.

He gave a slight shrug, made sophisticated by the perfectly tailored jacket he was wearing. "Ah, well—I had to try." I turned to the door and was reaching for the bright gold handle when he said, "But who knows? Perhaps in a few years, the younger generation."

I turned to face him. He must have been feeling triumph, but his smooth face didn't show it. He said, "For the right price, information is so easily come by."

I took a step toward him, so I could look into his eyes while he heard what I had to say.

"His name is Lucas. You know that, of course. He doesn't look much like Ned, but there are ways I see my brother in him. Ned would be so proud of him. Mr. Wyman"—I was trembling inside, but I could hear that my voice was very calm—"You're a rich man. You control people who will do your bidding before you've even finished telling them what it is you want. I'm an outsider, without any connections in California except a cop I'm not going to be talking to. Everything is on your side, except what I feel for that boy."

He was watching me, looking interested in how far I was going to go. I said, "Don't you or anyone you know ever come near him."

He seemed to be considering what I had said. Then he smiled, and reached past me to open the door.

"I'm sure it wasn't your intention," he said, "but you've increased my regret that we won't be working together." He stood back to let me out and said, with probably no thought of a second meaning, "I could have used you."

The cabbie got out and opened the back door for me. I leaned back, snapping my seatbelt, and looked in the rearview mirror at the man Luke hoped would have nothing but bad luck from his tainted treasure. For myself, I could only hope that what I'd done, and why I'd done it, would bring my brother's spirit peace.

I called Tom from the airport. "There was a delay, but we're ready to board. I'll be home tonight, but it will be pretty late."

"I'll wait up," he said.

# ─────── CHAPTER FORTY SIX ───────

I PICKED LUKE UP IN MAINE on an unseasonably balmy January day. I had spent the previous night in Freeport and had presents for the Abbotts, belated Christmas gifts for my nephew's other family. While I was in California Tilda had asked Luke herself if he would like to come to Maine for his February break, and he had decided he would. For now, we'd leave it at that.

Luke was turning the pages of the Graves book he'd given me—our overnight stay at Martha's was to include a pilgrimage to the cat shelter. From time to time I'd glance over and recognize in the illustrations some deity or metamorphosed human, and wait for him to ask me, the expert, about the story, but of course he didn't. He hadn't had any questions about my trip to California, either.

"My Mom took me there," he said as we crossed a bridge into Wiscasset. He was pointing at a boarded-up lunch wagon. "The first time she drove me to school. We got lobster rolls."

"We'll make it a Prentice tradition," I said. "You and I will go as soon as it's open again."

Woody didn't know who to greet first. His tail stood straight up as he circled Luke, then me, Luke again, and, in his excitement, Martha. "Hey," I said to my nephew—"Not fair. I thought you two were going to get a cat of your own." Woody was now standing on Luke, who was cross-legged on the floor.

"Right after lunch," Martha said. "There's chicken noodle soup and grilled cheese. I'll just get it on the table." Luke got up and started after her into the kitchen and I said, "Cat hair, honey. Could you please rinse your hands before we eat?"

He looked at his hands. They probably looked fine to him, but he shrugged and turned toward the bathroom. I joined Martha in the kitchen and said to her, "There must be something wrong with me. I actually think I'd like it better if he'd go back to giving me grief."

"Worry not," Martha said, setting out soup spoons. "He will."

I stayed at the house with Woody while Martha and Luke went to the shelter. They had borrowed his carrier, which caught his attention momentarily, but as soon as the door closed behind them he got in my lap and purred and listened to me tell him we'd be home soon and everything would be back to normal. It wouldn't, but I'd decided that the changes to my quiet life were good ones. Woody, of course, believes whatever I tell him.

It was almost four-thirty when I heard Martha's car in the gravel driveway. A door banged, and I looked out to see Luke standing beside the car, holding the carrier with both hands. Not empty, then. Martha got out of the other side of the car and they came up the walk together. I took a moment to carry Woody upstairs and shut him, protesting, in the guest room in case the newcomer was timid.

"Aunt Nell," Luke said as I came down the stairs. "We found Mrs. Hayes a cat."

"That we did," Martha said. "There were far too many cats waiting for a home and we wanted to take them all, didn't we, Luke, but then we saw this one"—she gestured to the carrier—" who is an older lady and had been there the longest and looked at us as if she knew we'd pick her."

"She really did," Luke said. "Wait until you see her, Aunt Nell." He set the carrier on the sofa and unlatched the door.

I said, "We should let her come out herself." After a moment she did, sniffing the air in a distinctly proprietary fashion. I said, "Look at those markings." The cat was snow white in parts, striped with gray in other parts, and had a spark-shape on her forehead. Thin white lines ran from it to outline her cheekbones.

"Isn't she splendid?" Martha said, "I know the people at the shelter meant well, but they were calling her by a most unfortunate name…"

"*Patches*," Luke said, making a face.

"And this young man"—she put an arm around Luke, who was grinning—"has come up with the perfect name for her."

I looked at Luke. "Well?"

"Iris." He sounded proud of his inspired choice, but I knew not to make a fuss. Instead, I looked back at the cat. She was exploring, sniffing the rug and furniture and Martha's plants, all harmless to animals. *Iris.* The queen of heaven's messenger. Carrier of news, both good and bad. Arcing down the sky with all life's improbable colors trailing behind her.

"I like it," I said.